TELL ME YOU'RE MINE

A BRITISH BILLIONAIRE NOVEL

Book One

J. S. SCOTT

Tell Me You're Mine

ISBN: 979-8-662623-64-4 (Print)
ISBN: 978-1-951102-32-6 (E-Book)

CONTENTS

CHAPTER 1

Damian

"OBVIOUSLY, YOU ALREADY know this wasn't me, Mum." I tossed the newspaper I was holding on a nearby table as I met my mother's concerned gaze.

Dammit! I'd gotten to her country estate in Surrey as soon as I'd seen the tabloids in London, but apparently, I hadn't been quick enough. My mother had *her own copy* of the fresh-off-the-presses scandal sheet right next to her elbow, and I was willing to bet she had read the *entire article.*

Possibly more than once.

I got her silent answer when she raised a brow, and pinned me with that all-knowing, parental stare that I'd hated since childhood.

Isabella Lancaster was pushing sixty-three years old, but she was still beautiful. Her dark hair had gone gray rather gracefully, and her dark-brown eyes were still as sharp as they'd been years ago.

She knew all...

Saw all...

And maybe I was an idiot to think that I could get to Surrey from London *before* she found out what was all over the tabloids this afternoon. Mum tolerated the gossipy, upper-class crowd much better than I did, so was it really surprising that she'd already gotten the news?

"You can't keep covering for him, Damian." Her voice was firm, but I could recognize the underlying distress.

I shrugged. "What do you want me to do? Dylan isn't in a good place right now."

Truthfully, my younger-by-fifteen-minutes identical twin brother hadn't been in his right mind for the last two years. Not that I really blamed him for that, considering all that he'd been through.

"It's been two years now, Damian. How long are you planning on taking the blame for Dylan's...misadventures?"

I shook my head as I began to pace back and forth across the large sitting room. I wouldn't *exactly* classify my twin brother's behavior as "misadventures." He wasn't some teenage party boy getting himself into a little trouble. Dylan was thirty-three years old, and well on a path to self-destruction. He didn't give a damn about anyone or anything.

"I don't care what people think of *me*," I told her defensively.

Okay, maybe *that* wasn't quite true. Dylan's latest indiscretion to be caught on camera was him *bare-ass naked*, surrounded by several women who were equally nude, and probably just as drunk as he was when that picture had been taken.

This time, I wasn't all that keen on letting people think I was ignorant enough to let *that* get caught on camera.

I was the *reserved* Lancaster brother, and I liked it that way. I wanted my competitors and my allies to take me seriously in the business world.

I had no idea how a reporter had actually gained entrance to Dylan's drunken orgy, but it wasn't surprising since my brother did very little to avoid bad press these days.

I stopped and picked up the paper.

Could it really be as bad as I remember? I only got a quick glimpse of the picture in London.

I grimaced as I looked at the image on the front page, and the cringe-worthy headline above it:

SORRY, LADIES! ONE WOMAN WILL NEVER BE ENOUGH FOR BILLIONAIRE DAMIAN LANCASTER!

Shit! It *was* as bad as I remembered.

I guess that I *should* be grateful that they'd blurred some of the explicit details on the nude bodies. I hadn't seen my brother naked since we were children, and I could have very well done without seeing his bare ass for *the rest of my life.*

Disgusted, I tossed the paper aside again without scanning the text. The last thing I wanted was to read a play-by-play of my sibling's sex life. *No, thank you!*

"You *should* care." Mum's voice was calmer now. "Everyone assumes it was *you.* That's *your* name above that photo. Dylan won't correct them. And Lord knows you won't, either, out of your misguided desire to protect your brother. It's going to be difficult for anyone to take you seriously after this. Do you really want to be sitting in a business meeting, trying to make a deal, knowing every executive in the room is *dying* to ask for the details about that orgy?"

Thank you, Mum, I thought. I'd never really considered *that* possible outcome, but no doubt I would in the future. *Every single time I have a business meeting from now on.*

While I didn't really care what people thought about me personally, I *did* give a damn about Lancaster International, and all of our subsidiaries. At one time, *Dylan* had cared about our company interests, too.

I rubbed a frustrated hand over the tension in my neck, very well aware that the headache that was starting to plague me was going to get worse. *Much worse.* "I'm headed to the States," I said. "I'll talk to Dylan when I get there." As usual, my twin had fled across the pond to avoid any media attention after doing something incredibly stupid.

Leaving *me* to take the blame, and do the cleanup.

So far, I'd done a pretty damn good job of burying most of Dylan's erratic behavior.

Like…the time he'd jumped up on a table in a popular nightclub with a microphone in hand, and tried to convince everyone that our current prime minister was trying to make England a communist country.

Or like…the time he'd gone to a poker game, and accused a well-respected championship poker player of cheating.

When Dylan got thoroughly pissed, there was no telling what would happen, or where his mind would go.

Luckily, most of my twin's drunken romps had never even hit the gossip columns. If there was one thing people liked more than a scandal, it was money, so I'd been able to pay to keep most of the incidents out of the press.

Really, there were only a few such incidents that I'd had to claim as mine.

Luckily, the prime minister and I rarely traveled in the same circles.

Regrettably, my twin had taken bad publicity to a whole different level this time, and for the first time since Dylan had started all of his lunatic behavior, I had no idea what to do about it.

Mum frowned at me as she insisted, "You need to do more than *talk* this time, Damian. You have to refuse to keep taking the blame and cleaning up after him."

"I can't," I said. "You know I made a promise to Dylan, and I swore I wouldn't break my word. I said that I'd give him time away from Lancaster, and everything involved with our corporation, including the press, so he could get his head together after what happened. I have no choice but to let people think his actions are mine, or to make sure they get completely buried."

The image of my twin pleading with me two years ago for time away from *everything* still haunted me. Dylan had been completely broken, and I hadn't hesitated to give him my vow that he'd have the space and solitude he craved.

I'd done everything possible to wipe Dylan's existence off the internet by hiring a highly skilled company who specialized in that type of thing. They'd even taken his name and photos off the corporation website so he could have his privacy. Anything that had come up in the last two years had been deleted as well. Granted, *I'd* taken the blame for a couple of things, but those articles had disappeared like they'd never happened.

Honestly, it felt eerily similar to that old Sandra Bullock movie, *The Net*, when her whole identity had been erased, like she'd never existed.

Okay, maybe it wasn't *that* bad. It was only his online fingerprint that had disappeared, and I still had a few business articles on there. I'd kept such a low profile that I'd never had much more than that in the news in the first place.

"Damian," Mum said softly. "When you gave your brother your word, I know you never had any idea he'd end up like this. He wasn't a drinker two years ago. You kept your promise, and he's had enough isolation. Unfortunately, Dylan hasn't used the opportunity you've given him wisely. He's avoided and escaped instead of using that quiet time to heal. This latest stunt isn't a good image for Lancaster International, and no decent woman will *ever* have you if you don't stop taking the blame for Dylan's behavior."

Great! Here we go again...

I raised a brow. "What makes you think there's a *decent one* who would have me now, Mum?"

I probably shouldn't bait her, but I was desperate for a change of topic. I wasn't prepared to lay out my plan to fix this current situation. Probably because I didn't have one…yet.

She grimaced. "I'd really like to see grandchildren before I die, Damian."

I loved my mother. I really did. But she was tenacious when it came to trying to marry all of us off so she could be surrounded by grandchildren.

Dylan certainly wasn't about to find himself a wife anytime soon.

And my younger brother, Leo, was rarely in one place long enough to have a good chat with a woman, much less marry one.

So naturally, all of my mother's matchmaking efforts had been put toward her eldest son.

"Don't hold your breath waiting for me to get married, Mum," I warned her.

Yeah, I liked getting laid as much as the next guy, but I kept those relationships uncomplicated by seeing women who liked their freedom as much as I did.

Lately, I hadn't even had time to pursue something with no strings attached. I'd been too damn busy running Lancaster by myself.

Leo had never been interested in taking over my father's business interests. When my dad had died, Leo had taken his portion of his inheritance, and was now probably the richest wildlife biologist in the world.

My mother released a long sigh. "I know you're worried about your brother, Damian. I am, too, but that doesn't mean you can't call him out for leaving you to pick up the pieces after every one of these incidents. He's gone way too far this time. You can't just write a check to make this particular article and photo disappear. They're already out there."

She was right. Dylan had done some idiotic things over the last two years, but this was the first time he'd done something *naked*, *with a damn harem.* "I don't think he cares anymore. I'm not even sure he knows that the press blames me for the things he does. Nor do I think it matters to him if he *does* know. He runs away to the States every single time something happens."

My brother had never once asked me *how* I'd kept his embarrassing conduct from catching up with him. He didn't have to. Dylan knew *me,* and he had my word that I wouldn't let anything touch him.

"Then *make him* see it, Damian. I know it's been a tough few years for Dylan, but it's hurting me to watch you work yourself into the ground running Lancaster International alone. You're doing your work and his, too. Not to mention the effort you've put into making sure that nobody even knows that you have a twin brother unless they knew about him before everything happened."

I shot my mum a questioning glance. "Have I ever complained?"

She shook her head. "No. You wouldn't. You never do. But I'm your mother. I can see how this situation is wearing on you. Do you think I haven't noticed that you aren't eating well, or that you have headaches that you've never had before? How much do you sleep at night?"

"I sleep," I assured her.

"A few hours, maybe," she scoffed. "You haven't looked truly rested and healthy for two years, Damian. You *need* to confront Dylan, make him understand that you need to move on with your life, even if he doesn't. You can't continue to run Lancaster International alone. He needs to come home. Or you'll have to restructure things and start delegating to make your high-paid executives actually earn their salaries."

Okay, so maybe I did have a hard time delegating responsibility to anyone who didn't have Lancaster as a surname. "Are you trying to say I'm something of a control freak, Mum?"

"Really? *Something of a control freak*, Damian? I swear, you'd rather die than give up some of your responsibilities, and that worries me. I think you're waiting for Dylan to come back and take back his obligations. In the meantime, the workload is killing you, and God knows how long it will take for Dylan to get his head together."

I was surprised by my mum's adamant tone. Over the last two years, she'd been extremely forgiving about Dylan's behavior, but apparently, her attitude had…changed.

Maybe she was right.

Maybe it *was* time to stop forgiving Dylan for every stupid thing he did.

I was perfectly fine with *her* change of heart.

I just hadn't figured out a way to do that myself *without* feeling guilty as hell.

Honestly, I understood why Dylan liked to spend so much time in California. The Lancaster family was rarely recognized there. Here in England, the Lancaster name was legendary, and had been for generations, so we avoided *any* publicity to keep our faces out of the media. In America, we had a lot more freedom because there were far better stories to chase there than the behavior of a couple of British billionaires. Their A-list movie stars gave the American press plenty of scandal to write about.

"He's still there, Damian." My mum's voice was soft and comforting. "Dylan *will* get through this. He's stubborn. It's always taken him a long time to accept something he can't change."

I was happy to hear her say that, glad *she* was still optimistic, because there were moments that I wondered if any of the old Dylan still existed at all. He wasn't the man I knew, the *brother* I knew, anymore. "I hope he works everything out."

Until Dylan got his shit together, I'd keep protecting him because that was just…what I did. Maybe I was only the oldest by a matter of minutes, but I *was* the eldest, and since my father had died, it had been my job to take care of my family.

Besides, my twin and I had been covering for each other since we were kids, and that instinct had never gone away. At least, for me, it hadn't.

Mum let out an exasperated breath. "Talk to him when you get to California. If anyone can get through to him, it's you. You two were always so close. He might open up to you."

Because I didn't want to crush her hopes that Dylan would eventually be okay, I simply answered, "You're probably right, Mum."

My mother sniffed. "I'm always right. And I know my sons."

Maybe she knew us *too well.* Mum was rather scary that way. "I better get moving. I have a flight to catch."

There was a twinkle in her dark eyes as she asked, "You're going *commercial* again?"

Actually, I hadn't flown commercial for over a year, but Mum liked to give me a hard time about the fact that I occasionally flew Transatlantic Airlines just to see how our company was performing. "How else would I know if we were having issues? Transatlantic is one of our more lucrative companies. I'd like to keep it that way. I'm not exactly going to suffer, Mum. I am booked in business class."

Yes, I wanted to see how our customers felt when they were flying on my airline, but there was no possible way I was going to stuff my six-foot-three frame into a seat with almost no leg room for twelve long, painful hours.

I was a concerned CEO, not a masochist.

My mother got to her feet. "Be safe. Try to take some time off while you're there. I'll miss you."

I nodded sharply as I kissed her cheek, and pulled her into a hug. "I'll come see you as soon as I get back, and I'll call you. Don't worry about the article. I'll figure something out."

I spent the majority of my time in my London home, but I got to Surrey as often as possible to see my mother. Jokes and teasing aside, we were pretty close, and she'd never really gotten over my dad's death, so she'd taken Dylan's abandonment of the family pretty hard.

Not that anyone could claim that Mum was *fragile*, but she *had* been through a lot in the last five years.

She hugged me tightly before she stepped back. "Everybody will forget Dylan's naked picture the moment one of the royals do something interesting."

I chuckled, even though I wasn't really in a laughing mood. "Let's hope the royals aren't in the mood to be well-behaved in the future."

It was rather pathetic to be hoping for a royal scandal, but the British media was fickle. They'd drop the news about Dylan's faux pas in a matter of seconds if someone in the royal family screwed up.

Mum nodded. "Something else will happen that makes the front page tomorrow, and the media will be one step closer to forgetting about today's article."

My mother had a strong backbone, and she always kept a stiff upper lip, but I knew that she was *truly* worried this time.

About me.

About Dylan.

About the reputation that generations of our family had tried so hard to keep squeaky clean and honorable over the years.

The Lancaster family was well-respected, and Mum valued *not* being in a position to encourage the gossips. So much so that she'd twisted herself inside out when she was younger to fit into my father's world with as little censure as possible.

Deep down, I cared about family honor, too. I knew that it was probably ingrained into my DNA.

However, my first priority was the *current* generation of Lancasters, and specifically, my brother, Dylan.

I really wanted to reassure Mum that I'd figure everything out, and that she'd get her wayward son back soon, without further scandal.

Problem was, it was really hard to convince *her* of something when I wasn't really sure what would happen *myself*.

CHAPTER 2

Nicole

MAYBE THERE'S A time in everyone's life when they wonder about the wisdom of their career choices.

Unfortunately, I was currently having *that* moment on foreign soil, in the middle of Heathrow International Airport, while I waited in line to board my flight so I could get my ass back to California where I belonged.

My business was done in London, and I was leaving with the knowledge that I'd managed to completely bomb my attempt to acquire my first, very large international client here in the UK.

I probably should have let Kylie do this pitch. But my second-in-command had some important meetings scheduled with our US customers, so I'd actually *volunteered* for this disaster.

I sighed as the line to board my flight crept forward at such a slow pace that I swore I was *never* going to get to my seat.

Behind me, I could hear a frustrated infant wailing.

I'm right there with you, little dude. I want to get the hell out of England, too.

Okay, maybe it *wasn't* exactly the end of the world if Ashworth Crisis Management didn't acquire clients in London right now, but I'd really hoped we could expand.

Wait! *Correction:* It had always been *my mom's* goal to go worldwide.

Unfortunately, I *wasn't* my mother, and ACM wasn't exactly flourishing and growing underneath my control.

I managed to smile weakly at the flight attendant as I finally boarded, trying to blow off my crappy mood, and not replay my London business failure over and over in my head.

Dammit! I'd been prepared.

I'd been ready.

I'd been completely certain of exactly what I was going to say to persuade Lancaster International that they *needed* a skilled crisis management team at their disposal.

Maybe it *was* a tough sell. Lancaster International had an entire department full of general public relations staff, but it wasn't *impossible.* ACM was different, highly qualified to deal with emergency situations.

Which was exactly why I blew it. I'd had the chance to prove to Lancaster, in real time, exactly what we could do, but I hadn't.

I'd maintained my confidence well…until the CEO of Lancaster had decided that *last night* had been an ideal time to make the tabloids explode with a naked picture of himself, and a bevy of nude females.

I hadn't had time to actually see the article or picture. The story had broken approximately *three minutes* before my presentation.

I'd had to face an entire conference room of suits, every one of them looking at me expectantly, like I should be able to come up with a solution for their mega-disaster on the spot.

I couldn't.

I hadn't been prepared for *that.*

Yeah, I knew the *basics* about the Lancaster family, but since there had never been a whisper of scandal about any of them, I'd focused more on the company and its very long history of acquiring failing companies and making them lucrative again.

The opportunity to pitch to Lancaster International had come up without much notice, so I'd focused on what I could do for *the company* as I'd prepared a hurried, but what I thought was a thorough, presentation.

Nowhere in my research had I come across the information that one of the Lancasters was still young enough to have sex.

Apparently, the eldest Lancaster male *was* still young enough if he'd been in bed with several naked women.

I should have switched gears, and gone to the rescue to solve their problem. I'm a crisis manager. That's what I do, for God's sake.

I'd had *nothing* for them. Not a single suggestion. Not a word to say about handling something I wasn't prepared to conquer. I'd been more focused on possible chemical spills, environmental hazards, sudden stock instability, etc.

How in the hell could I have known that one of the family members would suddenly do something to draw the attention of the entire country? Sure, I knew there *was* a Lancaster family behind the behemoth corporation, but I'd seen very little press about *any of them* while I was doing my research. The possibility of something like *that* happening hadn't even been on my radar.

Lancaster International had a sterling reputation, and had maintained that stature for generations.

Stop stressing, Nicole. You can't change something that's already happened.

I rolled my shoulders, trying to release the tension built up there. Usually, I was the kind of woman who could blow off a failure and move forward, but this one was sticking with me. The humiliation was still too fresh.

Thank God. This stupid line is finally moving.

Some passengers with seats in the front had stored their bags, and moved out of the aisle. As I looked for my own seat, I told myself that I needed to stop tormenting my psyche with all of the things I *could have* said or done.

It was over, and the opportunity to prove how flexible ACM could be to one of the largest, most powerful companies in the world had *already* flown right out of my grasp.

It's too damn late to worry about it...now.

I'd frozen, stumbling through my *prepared* presentation instead of finding a way to address Lancaster's immediate needs.

I wasn't exactly spontaneous.

Never had been.

I planned, I executed *that plan* to the letter, and then I conquered.

Throwing a very large wrench into my well-prepared pitch had entirely crippled me.

I liked everything neat and tidy, and my lack of flexibility had jumped up and bit me in the ass.

Sure, *they said* they'd be in touch, but the message of don't-call-us-we'll-call-you had come across loud and clear at the end of my presentation.

I'd *never* hear from Lancaster International, and honestly, if I couldn't sell our services to a company who needed a crisis manager as much as they did at that moment, who was I going to be able to convince in the future?

Mom could shift gears on the spot, and use new information to her advantage.

Problem was, I wasn't my mother, and probably never would be as sharp as she'd been in this business.

Me? I was a spontaneity failure, and I was just going to have to live with the fact that I'd bombed a critical presentation she could have skated through.

Relief flooded my uptight body as I flopped into my seat by the window, and glanced at the empty space beside me, hoping it would remain unoccupied. There was a large armrest between me and the recliner next door, but things felt a little awkward when I was traveling alone.

I never knew whether to talk to the person next to me, or just pretend that they weren't there. I hadn't really flown enough yet to know the etiquette of frequent business fliers.

My phone *pinged* just as I was awkwardly shoving my carry-on into the small cubby provided. I scrambled for my purse and rummaged through the contents until I found my phone.

I looked at the text.

Kylie: *How did it go?*

Me: *Don't ask. I don't have Mom's charm. I doubt Lancaster will be calling anytime soon. I should have taken the domestic clients and let you do this trip. We'd probably have our largest client yet if you'd done the presentation.*

Kylie: *It can't be that bad. Did you meet the president of Lancaster? I've never seen him, but I've heard he's pretty hot.*

Hot? The CEO of Lancaster International was *hot?* Obviously, Kylie knew far more about the family than I did. When I thought about billionaire CEOs who ran mammoth companies, it brought to mind gray-haired grandfathers who were older than dirt. Apparently, this particular CEO was younger than I'd thought. Either that, or my best friend had suddenly gotten a fetish for men old enough to be her grandparent.

Me: *I wouldn't know. He wasn't there. I imagine he was probably still sleeping after causing a scandal that I didn't know about until three minutes before the meeting. Long story. I'll explain later.*

I felt tears well up in my eyes, but I blinked them back. Part of me felt like I'd not only failed my company, but my deceased mother, too.

Kylie: *I'm sure everything went fine. You worry too much. Give yourself a break. You were used to everything being neat and tidy in corporate law. PR is really messy. I hope you at least managed to find a gorgeous Brit and have a fling. That sexy accent in the bedroom would be enough to make any woman have her first screaming orgasm.*

I rolled my eyes. Kylie Hart wasn't *only* the amazing director at Ashworth Crisis Management; she'd been my best friend since grade school. She, and our other friend, Macy, were the only ones who knew that I'd never had the elusive big O with any of the men I'd dated. The supposed monumental event that my misguided friend *just knew* was going to change my life and the way I looked at myself. Kylie was beyond eager to find my Mr. Orgasm.

I, however, didn't even think about it much anymore.

Me: *No fling. No orgasm.*

Personally, I was convinced that the female orgasm during sex was probably highly overrated. I'd had two sexual relationships. A woman didn't get to the age of thirty-two without sleeping with a guy. Okay. Yeah. Sex was *pleasant* with the right person, but I was convinced the screaming pleasure women talked about was like a unicorn: I wanted to believe it existed, but the proof was pretty damn elusive.

"You've never had an orgasm. Seriously? How is that even possible?"

I froze as a deep, *definitely British* male voice sounded right beside me.

Startled, I jerked my gaze from my phone to the previously empty space next to me, only to meet a pair of sexy green eyes that were staring at me in total disbelief.

When in the hell did this British Adonis sit down?

Obviously, the seat next to me *wasn't* going to stay vacant. In fact, there was one very muscular, very attractive body filling up the space that had been vacant just a few minutes ago.

All of my senses sprang to attention as I inhaled, and caught a whiff of the most alluring, masculine scent my olfactory receptors had ever experienced.

I fought the urge to just close my eyes and wallow in the fragrance that screamed hot, unbridled, deliciously dirty sex. I had no idea how I recognized that since I'd never personally indulged in *that* kind of sexual encounter. *Ever.*

I squirmed in my seat. The guy was close. *Too close.* In fact, he was leaning sideways in my direction so he could…

I flipped my phone over so he couldn't see it, and then leaned back to avoid whatever sexy pheromones this man seemed to exude in abundance. "You're reading my texts? Who does that?"

I swallowed hard as I put a hand on his shoulder to push him over, so he wasn't encroaching on my personal space.

He moved like he suddenly realized that he was being incredibly rude.

I flipped my cell phone over again, and my fingers fired off a brief message to Kylie.

***Me:** Gotta go. Taking off. Catch you at home.*

I quickly got out of the text window, put my phone in airplane mode, and shoved it back into my purse without looking at the jerk sitting next to me.

Like this entire day hasn't been crappy enough?

Of course the guy sitting next to me is a creeper! It's the perfect end to a really bad day. Perfect. Just. Freaking. Perfect.

He straightened up in his seat completely as he finally spoke. "You looked upset, like you were going to cry, so I read your messages to find out why you looked so unhappy. I found your texts… fascinating."

I turned my eyes to him again, and took a long, hard look at my offender, now that he was back in his own space.

I was angry, but I wasn't blind. The man was gorgeous, and judging by the way his peridot-green eyes were looking back at me, I could tell he was also slightly…amused.

I had to admit that he *was* the most attractive creeper I'd ever seen.

I gawked back at him because I could. *He* was staring at *me*, so I proceeded to evaluate him thoroughly, without a single ounce of remorse for blatantly checking him out.

He was probably in his early to mid-thirties. The way he wore his dark-gray custom suit made him seem…sophisticated. He appeared to be confident to the point of arrogance. Everything about him was immaculate, from his dark, thick hair to the way his subtle cologne made me want to lean closer so I could inhale the scent until I was drunk on it.

Everything about this man screamed hard control and self-discipline.

So why in the hell had he leaned over to read my text messages?

His appearance and his behavior just weren't jiving.

The only thing that made this man softer was the teasing look in his eyes right now, and that irritatingly pleasant baritone voice.

No doubt that sexy, low baritone with that appealing British accent could make most women drop their panties.

But I wasn't most women. I was Nicole never-had-a-flin g-or-dropped-my-panties-easily-in-my-entire-life Ashworth. I wasn't a victim to my sexual desires. At least I never *had been*…

I turned my gaze toward the window, determined to ignore the way my body felt completely primed and ready to crawl up this man's body and demand he satisfy what he'd created.

Dammit! I *hated* the way he made me feel, and I had to wonder if he was secretly laughing at me.

Honestly, I hoped he didn't say another word for the entire flight. Kylie was right. There was something about his low baritone and his sexy British accent that made me want to forget he was invading my privacy. Part of me actually *wanted* him to keep encroaching on my personal space so I could absorb his tantalizing scent again.

Suddenly, my brain overrode my hormone-stimulated body. What in the hell was I thinking?

I have to get a grip. Attractive or not, he's way too pushy, and he crossed the line from inquisitive to disturbing by reading my text messages.

I finally found my voice because I couldn't let him off scot-free with my silence.

"I don't know who you think you are, but I was having a *private* conversation. Invading my space to read my messages was just... weird and intrusive."

He shrugged a set of very broad shoulders. "Not very private if you're having that discussion on a jet with several hundred other passengers, beautiful."

I opened my mouth to give the jerk a lecture, and then closed it again.

Beautiful? He called me beautiful.

I wasn't used to hearing *that*, and he'd stunned me into silence.

Was he actually hitting on me?

No! Of course he isn't. He's using me for sport. He's getting some kind of twisted amusement out of this whole situation.

I'd never been a woman who would make any guy look at me twice. Hell, they didn't even linger the first time. I *was* a blonde, but more often than not, I tamed the curly locks into submission by wearing them in a contained style away from my face. Other than my light hair, I had very few memorable physical assets.

I'd gained my freshman fifteen even before I'd started college, and then that weight gain had turned into a sophomore twenty.

My five-foot-ten height scared most men away. In heels, I was taller than most any guy in a room. *Okay, okay.* Even in flats, I matched or towered above a room full of people. I felt big, awkward, and I had to remind myself often not to slouch so I felt more comfortable.

I was wearing flats today, and I hadn't bothered with much makeup since I'd been getting ready to board a twelve-hour flight. I'd braided my crazy hair, thrown on a pair of jeans with a casual blouse, and headed toward the airport, feeling utterly gutted.

I was as far from *beautiful* as a woman could get. Especially today.

I wasn't exactly down on myself. I was intelligent. I knew that. I'd gotten a ton of scholarships to help get me through college, and then law school at Harvard.

However, I'd gotten totally screwed in the gene pool lottery, but was there really any harm in being realistic? I was frightfully tall, big-boned, and bordering between curvy and plump. In all honesty, it wasn't exactly a shocker that no guy had ever been complimentary about my physical appearance.

I was really annoyed that the quintessential Mr. Orgasm sitting next to me was using me to play some twisted game.

"Don't call me *beautiful.* Don't try to distract me from the point I was trying to make. It *was* rude and very creepy that you were reading my messages." I shifted uncomfortably in my seat as I spoke. For some unknown reason, I was looking at his startling green-eyed stare again, like his perfect features were a magnet that drew my eyes to him.

Angry with myself for drooling over a man whose only intention was to needle me, I sharply turned my head to look out the window again.

It doesn't matter if he's the most attractive man I've ever seen. Ted Bundy had been attractive and charming at times, and look how that had turned out for almost every woman who crossed his path. This guy is obviously a psycho wrapped up in a very desirable package, which makes him all the more dangerous.

He cleared his throat. "I'm not trying to…distract you. I'm just trying to figure out why a woman like you has never had an orgasm."

I huffed. "That would be none of your business."

He's definitely a creeper if he's digging for information about my nonexistent sex life.

"Maybe I *want* to make it my business. Maybe I *want* to understand," he answered in a deceptively casual tone. "And I'd love to know what happened with Lancaster International."

I kept my head turned toward the window as I snapped, "Do you always get what you want?"

"Yes. Almost always," he answered.

I ignored his arrogance as I realized that he'd asked about *Lancaster International.*

Holy shit! Had he been reading my texts for *that long?* The knowledge that he'd been surveying my conversation with Kylie since the very beginning made me livid. "Lancaster International would also be none of your business," I said in a snippy tone that I hoped would shut him up.

God, he really *had* to stop talking. I didn't want to hear another word spoken in that annoyingly hot accent.

Not that it's really getting to me. Because really, how could there be anything sexy about a man who wants to play me like I'm an idiot?

The bastard could just use the in-flight entertainment system if he wanted some kind of distraction to pass the time on this ridiculously long flight.

Gorgeous or not, this man was trouble, and I needed to just stop holding a conversation with him. *Period.*

I felt his body shift, and I peeked sideways as he stood up to take off his suit jacket to hand it to the flight attendant to hang up in a closet.

Sweet Jesus!

I hated myself for feeling breathless because he was so incredibly tall, bulky, and built like a Greek god. Broad shoulders tapered down to a very fit waist. I was almost certain that he had some mouthwatering six-pack abs underneath the expensive linen of his stark-white dress shirt.

Put your tongue back in your mouth, Nicole! He might be physically stunning, but he's also a crazy man, and not in a good way.

I forced my eyes away from the Adonis, disgusted with myself as my hands fumbled with my seat belt to get it fastened. The huge jet had started moving, but I'd been too caught up in lust to notice that immediately.

I kept my eyes glued to the window as we prepared to lift off.

Once the plane was in the air, I could pull out my laptop and try to get some work done. It would be as if the smoldering-hot man beside me didn't even exist. Once I was buried in work, I could block out *everything.*

I felt his movement as he took his seat again. I heard him fasten his seat belt as he said, "We do have twelve hours for me to get the information out of you."

His highhanded tone set my teeth on edge, and it pissed me off that he hadn't just kept that gorgeous mouth closed. "I don't like to talk when I'm traveling. I have work to do."

He let out a long, masculine sigh. "As a matter of fact, I have a rather large amount of work to accomplish myself. But I'm afraid that my laptop isn't as intriguing as you are right now. Care to satisfy my curiosity so I can concentrate on my own work?"

"No," I answered sharply. I decided to keep things simple. "I'm tired. My business in London was a failure, and I'd prefer a *silent* plane ride back home to contemplate my utter humiliation, if you don't mind."

I had no idea why I'd decided to tell him that my London venture had been a gigantic fail. Maybe I was hoping it would make him mind his own business.

"You know you want to talk about it," he said persuasively—in that damnably sexy British accent. "I'm a stranger, right? You'll never see me again. Why not vent to somebody you *don't* know, and will never see again?"

Ugh! Didn't this guy have an *Off* switch attached to those sensual lips of his? "Has it occurred to you at all that maybe I just don't like you? You were reading my text messages, for God's sake. It's nearly impossible to like or confide in a disturbed individual who does something like *that*."

I hoped *that* comment would offend him just a little, that he'd... *Just. Stop. Talking.*

Oddly, I seemed to have *absolutely no filter* when it came to my frustrating seatmate. Usually, I could ignore what was going on around me, especially when I was working, but I couldn't seem to keep my own mouth shut at the moment.

When I heard a low rumble of laughter next to me, it was pretty annoying to admit to myself that my tactic to silence him had been completely unsuccessful.

Hadn't he just said he almost always got what he wanted?

The obnoxious man obviously wasn't going to give me the peace I now craved until he was satisfied.

I sighed. He was right about one thing. Underneath my anger, I really *did* want to vent about what happened at Lancaster International because I wanted to make sense out of why a perfectly intelligent woman had managed to screw up a presentation that meant so much.

I just didn't want to do it with a guy who got a kick out of using me as a source of entertainment.

Maybe, if he was a decent guy, I *would have* spilled my guts to Mr. Orgasm. The fact that I'd never see him again made the prospect pretty damn tempting.

If only he wasn't the most annoying guy I'd ever met.

CHAPTER 3

Damian

IF THIS WOMAN had done some kind of business with Lancaster International, I was surprised that she didn't recognize me.

Even stranger, I'd never seen *her* before, and I *never* forgot a face.

Granted, I wouldn't recognize every one of my employees since Lancaster International had hundreds of thousands of them around the world. However, she'd obviously just come from my headquarters in London, and I *was* familiar with every upper-level executive who had an office there. I made it a point to know their business because it was ultimately my business, too, and I'd never seen this gorgeous blonde American woman strolling around the executive floors to meet with any of them.

I definitely would have remembered *her.*

So here I was, in a position that should have been awkward, but it really wasn't. Not for me, anyway. It was just...different. The woman had no idea who I was, nor did she seem to care about getting to know me.

To her, I was just some totally random, unpleasant guy who was sitting next to her on an airplane.

Not that I blamed her for having *that* initial impression of me. Reading her text messages had been way out of line, and obnoxiously intrusive, but she was so damn intriguing that it had been impossible to resist finding out why she'd looked so defeated when I'd taken the seat next to hers.

My actions had been so out of character for me that I was still trying to figure out *why* I'd invaded her privacy.

I'd never felt like I had to solve all the world's problems like my brother, Leo.

Normally, I never had *any* desire to carry on a conversation with a stranger when I was traveling. Like her, I preferred to keep to myself on the rare occasions I flew commercial.

I should be satisfied that no one had recognized me, and eager to pull out my laptop so I could get to work. I could knock out a significant number of things that had piled up on a long flight like this one.

I was nothing if not disciplined, to keep my focus on Lancaster International at all times.

I'd *never* been distracted from my single-minded purpose...until I'd taken my seat next to the most intriguing female I'd ever met.

This time, for some unknown reason, all I wanted to do was watch *her.*

Damned if I knew where that *beautiful* comment she'd disliked so much had come from, or why I'd said it. I wasn't exactly a slick operator. Dylan had always been the charming one. And me? I'd always been the quiet, keep-to-myself Lancaster who followed a meticulous schedule that left little or no time for anything else but my obsession to make Lancaster International stand out from any of my competition. My twin had been the one who could lavish people with outrageous flattery without making it sound insincere or cheesy.

Honestly, I hadn't meant to *flatter* the female next to me, exactly. She was, in fact, beautiful, and it was incredibly provocative that she didn't seem to know it.

I was a big man who appreciated a statuesque, curvy female like her, so I'd noticed her from the first moment I'd sat down in the seat next to her.

Generally, I could blow off a mild attraction and get back to whatever business was at hand.

I didn't have time to flirt. I'd never even had the inclination.

I didn't push anyone for any kind of conversation because I wasn't exactly a talker myself.

I used my available time wisely, which meant I focused on Lancaster International.

Normally, I didn't even *notice* who occupied the seat next to me on one of my rare commercial flights.

But things weren't exactly *normal* this time. Not with *her* sitting next to me. Something about this particular female completely fascinated me. I felt like she'd curled those elegant fingers around my balls the second I'd found my seat, and now she refused to let go.

I wanted to know more about her.

And hell, yes, I wanted to know what kind of idiots she'd dated who had been unable to satisfy her.

No orgasm? Ever? Not once?

My cock had immediately stood up for the challenge. Literally.

It didn't seem to matter that she'd just professed *not* to like me.

In fact, her attempt to dissuade me had completely backfired.

There were very few people in the world who would actually call out Damian Lancaster for *anything*, and I was discovering that I actually...liked it.

I wanted to know how she was connected to Lancaster International. It was my company, after all.

Granted, her sex life was probably none of my business, but I wasn't going to be satisfied until I knew why she'd dated so many wankers.

I cleared my throat. Since I'd never had to ask twice for much of anything, I wasn't exactly sure how to be more persuasive. "You'll like me more once you start talking. Tell me about Lancaster. What business did you have with them? But before you start, tell me your name."

My dick twitched as she folded her arms across a pair of very ample breasts.

I wasn't sure she'd answer. Her internal war between the need to talk and her desire to stay silent was evident in her expression.

I *wanted* to win. I always did.

I waited…

And waited…

"Nicole." She sounded exasperated. "My name is Nicole."

I released the air in my lungs. Maybe she *hadn't* shared her last name, but I was relieved that she'd said *something,* because I was certain she still thought I was a complete tosser for reading her texts.

"Damian." I hadn't even thought about the wisdom of using my real name, which was a little concerning since I made it a point to never do anything impulsively.

Luckily, I didn't see any obvious signs that my name meant anything to her.

"I'm not sure I really want to talk about the Lancaster disaster," she said. "And talking about my failures with a man I don't know, and who seems to love making fun of me, would be a pretty bad choice of people to discuss my disappointment with, don't you think?"

I frowned. "I never made fun of you, Nicole. If you were under any impression that I was insincere, you're wrong." What kind of asshole would do something like *that* to her? "If I didn't honestly want to listen, I wouldn't have asked."

Her voice had been reluctant, but I could tell she really *did* want to talk to someone, and I really wanted to be that confidant right now. Especially if the story had *anything* to do with Lancaster International. "Like I said, I'm a stranger. Shoot. I'm not about to judge."

I could feel the jet lifting off, but I ignored it. I was too eager to hear what Nicole had to say, and being in an aircraft was like a second home to me.

She let out a sigh of submission, and I wanted to celebrate because I knew that sound meant she *was* going to talk, whether it seemed like a wise decision to her or not.

I calculated that my best course of action was to stay silent until she spoke, which she eventually did.

"My mom passed away from cancer a year ago. Her company...my company now...was her baby. She built Ashworth Crisis Management from the ground up, and she was really, really good at it. I came to London to pitch our services to Lancaster International. I had no idea that the owner is some kind of man-whore, and that I'd only find that out a couple of minutes before my presentation. Because I wasn't prepared for some real-time scandal to happen, I completely blew it. I froze instead of changing things up to address the imminent problem they were facing."

I didn't speak. I waited for her to go on. I sensed that she needed to keep venting, and I was a very willing audience.

"I bombed my presentation in front of the Lancaster executives. I just...choked. I'm a planner. I'm not good at just...winging things. I was all over the place, and I never got to really tell them what we could do for them in their current situation."

She looked so forlorn that it made my damn chest ache. I could relate to what had happened to her. I wasn't exactly Mr. Spontaneous. I was a meticulous planner, too. "Something came up suddenly that you weren't prepared to handle at that meeting, Nicole. It's not your fault."

She shook her head. "I doubt it's *ever* going to come naturally to *me.* I went to school to become a corporate attorney, and I was a damn good one. Sure, I had to talk to executives, but it was normally a few at a time. And I knew what I was doing. Trying to step into my mother's shoes is just so...difficult."

God, could I relate to *that.* "Believe it or not, I get that, too. I stepped into my father's shoes five years ago when he died unexpectedly from a heart attack. They were big shoes to fill, and I didn't feel like I was ready. It's going to take some time for you to feel comfortable. Why did you leave corporate law?"

Nicole was obviously intelligent and highly educated. She'd just stepped into a world she knew nothing about after her mother's death. I had to respect the balls it took to take that leap. Dylan and I had had the benefit of being groomed to step into my father's shoes one day.

I had to admire this woman's strength and determination. She'd dropped everything in a world where she was comfortable to enter an entirely different universe. My question would be...*was she happy where she was right now?*

She started to speak before I could ask. "I suppose I just didn't want to let go of ACM because it was so successful, and I was there to see her fight for that success. I wanted to keep it going because she...couldn't. I couldn't sell something that was that important to her."

Nicole had wanted to keep some part of her mother alive, even after her parent was gone. I understood that. "Did she ask you to do it?"

She shook her head slowly. "No. She knew I was happy as a corporate attorney. My mother wasn't like that. All she ever wanted was for me to be happy. She expected me to sell, but I couldn't do it. So I moved from New York back to California permanently after she died to see if I could make a go at ACM."

I really fucking hated the crushed look on her face. I wanted to say the right words to make it go away, but I wasn't Dylan. The right words weren't always there for me, and I wasn't really good at blowing sunshine up anyone's ass, but in Nicole's case, I wanted to try. "It's just one botched presentation. You'll get another chance."

What I definitely *couldn't* tell Nicole was that I *should* have been at her presentation. The meeting had been on my schedule. I'd had to bail out of that commitment because I'd wanted to drive to Surrey to see Mum after I'd seen the tabloids with Dylan's bare-naked ass exposed to the entire country.

Nicole's voice sounded desperate as she told me, "You don't understand, Damian. It wasn't about getting *another deal.* It was about accomplishing something my mom always wanted. I got the opportunity that she didn't, and I fucked it up."

Ahhh...so it wasn't about the money for her at all. It wasn't financial; it was personal.

I hated the fact that I hadn't been at that meeting, and she'd left Lancaster International headquarters feeling like she'd failed.

For some strange reason, I wanted to reach out my hand and turn her face to me so I could see her expression, but I didn't.

Number one...I wasn't sure that seeing an injured look in her gorgeous blue eyes wouldn't be akin to a swift kick in the gut for me.

And number two...I didn't want to invade her space again. Okay, maybe I *did* want to invade her space, but I didn't want her to feel uncomfortable. I'd probably already done enough to make her wary, and the last thing I wanted to do was shut her down for the rest of the flight.

I wanted her to keep talking to me, which meant I needed to stop doing impulsive shit that was so contrary to my normal personality.

Hell, just wanting somebody to talk to me was highly abnormal.

What in the fuck can I do to make her understand that what happened at Lancaster isn't the end of the world?

Maybe she just needed some kind of…do-over. "Then tell *me* right now, Nicole. Tell me what you could have done for Lancaster. What would you say if you got the chance to do that meeting all over again?"

She didn't hesitate to answer. "I'd tell them that what the CEO is doing will probably catch up with them if they don't try to fix this right now, and put a kibosh on anything else similar happening in the future. I'd say that they'll eventually see a decrease in their business if it continues because people don't always buy with their wallets. Sometimes, they buy with their instincts and their heart. At some point, if the owner of the corporation doesn't stop the bullshit, Lancaster is going to become a company with an 'ick factor.' Some people will be turned off, and buy the product right next to *their product*, one that *doesn't* sport the Lancaster name."

I had no desire to defend my brother, but I did feel the need to champion Lancaster International. "What if they don't see a decrease in sales trends? It's the twenty-first century, for God's sake. Not everyone is a prude."

Nicole turned toward me and lifted a knowing brow. "They haven't seen the social media backlash yet. Maybe it will be brief and die out quickly, but there is going to be plenty of criticism. I'm sure you know that people have called to boycott companies on social media for less. The guy isn't just a womanizer, or a serial dater of lots of women. Nobody really cares much about that. But showing up naked on the front page of a well-read newspaper with a bunch of nude women *can* smack of general disrespect and disdain for the female gender. People will assume he bought those women, and that he was able to use them because they needed to support themselves, and he has endless funds."

I gritted my teeth, knowing there wasn't a damn thing I could say in my brother's defense. More than likely, he *had* rewarded those women handsomely, even though they'd been with him willingly.

She was right, of course. A lot could be made of a salacious picture and a sensational, lewd story. "Then tell me what *you'd* do to prevent all that from happening," I requested grimly.

She snorted. "I'd kidnap the CEO and ship him to someplace in Siberia for a decade or two so nothing else happens."

Agreed! I would have been happy to buy Dylan a one-way ticket, but knowing my brother, he'd find a way back to England.

She hesitated before she continued. "Honestly, I'd try to get in front of the whole thing. Find the man-whore a girlfriend who doesn't have any skeletons in her closet, and book some positive publicity to let the public know that it was a one-time drunken incident. When I was researching, I did see something about Mr. Lancaster being single. I guess I just assumed that he was a widower. But if the old guy is healthy enough to get it up for an orgy, he can certainly get himself a nice girlfriend. He'd have to take responsibility for doing some skanky things, and then show the public that he's changed."

I raised my eyebrows. Was she under the impression that I was an...old man? "How old do you think he is?"

I couldn't help myself. I *had* to ask. Obviously, she'd never managed to dig up a picture or she wouldn't be talking to me right now.

It hadn't been cheap to get experts to remove all that info from the net, but it had been worth it. Perhaps if she'd dug a little deeper into the family, she might have found a photo of me, but there wasn't a whole lot there to find.

Nicole shrugged. "I don't know. I've never seen pictures or articles about him. Initially, my presentation had nothing to do with the family. It was about improving Lancaster's image overall as a company, and handling anything that came up in the future that might make them seem negligent to the general population. I didn't know any of the *family* was even prone to bad publicity until I heard about this recent orgy thing. Doing damage control on a sleezy billionaire wasn't even on my radar."

"He's actually not *that* old." I hated the defensiveness I heard in my voice. "I've seen his pictures. Thirties, maybe." I had to keep my comments vague. I was treading into dangerous territory. But I was *British*, so it had to make sense to her that I knew more about British billionaires than she did.

"That young?" She sounded completely caught off-guard. "Then they really need a fixer. They definitely can't blow off the incident as some kind of dementia. Look, the guy is single, and I really don't care what he does, but some people *will* care. Overall, Lancaster has always had a great reputation. I just wanted to be the PR company that was able to keep it that way. I wasn't ready for the big sex scandal."

"It was a stupid thing to do," I grumbled, knowing I had to abandon the discussion about my family before I got myself in trouble.

She nodded her head slowly. "It was, but I've learned not to judge. I don't know the circumstances. It could have been some kind of trap, and the guy does have a right to his kinks. But maybe he should have checked the lock on the door. When you're at the helm of one of the most powerful companies in the world, private things need to stay private."

Of course, what she just said made me wonder if the woman had her own kinks, and exactly what *those* might be.

I'm a red-blooded male who hasn't gotten any for a while, so don't judge me about my sexual curiosity.

I decided it was probably best *not* to ask her about her sexual fantasies at the moment. "There was no way you could have known what would happen while you were there. And I highly doubt that you really bombed that presentation. I'd say that you were presenting the wrong thing at the wrong time—through no real fault of your own."

I knew *that much* was true. The entire corporate office had been bombarded by the media even before I'd left to get to Surrey.

My employees had been trying to put out fires, and Nicole had been unprepared to be a firefighter.

"That's possible, I suppose." Her tone didn't sound like she was quite convinced.

"Feel better now?" I asked.

She put her feet up in the recliner and leaned her head back. "Not really. But thanks for trying."

I ignored her denial. She *sounded* better, and that worked for me.

"Should we talk about your other little problem?"

She closed her eyes. "What problem?"

"Is it really true that you've never had an orgasm?"

Her eyes popped back open. "I think I need a drink."

I grinned as I pushed the call button to get us some cocktails.

CHAPTER 4

Nicole

IT TOOK FOUR rounds of alcohol and a belly full of airplane food before I'd even entertained the idea of answering Damian's questions about my sex life.

However, by the time I *emptied* cocktail glass number four, I had absolutely no inhibitions about telling him anything.

I handed my empty glass to the flight attendant and leaned back in my comfortable seat, thinking about everything Damian had shared with me over the last few hours.

Unlike most gorgeous men, Damian didn't seem to *want* to talk about himself. *At all.*

I felt like he'd pried every detail of my life from me, but he never said a whole lot about himself. His answers to *my* questions about *him* were brief, and he hadn't volunteered anything more than what I'd asked.

If he thought he could just give me a *yes*-or-*no* answer, that's exactly what I'd gotten, but one-word answers hadn't worked every single time.

I did find out that he'd grown up in Surrey, and had taken over an already successful family business after his dad's death five years ago.

His mother was originally from Spain, but she'd been in England since she'd married Damian's father decades ago, who'd been an Englishman. She still lived in their family home in Surrey.

He'd attended Cambridge for college.

He was well traveled, a fact I'd picked up myself after I'd asked him where he'd been in the world. His answer to that particular inquiry was probably the longest answer I'd gotten.

He definitely got around.

I'd gotten little tidbits of his life during our conversation, but I *still* didn't feel like I knew that much about *him.*

Me? Well, I'd pretty much spilled my guts right after my second cocktail. If he asked a question, I'd answered it with a lot more information than I really needed to tell a virtual stranger.

That's what I get for having more than one drink.

I got pretty damn chatty after a couple of cocktails.

After four of them? I was pretty much in an ask-me-anything-and-I'll-tell-you mood. *Anything at all.*

"Would you like another one?" the smiling brunette who had taken my cocktail glass queried politely.

I shook my head, smiling back at her before she retreated. If I didn't stop, Damian would probably know my whole life story from birth to the present.

I'd noticed that he had downed a single beer before he'd switched to some kind of tea.

I'd probably *never* understand the obsession that British people had with their tea.

I turned my head to look at him, and he raised his brows as he lowered his teacup. "So let's get back to the subject I originally asked you about," he suggested.

"What subject would that be?" I tried to act like I had *no idea* what he was asking.

"Is it true that you've never had an orgasm?" His question was firm, but low enough that not everyone in business class could hear him.

Really, I wasn't sure how many of our fellow passengers were still awake. The lights had been dimmed after dinner, and it looked like most people had lowered their seats flat to sleep.

He was so persistent when he wanted to know something, and in my... ummm...alcohol-induced relaxed state, I wondered if it was *really* that big of a deal to tell him what he wanted to know.

Like he said, I'd never see him again.

I took a deep breath. "It's true. I haven't. End of discussion."

Okay, so maybe I *wasn't* all that comfortable admitting that my sex life sucked to a guy like Damian. I doubted he'd be able to empathize. Something told me that Mr. Orgasm had never left a woman unsatisfied.

"Wait a minute. You can't just leave it like that. You have to tell me *why*," he insisted.

I let out a long sigh. "I'm not a virgin, if that's what you're asking. I've had two serious, long-term relationships, and it just didn't happen for me. Maybe some women just aren't...orgasmic."

"Or *maybe* the men you were seeing were absolute morons," he grumbled.

Damian sounded so indignant that my lips curved up in a smile. "So what if I've never had an orgasm with a guy? Is it really *that* big of a deal?"

His voice got louder and a little more annoyed. "Hell, yes, it's a big deal. If you'd ever *had* an orgasm during fantastic sex, you'd know how big of a deal it really is. Why even bother to have sex if your partner can't get to the finish line?"

I wanted to tell him that my male partners had never had an issue getting to *their* finish line, but we were sitting on a plane full of passengers, and I didn't really want them to hear us discussing my sex life.

I might be pretty tipsy, but obviously not to the point where embarrassment wasn't a possibility.

"It's not that important to me, Damian. Keep your voice down."

"Sorry," he rumbled apologetically. "But I think you should insist on more."

I rolled my eyes at him. "Great. Now I'm sitting next to Dr. Phil." I was starting to get a little offended, but Damian was probably right. I *hadn't* ever demanded much from either of my previous long-term love interests.

I'd met my first boyfriend in college, and we'd both put more effort into our studies than our relationship, not to mention the fact that we'd both been pretty young and inexperienced.

The second one had come along just when I'd been starting my previous job in corporate law. We'd worked in the same company. He'd been climbing the ladder to get to an executive position, and I'd been career-focused, too, so neither of us had really given our relationship our best efforts.

We'd finally broken it off when I moved to California to take over ACM. We'd probably both known that there was really nothing there anymore, but we'd gotten comfortable after several years together, kind of like roommates who were friends with benefits.

When we were both home…

And not too exhausted…

Okay. Yeah. Well. Maybe we *hadn't* reaped the benefits *all that often.*

Still, we'd seen no reason to break it off until I'd decided I was moving to the other side of the country.

"Hey. I didn't mean to upset you, Nicole." Damian sounded *almost* contrite. "You're absolutely right. It's not my place to give you advice. I just think you should demand something...better."

I did a major eyeroll. *Sheesh!* He'd done so well with his first few sentences. And then...he'd just *had* to go there with his personal opinion during the last one. *Again.*

I lifted a brow as I asked him, "Why do I think you have a very hard time *not* giving your opinion?" I wasn't really angry with Damian. In fact, it was kind of sweet that he was trying to be my champion.

Damian frowned at me. "Honestly, I usually don't give *anyone* my personal opinion on *anything*. I'm the boss at my company. I give orders, not opinions."

I turned my head to look at him. I recognized a hint of a hardcore authoritarian in his tone that I hadn't heard before.

For some reason, I bought the fact that the Damian I'd been talking with for the last three or four hours wasn't the face he *usually* showed to the world.

Maybe it was intuition...

Or the seemingly genuine bewilderment I saw in his beautiful green eyes right now.

Whatever it was, his chagrin was real.

I reached out a hand, but I couldn't quite touch him, so I just kept it on the armrest between us. "Hey. Are you okay, Damian? Yeah, maybe I didn't *ask* for your opinions, but now I'm kind of glad you made me think. You're right about the fact that the men in my life never put much effort into a relationship. But then, neither did I. It worked both ways."

His eyes grew clearer as he asked gruffly, "Why were you even together?"

I shrugged. "I guess they were my okay-for-now boyfriends, just like I was their okay-for-now girlfriend. Haven't you ever had someone like that? Somebody you don't mind being with, even if they don't set your body on fire or anything."

He quirked an eyebrow, the amusement back in his eyes again. "Yeah. I call them my mates, and I don't sleep with any of them."

I made a face at him. "I meant haven't you had that kind of relationship with a female."

"No," he answered. "It seems rather pointless. I think I prefer hooking up with a woman I like for amazing sex, and then going home when the evening is over. No strings attached."

Really? "So all you want is good sex from a woman?"

He hesitated before he answered. "I'd prefer incredible sex, if you don't mind. And it's just never gone any further than that. Most of the women I've dated aren't looking for anything more intense. So it's always worked out well for me."

I was ready to call bullshit on his statement about nothing ever "going further" for him. That it had just never happened.

Somehow, I knew that he sought out women who wouldn't ask for more. It had never gone further because he designed it that way.

What I didn't know was *why* he did it.

"That sounds...pretty cold," I observed aloud.

"Is it really any worse than being an okay-for-now girlfriend?"

I thought about his question before I replied. "Probably not."

"At least I've never left a woman unsatisfied."

I shot him a dubious look. "How do you *know* that? Women fake it all the time."

He glared back at me. "I assure you that *no woman* has ever had to fake it with *me*."

Did he *not* know that every guy in the entire world thought that, too? I was sorely tempted to do the Meg-Ryan-I'm-faking-an-orgasm scene from the movie *When Harry Met Sally*, but I knew nobody could ever fake it as well as Meg did.

I certainly couldn't.

I never even *tried* to fake it, and my boyfriends had never really cared.

Done with the entire conversation, I reached for my carry-on bag and sifted through the contents for a pair of sweatpants and a T-shirt. "I need to change. I want to try to get some sleep."

Damian was reclined, so there wasn't enough space in the pod for me to avoid swinging a leg over his to get to the aisle.

It shouldn't have been a difficult task.

It wasn't like I had to *crawl* over him.

It was just his lower legs, for God's sake.

It was just a little...*hop*!

Unfortunately, the small leap was a whole lot harder than I anticipated after all of the cocktails I'd swilled down over the last few hours.

I got dizzy from getting up too fast, and then tried to catch myself by grasping Damian's seat behind me after I'd jumped over his long, stretched-out legs.

I failed to catch myself, and I panicked for a moment as I started to fall backward.

Strong arms wrapped solidly around me, pulling my upper body against a very solid chest as my ass landed very inelegantly in Damian's lap.

CHAPTER 5

Damian

I KNEW I WAS completely fucked from the second her statuesque body collided with mine, and I smelled a faint, mouthwatering scent of…strawberries.

Christ! When in the hell had *fruit* become an aphrodisiac? Yeah, I liked strawberries, but they'd never exactly gotten my dick hard.

I'd been aware that Nicole was tipsy, but she'd gone into motion so fast that I hadn't had a chance to move my legs so she could be more careful once she got to her feet.

Transatlantic Airlines prided themselves on their extra-wide, reclining, lie-flat seats in business class, and I was just figuring out how very convenient they were as I steadied Nicole's curvy figure in my lap.

I'd wrapped my arms tightly around her as she'd fallen to keep her upper body from flopping over the armrest between us, which allowed her beautiful ass to plop directly into my lap. Her lower legs dangled naturally over my armrest next to the aisle.

I closed my eyes and stifled a tormented groan as the feel and the tantalizing scent of Nicole wafted over my senses. I'd *wanted* to know what she'd feel like in my arms, and now, I knew.

I guess I'd never known that a guy could feel ecstasy and torture at the same time.

My cock had responded immediately by pushing eagerly against her shapely ass.

Jesus!

She smelled so damn sexy.

She felt like she was made to be plastered against me just like this.

Every primal male instinct I had said that this woman was... mine. That she and I should always be just like this...

Wait a minute! That's totally ridiculous. I hardly know her.

I shook my head slightly, knowing my brain wasn't going to win the battle between my body and my mind.

Not now.

Not with her.

Not when this gorgeous female was as close to me as she could get with our clothes on.

"Oh, God. I'm so sorry," Nicole muttered as she started wriggling to get up.

"Don't!" I insisted. "Don't. Move."

The more she squirmed, the more my cock responded to that motion. Maybe I was a masochist, and I liked being tortured, but I knew I hadn't had my fill of anguish just yet.

"Damian, I have to get up," she said firmly. "I'm sorry. I guess I got dizzy from the cocktails. I don't usually have more than one."

Fuck! I loved the breathlessness of her voice, a sound that told me that she wasn't totally immune to the insane sexual attraction between us.

"You're fine right where you are," I argued. "Are you okay?"

"I'm not hurt," she answered softly. "But I feel ridiculous."

Strangely, it bothered me that she felt uncomfortable. "It's not like anybody noticed except me, Nicole. And I'm sure as hell not complaining." The business section was dark. Most of the passengers were sleeping, or resting with earbuds in as they watched their small television with their overhead lights off.

The flight attendants were unobtrusive and quiet somewhere in the galleys to give passengers their sleep time.

Nicole's arm crept around my shoulders to steady herself as she said, "I'm heavy, Damian. I need to get up."

Heavy? She felt incredible to me. "You're perfect, Nicole." My voice was far hoarser than I'd like.

"You're insane," she accused.

"I think you're making me that way." I blamed *her*, only *half* joking. I'd never experienced this kind of chemistry with anyone, so it was, in fact, fifty percent her fault, right?

I had no idea *why* I was reacting to Nicole this way, and quite honestly, I wasn't sure I liked it. I wasn't an insta-lust kind of guy.

Before she'd fallen into my lap, I'd been trying to figure out why the real Damian Lancaster had fled my body, only to be replaced by a guy who couldn't control his reaction to some random female sitting next to him on a plane.

Bloody hell! I'd certainly never felt any kind of instant desperation to shag *any* female. I planned my liaisons carefully, and never with a woman I *didn't* know.

Normally, I'd be on my laptop right after we'd gotten airborne. It didn't usually matter if my seatmate was male or female, young or old, attractive or unattractive. I simply...didn't notice.

This particular flight had been different since the second I'd laid eyes on Nicole. I hadn't been myself since I'd given in to some strange compulsion to look at her texts.

For fuck's sake, I'd actually read those messages like they were the most fascinating reading material I could find. And then, to make things even worse, I'd actually tried to make her feel better because she'd looked so damn disheartened.

Oh, and let's not even mention the fact that I'd cajoled her into telling me about her sex life.

I released a heavy breath as I tried to figure out what in the hell was so different about Nicole.

I was attracted to the female I was holding in a way I'd never experienced before, and honestly, wasn't comfortable with, either.

It was something instinctive.

Like a hard kick to the gut that I couldn't ignore.

My *brain* hadn't functioned properly since I'd gotten on the flight.

And my *cock* was in overdrive.

Shit! I wasn't a guy who let his cock rule his goddamn brain!

"I can't just sit here for the entire flight," Nicole whispered loudly next to my ear.

She sounded nervous, but not in a *frightened* sort of way. "A few more minutes," I persuaded as I pressed my face against her hair like a man fucking desperate for the scent of a woman. But I wasn't frantic to breathe in *any female. Just. Her.* "You smell so damn good, Nicole."

She snorted lightly. "I'm not wearing anything. It's probably my shampoo or body wash. I showered right before I came to the airport, thank God. I had no idea I'd get drunk and fall into the lap of the attractive man right next to me."

I wrapped my hand around the fat braid of her hair, and gently turned her face toward me. "Are you attracted to me, Nicole?"

I already knew the answer to my question. There was no possible way I was in crazy-town alone. As our eyes met, I could feel the red-hot chemistry flowing between the two of us, but for some reason, I wanted to *hear* her admit that she felt the same damn indescribable pull toward me that I was experiencing with her.

She nodded slowly. We were so close I could see her swallow hard before she answered. "Yes. How could I not be? You're the entire package, Damian. Tall, dark, and handsome. With a sexy British accent, too. Okay, maybe you're a little arrogant, but as long as you're not doing that really bossy thing you do, even your ego is kind of hot."

I felt a smile tug at my lips as I insisted, "I don't do a bossy thing."

Her snort was louder this time. "You're seriously bossy sometimes."

I had no doubt that she was probably right. I was used to being the boss. The fact that she didn't seem the least bit daunted made the woman *even more* attractive.

I was Damian Lancaster, and all I heard was *"yes, sir"* from all of my employees as they scrambled to do what I needed done, every single day.

It was probably a little twisted that I actually liked the fact that Nicole had no idea who I was, or that my life was far from normal. I knew her attraction to *me* was real. It had nothing to do with the obscene amount of money or power I had.

I toyed with a lock of her blonde hair that had escaped from her braid. "I'm just a guy with all of the regular faults."

I wasn't sure if I was trying to convince *her* that I wasn't different, or *myself.*

She smiled. "Just a guy who can get any woman to drop her panties because he's way too attractive to ignore, and very charming when he wants to be?"

I shook my head. "I've never been charming, Nicole. You probably just think I'm charming because you're more than just a little pissed."

She wrinkled her brow. "I'm not pissed at you."

I chuckled. "Not pissed as in…angry. Pissed as in…drunk."

I'd forgotten that she wasn't exactly a world traveler, so she might not recognize some British-isms.

She nodded. "Shitfaced. Definitely."

I grinned. "I think I like 'pissed' better."

She tilted her head adorably. "I think I like that word better, too. So I guess I am...pissed."

I had to wonder just how open she would have been if she was completely sober right now. Nicole was at the perfect point of drunkenness, when her inhibitions were low and she wasn't quite steady on her feet, but she wasn't completely out of touch, either.

I stroked the flawless skin of her cheek, mesmerized by how incredibly soft she was...everywhere. "You're so damn beautiful."

She slapped my shoulder. "See. I was right. You're *totally* charming. I'm not beautiful. My mother was beautiful, though. I always wished I looked more like her. She was petite, and never carried an extra pound—"

I put a finger to her lips to stop her from saying anything else negative about herself. "You're fucking perfect."

I knew she wasn't fishing for compliments. She really thought she was highly flawed, and I hated that. What kind of tossers had she dated who had made her feel like she was anything less than wholly desirable? Some primitive instinct made me want to punch every single one of them for not appreciating Nicole.

She made a face at me. "No need for flattery. I decided a long time ago that I'd rather be smart than hot."

I ran a thumb over her luscious mouth, tracing her lips. "Lucky for you then that you're both of those things."

She opened her mouth to voice what I already knew would be a denial.

Since I didn't want to hear it, I knew I was about to do what any red-blooded man would do with a smoking-hot blonde sitting in his lap.

I put my hand firmly behind her head and did exactly what I'd wanted to do since the first moment I'd laid eyes on this woman.

I swooped in and captured her mouth so she couldn't say anything at all.

CHAPTER 6

Nicole

IT WASN'T LIKE I'd never been kissed before. I had. Plenty of times. I'd had boyfriends, and dates that had never turned into anything more than a goodnight kiss.

Kisses could be pleasant.

Kisses could feel good.

Kisses could make a woman feel wanted.

But holy hell, kisses had *never* felt like an all-consuming claiming of my body and soul.

Not until…now.

Not until…him.

Not until…this.

Not until…Damian.

Yeah, an embrace could *lead to* a sexual act.

But with Damian, his kiss *wasn't* a subtle prelude.

It was raw, hungry, and sexy as hell. It was a main event.

He ravished my mouth like it was something he had to do or die.

I was so stunned that it took me a moment to react, but when I did, I had no choice but to give back exactly what he was giving.

His hungry mouth was way too compelling to do anything else.

I released a small moan of surrender against his lips, closed my eyes, and allowed myself to fall into the molten embrace. It was so irresistible, so urgent, that I couldn't possibly stop it.

I let my tongue duel with his, absorbing the taste of Damian like he was a highly decadent dessert.

When he pulled back a little to nibble on my bottom lip, I whimpered from the loss of all of that male passion, craving it like a drug until he stopped teasing and covered my mouth again.

I speared my hands into his hair, luxuriating in the feel of the coarse, short strands sifting between my fingers.

Maybe I was a little…pissed. But I was downright drunk with the scent, taste, and feel of this man, who was completely devouring me like I was the tastiest thing he'd ever sampled.

Heat flowed between my thighs as he stroked one of his large hands up and down my spine, and I was stunned by my reaction. I wanted him so much that I wanted to crawl inside him, be surrounded by his essence, and never come out again.

My instincts felt like they were being guided by some kind of feral desire I never knew existed.

It was as frightening as it was exhilarating.

I didn't know what in the hell was happening to me, but the sensations he was wringing from my body were so exquisite that I didn't want them to end.

He pulled away abruptly, and I squeaked from the loss. "Damian." I said his name, breathless and panting as I leaned back to look at his face.

"For fuck's sake, don't move." His voice was a husky demand.

The light was dim, but I was so close that I could see his face.

His eyes were a deep, swirling green, a color way different from the light peridot they'd been earlier.

Damian was breathing just as heavily as I was, and his tormented expression made my heart ache.

"Are you okay?" I asked softly, my pulse still racing.

He pinned me with his gaze. "Give me a minute. It's not like I can get you naked and shag you right here in this seat."

My eyes grew wider. I knew what it meant to shag someone. Was that really what he wanted to do? Did Damian really want to fuck me right here, right now? "You want to do that?" I asked hesitantly.

"Do you really have to ask that question?" he queried in a dangerous tone.

I took a deep breath that came out in a shaky exhalation.

No. I probably *didn't* need to hear him confirm that. Not after a kiss that had shaken me to my core.

"Never mind," I said hastily.

Maybe it was just really hard for me to understand how a man like Damian could kiss me like that, like he really...wanted me.

Like he needed me, even.

What the hell?

Granted, my head was a little fuzzy from too many cocktails, but I knew no guy had ever consumed me with a single kiss. In fact, no man had ever moved me that way with *any* kind of touch, sexual or not, like Damian had just done.

When had anybody ever wanted me that much?

Umm...the answer to that would be...never. Ever.

I looked around the business section. All of the other pods were dark, or the occupants busy with their own distractions.

I'm sitting here, shaken and destroyed, and not one single person in the area even noticed that Damian was rocking my entire world.

"Hell, I'm sorry, Nicole," Damian said gutturally. "I'm acting like a tosser."

I shot him a small smile. "I take it a *tosser* is a bad thing?"

"An asshole in American terms," he informed me. "A huge asshole."

There was no way for Damian to know that I was actually kind of flattered that he wanted to rip off my clothes and fuck me.

I shrugged. "It's okay. I guess it's just strange. Nobody has ever really wanted me that much."

Okay, maybe that sounded pathetic, but my mouth hadn't really had a filter for the last few hours. I'd probably said quite a few things I wouldn't normally say to a near stranger.

But was Damian still a stranger, though? After we'd had our tongues down each other's throats and all?

"I'm fairly certain you can feel the proof of my attraction against your ass," he said dryly.

I nodded. He'd been hard since the moment I'd landed in his lap, but I'd chalked that up to surprise or an involuntary reaction to *any* woman landing on top of a man.

He rubbed a hand over his face, and responded like he'd read my mind. "I want *you*, Nicole. I'm not some randy adolescent who can't control my dick."

I nodded again. "I think I'm starting to get that now."

And it was kind of scary.

Men who looked like Damian generally were not attracted to a woman like me.

In my thirty-two years of existence, no one, not even an average guy, had looked at me the way Damian did.

"I was frustrated," he admitted. "And I normally don't get frustrated."

His voice sounded like he'd found some leashed control, and I wasn't certain if I was sad or relieved about that. "I really need to get up now," I told him.

I had to be squashing the crap out of him, and I really, really needed to pee. All of those cocktails had found their way to my bladder, and it was getting *very* uncomfortable.

He looked resigned. "I'm not going to apologize for kissing you. Just for the way I acted afterward."

"I really don't want you to be sorry for something that felt that nice."

He lifted a brow. "Nice? That's it? It was just…nice?"

He looked so disgruntled that I had to hold back my laughter. Really, the man *was* arrogant. "Okay, so maybe it was a little more than nice," I considered.

He rested his forehead against mine. "I'm totally deflated."

I laughed because I couldn't hold it back this time. "What do you *want* me to say about it?"

He kissed my forehead. "Something a little more complimentary than just…*nice*. That word practically made my balls shrivel up and fall off."

I squirmed just a little. "Nope. They didn't. They're definitely still there."

He cupped my face and looked at me with a fiery gaze that sent a shiver of need down my spine. "Shall we try again so you can look for a better word?"

"No!" I squeaked. "Not that it wasn't lovely, but I don't think that's a good idea."

"Lovely?" he said in a disgusted tone. "Is that supposed to be a step up from *nice*? Because I have to tell you, sweetheart, it really isn't an improvement. I think we should try again."

My heart skipped a beat just from hearing a term of endearment aimed at me escape from those sexy lips of his. It sounded so natural. So unpracticed. I wasn't sure if he'd even noticed that he'd said it.

It was probably pitiful that I'd nearly melted into a puddle at his feet when he'd uttered it. "Once was more than enough," I said firmly.

No matter how much I wanted him to kiss me, I did *not* want to feel like I was about to spontaneously combust again on a crowded airplane, whether most of the passengers were sleeping or not.

I'd gotten so lost in Damian, to the point where I'd wanted to straddle the gorgeous man and ride him into oblivion. And I didn't *ride* anyone. It was *way* too awkward for a bigger woman like me.

He moved closer, his lips barely an inch from mine. "Are you certain?"

My body started to tremble as his husky baritone sent my female hormones into overdrive.

He was so close I could almost taste him, and I wanted Damian so badly that I nearly threw caution to the wind and breached the tiny distance between his mouth and mine.

"I'm sure," I told him, my tone desperate.

He kissed me softly, an embrace so brief that I barely felt it, and then leaned back with a masculine sigh. "You're right. This isn't the time or the place."

My heart sank with disappointment, even though I'd been the one to refuse. "I have to get up, Damian," I insisted.

"You will, just as soon as you admit that our attraction goes both ways."

"So I can feed your arrogance?" I was *sort of* joking, but there was a part of me that really didn't want to be just a woman he'd kissed on a long-haul flight. A female who had been mesmerized with a single kiss, and then *told him* how incredible that encounter had been.

He searched my face as he answered, "No. I just want to know that I wasn't the only one who just experienced the hottest kiss I've ever had in my entire life."

And...I melted. I just gave up, gave in. His eyes were so sincere that I instinctively knew that it wasn't his arrogance talking right now.

In fact, I almost sensed that he was…insecure? Was it possible for a male like Damian to be vulnerable to *any kind* of self-doubt?

I blurted out the words I knew he wanted to hear. "Okay, here's the truth. It was the most amazing kiss I've ever had, too. Every kiss I have for the rest of my life will probably be compared to the one we just shared, and come up wanting. You completely rocked my world, Damian." I hesitated before I asked, "Happy now?"

He grinned at me. "Completely ecstatic," he drawled.

"I have to pee really bad, so I have to get up now," I informed him.

"Right," he said as he put a hand under my ass and pushed until I moved toward the armrest next to the aisle. "Up you go."

My toes touched the ground as I finally became perched on the armrest.

His arm went supportively around my waist. "Go slow," he instructed.

I stood up and put a hand on the back of his recliner. "I'm good," I told him.

Once my head stopped spinning, I cautiously bent to pick up the change of clothes that had landed next to his seat when I'd fallen.

Damian kept a hand near my waist, probably just in case I decided to swan dive into his lap again.

I turned toward the rear of the plane. The restroom wasn't far away, and I was feeling more confident that I could get there safely, when Damian spoke.

"Need help?"

"Nope. I'm good. No more falling into the laps of gorgeous men." If I was still shaky, it wasn't from the alcohol.

It was *that damn kiss.*

He frowned as he looked up at me. "No falling into *any other* men's laps," he grumbled, like the thought of me kissing another guy was completely unacceptable to him.

He almost sounded…jealous, but I quickly removed that possibility from my mind. I'd never inspired any kind of protectiveness or possessiveness from any man.

"Seriously. I'm okay," I assured him as I moved toward the bathroom.

It was a short walk, but I swore that I could feel Damian watching me until I slipped inside the restroom door and locked it behind me.

CHAPTER 7

Damian

"I HOPE YOU HAVE a pleasant visit to the US," Nicole muttered as she was drinking her coffee near the end of the flight.

She'd put her seat down flat after she'd changed clothes earlier, and had fallen asleep almost immediately.

I'd envied the fact that she could pass out so easily, even though I knew it probably had a lot to do with the amount of alcohol she'd consumed.

Me? *Dammit!* I hadn't slept for a single moment. My mind had been racing to figure out exactly *how* I could dig myself out of the dark hole I'd landed myself in.

I *had* gotten my laptop out after Nicole had gone to sleep, but I'd done absolutely nothing productive, which was a rarity for me. If my computer was out and turned on, I was working, churning through things that needed my approval or input.

I wasn't used to not being productive, and I sure as hell wasn't accustomed to a woman getting me so damn distracted that my priority wasn't Lancaster International.

But there it was…the first time I'd ever put my thoughts about a woman over my business interests.

I'd pondered my dilemma for hours, and I still hadn't come up with a solution.

Problem was, I could hardly tell Nicole that I was Damian Lancaster now. She'd probably hate me for lying to her, and for initiating that whole tell-me-what-you-would-have-said-if-you-had-the-opportunity-to-do-the-presentation-again discussion.

I'd been so eager to hear her talk that I hadn't taken a moment to think about the fact that I might want to see her again. I hadn't thought about the future, but I'd known that she would have never said a word to me if she'd known my true identity.

Can I blame her for that, really? In the public eye, I'm a hedonistic bastard who apparently loves gigantic orgies.

I *couldn't* tell her the truth, even if I wanted to spill it. I couldn't possibly out Dylan, and I'd have to if I ever wanted Nicole to speak to me again.

A few days ago, I couldn't have cared less about what the public thought of me.

Now, I cared. I cared a lot. All because of the woman sitting beside me who had been treating me like a total stranger from the minute she'd woken up a quarter of an hour ago.

I hope you have a pleasant visit to the US…?

What was *that* statement all about?

I was fairly certain it was a brush-off, but I couldn't say for sure since nobody had ever brushed me off before.

Maybe Nicole was embarrassed about our discussions and *that damn kiss*, now that she was sober.

"I'm hoping it will be," I answered vaguely, stalling for time to think as I made myself a cup of tea.

What exactly were my choices here?

I could either spill my guts, or just walk away from Nicole like I'd never experienced this mind-blowing attraction I had to her.

I'd forget about her, right?

Oh, hell no. Who in the hell was I trying to convince? This *wasn't* going to be an out-of-sight, out-of-mind situation. I'd remember her, the way I'd felt when her gorgeous body had been plastered to mine, the frank discussions we'd had, and that kiss. *That damn kiss!*

"How long are you staying?" she asked in a polite voice that I instantly decided I hated.

Jesus! What had happened to that sexy, breathless voice that had gotten my cock so hard that I'd been desperate to fuck her?

Really? Like I'm still not trying to control my dick, sexy voice or not?

"I have no idea," I told her honestly. "However long it takes to get my business done here."

Dammit! Having this superficial discussion grinded on me after we'd been so damn close the night before, but what fucking choice did I have?

Obviously, she wanted to put distance between us, maybe because she was embarrassed, but there was also the distinct possibility that she'd woken up, looked at me, and decided I just wasn't her type.

Her comments had been short and disinterested since she opened her eyes earlier.

Was it possible that she'd only confided in me, kissed me like I was the only man in the world for her, because she'd had one too many cocktails?

Let it go, Damian. It was one kiss. Okay, it was one extraordinary kiss, but it's not like you formed some kind of relationship with this woman in a matter of hours.

Besides, I couldn't find a way out of my current situation, and I'd rather see a polite look on her gorgeous face than one that said that she completely hated my guts.

In any event, *now* was not the time to become infatuated with a woman. I had Dylan and my corporation to worry about, and those two things consumed every waking moment of my day.

Not that I'd *ever* experienced an infatuation with *any* female, but if it was going to happen at some point in my life, I'd like it to happen *later*, when all of this mess with Dylan was resolved.

I was the sole partner in Lancaster who *didn't* have his mind all screwed up right now, so it was important for me to stay rational.

I was silent until the flight attendant came around to pick up all of the plates, utensils, and trash in preparation for landing.

Ignoring the fact that saying goodbye to Nicole didn't feel right, I buckled my seat belt and brought my seat into landing position.

But as the jet descended, I couldn't seem to keep my mouth shut. "Can I offer you a ride home?"

Now why in the hell did I just say that?

Hadn't I already convinced myself to let this whole encounter go?

Yeah, I had, but instinct had overridden my rationale for just a moment.

"No, thank you," she said in a courteous, aloof voice that irritated the hell out of me. "My friend is picking me up. I don't live in Los Angeles."

"You don't?" I asked with more curiosity in my tone than I would have liked. "Where do you live? Isn't your office in Los Angeles?"

"Newport Beach," she replied. "But since there's a nonstop through Transatlantic, it's easier to do the drive to LA from Newport than deal with layovers to get out of a smaller airport."

I wasn't familiar with much of California outside of Los Angeles. "Where exactly is Newport Beach?"

"Orange County. A fifty-minute drive from LAX in good traffic. Of course, decent traffic on the 405 Freeway doesn't happen all that often."

I turned my head to look at her. She sounded a little more relaxed, but she still wasn't looking in my direction. Her entire focus seemed to be looking at whatever was outside her window.

Honestly, I should be *grateful* that she'd refused a ride. I had a car and driver picking me up, which would have looked a little weird for a normal guy. Unfortunately, I *didn't* feel overjoyed that she'd refused. In fact, it was more than a little depressing that she hadn't hesitated to turn me down flat.

"Still feeling unhappy about the way your meeting went?" I had to ask. The whole situation at Lancaster wasn't her fault.

She turned her head to look at me, and the sad smile on her lips hit me like a sharp kick in the balls. "I'll live," she answered flatly. "Eventually, I guess I'll see it as a learning experience."

"The circumstances were out of your control, Nicole. Don't blame yourself." *Dammit!* For some reason, I *still* wanted to console her.

She leaned back against the headrest, her eyes still on me. "Thanks for letting me talk about it earlier. I'm so sorry I…had a little too much to drink."

Ahhh…so she *was* embarrassed about that. "Don't be sorry. It was a fascinating…discussion."

Her cheeks flushed a rosy red, so I knew damn well she hadn't forgotten that kiss. *That damn kiss!*

She shook her head. "I wasn't myself. At all."

"Meaning that, as a rule, you don't kiss a man you barely know during a long-haul flight?"

"Never," she said adamantly. "I'm so sorry, Damian. I don't know what I was thinking…"

"Don't," I said gruffly. "Don't regret it."

She tilted her head as she gazed at me curiously. "I don't. Not really. It's just a little mortifying that I got tipsy enough to fall into your lap and let it happen. Just tell me that you're not married or seriously involved with someone."

I felt a little insulted. "Do you really think I would have kissed you if I was?"

She lifted a brow. "Do you really need to ask that question? Guys do it all the time."

I pointed a finger at my chest. "Not this guy."

Okay, so now I *knew* that I definitely couldn't tell her that I was Damian Lancaster, apparent thrower of large orgies and a guy who needed more than one woman in his bed.

At least, that's what she'd think if she knew.

She nodded slowly. "Then I guess I can say it was nice meeting you."

I grinned. "It was more than *nice* meeting you, Nicole Ashworth," I responded.

The wheels hit the runway, and I was suddenly slammed back into reality.

Nicole would go her way, and I'd go mine.

It was time for this pleasant little interlude to end.

I *was* Damian Lancaster, and there wasn't a single thing I could do about that fact.

Like it or not, I was never going to see this mesmerizing woman again.

This flight couldn't end any other way.

I stood to take my suit jacket from the flight attendant once the jet got to the gate.

"Oh, my God. You *are* tall," Nicole said in a slightly awed voice as she got up from her seat.

I lifted her suitcase to bring it into the aisle for her. As she stood beside me, I realized just how much height those long, beautiful legs added to her stature.

The woman was beautifully statuesque, but she was *at least* half a head shorter than me.

I had no idea why she thought being tall and curvy was a negative thing.

I shrugged. "Being tall has its advantages."

"Not when you're taller than most of your dates," she answered wryly.

Dates?

Dates?

Why did it bother me to think about Nicole being with any other man? It wasn't like we were an item.

I had to remind myself that we hardly knew each other.

I looked down and our gazes locked as we waited for the doors to open so we could disembark.

For an instant, I could barely ignore the urge to swoop down and kiss those gorgeous lips of hers again.

Opportunity was knocking, and I wanted to fling that door wide open, and say to hell with the consequences.

Fierce need to claim this woman was eating my guts out.

We were so close that I could literally feel the warmth of her breath on my face.

I clenched my fists, trying to fight the powerful urge to touch her, to kiss her again, until a voice of caution rang pretty damn loudly inside my head.

And then what, Damian? Provided she lets you paw her in public, what happens after that? You have to let go, man. Seeing her again, hiding your true identity, wouldn't be fair to her. Just. Let. Go. It's better that way.

And just like that, the aircraft door opened, and that fleeting moment of opportunity was gone.

I shrugged off my disappointment.

I didn't want to be the tosser who hurt her feelings.

I'd rather just be...nothing. A brief encounter that she'd soon forget.

Waving her in front of me, I watched as she gripped her suitcase and went toward the exit.

The woman moved with purpose, her ample hips swaying, a fact that made her look elegant, even though she was still dressed in a pair of sweatpants and a T-shirt.

I followed behind her as we both headed toward the baggage claim, wondering if I was going to regret not getting one last taste of Nicole before we parted.

"Bloody hell. I regret it already," I grumbled under my breath as Nicole's long-legged strides carried her into the crowd and out of sight.

CHAPTER 8

Nicole

Kylie: *Waiting in a no-waiting zone. Hurry!*

I SMILED DOWN AT the text. It wasn't unusual for Kylie to be parked illegally, but she'd gotten so many parking tickets in the last year that she was actually starting to be more cautious.

I spied my bag the moment I got to the baggage claim, and hefted it off the belt.

Two seconds later, I was sprinting, two suitcases in tow, to get to the pickup area. If Kylie was forced to circle the airport, it could take forever for her to get back to me again. It didn't matter that I had an evening arrival. LAX traffic was pretty much a nightmare at any time of the day.

I was breathless by the time I got outside and to the curb, but I kept moving toward the median since there was no curbside pickup.

Even if I'd wanted to, there hadn't been time for me to find Damian and say goodbye.

Part of me was relieved that the farewell opportunity hadn't been there. No doubt it would have been awkward, and since I was the queen of being ill at ease, *that* moment was better off avoided.

"Nic! I'm here!" The forceful female voice called out just as I spotted my best friend.

Kylie was waving a hand in the air at the back of her older Honda Accord, the trunk already opened for my luggage.

"Welcome home," she said jovially as I tossed my suitcases in the trunk.

We hugged hurriedly before we jumped into the vehicle. "I'm glad to be home," I said with a sigh.

"Bad flight?" she asked with a frown.

I shook my head as I put my seat belt on. "No. It was fine. I just…"

"Come on, Nic. Tell me. I've known you since kindergarten. It's not like I can't tell when something's wrong. I know the presentation didn't go the way you wanted it to go, but you'd normally be over something like that pretty fast."

"Not necessarily. It was bad. And it was a very large deal to blow. It would expand the entire company if we went international. Especially with an initial client like Lancaster International."

Honestly, I hadn't actually thought much about my botched presentation after I'd told Damian about it.

He had completely distracted me.

The loss of the deal hadn't even crossed my mind when I'd woken up near the end of the flight, either. I'd been too mortified about what had happened *before* I'd fallen asleep.

Kylie put the car into gear, but we didn't move very far. The entire area was like a very large parking lot, so we were going to be inching along until we got outside the pickup area and onto the freeway.

"Spill it," she demanded. "I heard about the scandal that happened right before your presentation. But I know this isn't about the meeting."

Sometimes I really hated the fact that Kylie could read me like a book. "It's nothing really bad. I just met this guy on the plane. I'm not sure what happened, exactly. I just had this...weird instant attraction to him. That's never happened to me before."

She snorted. "It's happened to me plenty of times, and it never ends all that well. After you satisfy your insta-lust, you usually find out the guy can't carry on an intelligent conversation. So what was he like?"

"Very tall. Dark. Handsome. British."

Kylie squealed. "See, I told you. That sexy British accent will turn a woman on every single time. Did you join the mile-high club with Mr. Orgasm?"

I turned my head to glare at her, but it was hard to see her face clearly in the dark. "You're kidding, right?" Like I was really going to squeeze into one of those tiny restrooms on the plane with a guy as big as Damian to have a quickie. "He's a big guy. Even if I would have been inclined to screw some man I barely knew in a tiny bathroom on an international flight, we never would have fit."

"Did you get his number? Did you give him yours?" Kylie's voice was enthusiastic. "He might be the one to end your no-O problem."

I rolled my eyes. "Can you get off your orgasm obsession? I was attracted to him. That's it. We were sitting together on an airplane. We talked a lot."

"And he was smoking hot," Kylie added.

"Okay. Yes. He was incredibly attractive. And while everyone was sleeping, I kissed him, but there was no sex involved." Never mind that Damian's kiss was hotter than any of the sex I'd ever had. I wasn't sure I wanted to share that with Kylie. She'd never stop digging at me about not giving him my number.

"You kissed him?" Kylie's voice sounded shocked. "Way to go, Nic. I'm proud of you. You're about the biggest prude I know, but you stepped outside your comfort zone."

"I am not a prude." I was a little offended.

"Oh, pleeeaze! Miz I-won't-sleep-with-a-man-unless-I'm-in-a-committed-relationship," Kylie teased. "You've never had a fling in your entire life."

I shifted uncomfortably in my seat. "And you've had a million of them?" I shot back at her.

"No. But I've had a few, and I was married for a couple of years."

She didn't have to mention that she'd never been unfaithful during the years she'd been married. I heard that shift in her voice, that infused sadness I could always recognize when she said anything about her marriage.

I changed the subject. "I didn't give him my number because he didn't ask for it."

"You could have asked for his," she suggested. "Or maybe you could have just given him yours anyway."

"I suppose. But he's not the shy type. I doubt he would have had a problem asking for mine if he was interested." I had no idea what I would have done if he'd wanted to see me again, but I was fairly certain I would have given Damian my number if he'd asked for it.

Maybe I *had* made a fool of myself while I was under the influence of too many cocktails, but I still would have jumped at the chance to see him when my head was clear.

"Now you'll never know what would have happened," Kylie said, like not seeing Damian again was a major tragedy. "Did he say why he was here in the US?"

"Business. He said he was here on business. He has his own company. A family business that he took over when his father died. It's weird, but he spent more time listening to me than talking about himself. He tried to give me a pep talk about what happened at Lancaster, too. He said it wasn't my fault."

Kylie let out a dramatic sigh. "And he's smart in addition to being hot. It wasn't your fault, Nic. Anybody making that presentation would have been screwed. It just happened to be you. Who could compete with the adventures of a nymphomaniac? Lancaster could seriously use a fixer right now. If you ask me, they blew their chance to grab the best crisis management agency in the world. Don't let it get to you. We'll get other chances to go international."

I smiled. Kylie was hard on herself, but quick to try to comfort anybody else. "How are things at the office?"

"We picked up several new accounts," she informed me, her voice upbeat. "They weren't huge, but we're conquering the entire country one client at a time."

God, I wished I could be as enthusiastic as the director of my company. Kylie lived for this stuff. She'd actually worked for my mother before I'd taken over, and her talent and expertise had been the only things that had kept me sane when I'd decided to keep my mother's business. "That's fantastic," I told her, and I meant it.

"Now if Macy and I can just find your Mr. Orgasm," Kylie said impishly.

God, the last thing I needed was my two best friends putting their heads together to find me a man. There was no telling what they'd decide was orgasmic.

"I think I found him, but he wasn't interested enough to ask for my number," I mumbled.

I let myself feel the disappointment I'd been holding back because Damian *hadn't* asked for my contact information.

Deep down, beneath my mortification about acting like a twit because I'd been intoxicated, I'd wanted him to want to see me again.

"He was *that* hot?" Kylie questioned as we continued to move at the pace of a very slow turtle to get out of the pickup area.

"He's…" My mouth snapped closed as I saw a guy putting his suitcase in the back seat of a dark luxury vehicle. "Oh, shit! He's here."

"Where?" Kylie asked as she craned her neck to look around. "Is that him?" She pointed at Damian as he opened the front passenger door to get inside the car.

I nodded. "That's him."

I groaned as we drove past the vehicle, and I tried not to wonder who was in the driver's seat.

What if he was lying? What if he really is married?

"Um…he's definitely hot," Kylie said slowly. "But it couldn't possibly have been *that guy* who was riding with you in the business section of Transatlantic Airlines."

"It was," I insisted. "That was Damian. I never did get his last name."

"Holy shit! He actually *told you* that his name was Damian?"

I shot her an exasperated look. "Of course. That's his name. Why are you acting so weird?"

"Because *he's* the last person I thought your mystery man might be."

I wanted to study her face, try to gage what Kylie was thinking, but the inside of her vehicle was too damn dark. "You *know* him?"

It was possible, I supposed. Kylie had lived in Los Angeles for a couple of years while she was married. But what were the chances of her running into someone she knew here? There were literally millions of people in this city and the surrounding areas.

"I don't know him *personally*, but I know of him," she answered carefully.

"Then tell me what you know." Even though my chances of meeting up again with Damian were nonexistent, I still wanted to know more about him.

Kylie took a deep, audible breath. "Once you told me about bombing your presentation, I got curious and started to do some digging about the family."

"Did you see the scandalous picture?"

"Oh, I did. The guy might be a disgusting man-whore, but he's got a really nice ass," she said mischievously. "It's weird, but there's almost nothing else about him on the net. I had to dig pretty hard, but I finally found a photo of him on a business website. But it wasn't a *naked* picture."

"So what does all of this Lancaster research have to do with Damian?"

"Turns out, Damian Lancaster is just as hot as that guy you met on the plane."

"He is?" Okay, maybe it was a little hard to believe that the CEO of Lancaster International was *that* attractive, but sometimes Kylie and I had different tastes.

"Yep. As a matter of fact, that man by the car back there *was* definitely Damian. His full name is Damian *Lancaster.* If you're totally certain that *he* was the guy who sat next to you, then you shared a hot kiss with the Lancaster man-whore."

CHAPTER 9

Damian

I WAS COMPLETELY KNACKERED as I pushed open the front door of the Beverly Hills house that was owned by Lancaster International.

My corporation owned homes in many locations, mostly the places that had a Lancaster office nearby, which meant that we had residences in almost every country in the civilized world.

"Dylan!" I barked in a loud voice that carried through the ultra-modern home.

I was exasperated when I got no reply.

"Let me take your bags to your room so Anita can get you unpacked, sir," my driver's voice insisted from behind me.

I nodded gratefully at the older man. "Thank you, Clarence. Do you have any idea where my wayward twin brother might be?"

Clarence and Anita had been the caretakers for the Beverly Hills mansion since it had been acquired several years ago, and the husband-and-wife duo were more like family than employees. The two of them had been with the Lancaster family in some capacity for as long as I could remember. I'd grown up with the two of them working at our estate in Surrey. When the opportunity had come up for them to relocate to the warmer climate of California to be the caretakers for our residence here, neither one of the British natives had hesitated to move. They'd left England without a backward glance.

"He was in the pool area before I left for the airport, Mr. Lancaster. You may still catch him there. But if you don't mind my saying so, your brother seems to be...in a mood." Clarence's voice was cautionary, but I didn't give a damn whether or not Dylan *wanted* to talk.

I was tired of tiptoeing around his state of mind.

We *were* going to talk about what happened in London, and how it could affect Lancaster International in the future.

I shrugged out of my suit jacket as I strode toward the pool area.

I was hot.

I was tired because I hadn't slept at all on my flight.

But mostly, I was annoyed because Dylan's actions had kept me from pursuing a relationship with the most attractive, fascinating woman I'd met in...well...maybe in my entire life.

If he hadn't created a huge scandal, I would have been at that meeting with Nicole, and I would have been every bit as mesmerized as I'd been sitting next to her on an airplane.

I would have hired her on the spot, and talked her into staying in London longer so we could discuss the details, right after I'd taken her to my place so I could fuck her until she begged for mercy.

Christ! I *had* to stop thinking about Nicole Ashworth.

I saw Dylan sprawled out on a large lounge chair before I even entered the outdoor pool area. The outdoor space was enclosed in glass on the three sides, so one could admire the view of downtown Los Angeles from the inside if they didn't care to step outdoors.

The home sat high on a hill, with all of the lights of the city spread out in a seemingly endless area below.

It was an amazing sight at night, but I ignored the splendor of the view.

My mind was on one thing and one thing only: threatening my brother with his life if he didn't get his shit together.

I pushed on the glass door that led into the pool area as I yanked at my tie. It was a warm night, but I wasn't sure whether it was my state of dress or my irritation that made me feel like I was fucking suffocating.

"Dylan," I growled as I strode to his lounge chair. "We need to talk."

My identical twin opened one eye and groaned. "Sod off, Damian. I don't need a lecture."

He needed a lot more than simple censure, which was the *only* thing I'd been capable of doing…until right now. "You're completely pissed," I accused.

Dylan and I had shared more than a few drunken hours together when we were younger, before we'd had to grow up and face the multitude of responsibilities that had been left to us after our father had died.

"Not pissed, exactly," Dylan said, his words slurred. "Just… relaxed."

"Yeah, well, you've been pretty damn relaxed for the last two years then." I went to the bar, dropped ice in a glass, and poured myself a generous portion of a good Irish whiskey.

I didn't normally drink to excess like Dylan obviously had tonight, but I knew I could use a good single malt as I tried to pull the reins in on my brother.

"Why do you have to be so stiff and buttoned up?" Dylan asked as he leisurely opened a second eye to look at me.

I tossed back a swig of my whiskey before I said dryly, "I'm British. It's in our DNA."

He lifted a brow as he sat up in the lounger. "We have very similar DNA, and I know how to loosen up."

I rolled my eyes. *Of course* we had similar DNA. We were identical twins. And he wasn't "loosened up." Dylan was thoroughly pissed. Big difference there.

I took a deep breath, and let it out as I took a chair close to my brother's lounger. "All of this has to stop, Dylan. The orgies. The eccentric behavior. Getting pissed until you have no idea what you're doing. I realize that you didn't exactly hang around in London to see the fallout of showing your bare ass in the middle of an orgy, but it was front-page tabloid news. You hurt Mum, and the entire country now thinks it's me, not you, who needs multiple sex partners. What do you think some of our worldwide partners are going to think, the ones who are *really* buttoned up and conservative?"

Dylan shook his head as he argued, "That was all a setup, Damian. I swear. One of those women slipped me something in my drink, and then took me somewhere. I had no idea what I was doing. Hell, I don't even think I had sex with any of them. And I sure as hell never *claimed* to be you."

My brows narrowed as I studied him. "Did you introduce yourself as Dylan?"

He shrugged. "Didn't say anything. I think they *assumed* I was you."

Okay, maybe I could buy that it *was* actually a setup, possibly by one of our competitors who wanted to swoop in on a deal we were competing on with a religious-minded company somewhere. Since we did deals on a daily basis, it would be difficult to nail down *exactly* who was responsible.

However…

"You're not an idiot, Dylan. If they slipped you something, evidently you were already…impaired." My brother had a genius IQ and an almost scary intuition. Sober, he would have been wise to a possible setup.

"Okay, I made a mistake," Dylan grumbled as he ran his palms across his face. "What happened to the Damian who doesn't give a damn what the tabloids say about him?"

"I don't care," I snapped. "Not when the only one who's affected is *me*. For fuck's sake, *Dylan*, Mum saw that damned front-page photo, and so did our competition and partners. You've done some ridiculous things in the last two years, stuff I've been able to cover up or take responsibility for, but I can't just make this one go away. The photo is out there everywhere until I can get it scrubbed from the net. Whether it was a setup or not, putting yourself in that position was a juvenile stunt."

I loved my brother, and I hated having this conversation. At one time, Dylan and I had been close, and we'd respected the hell out of each other.

But that had been *another* Dylan, not the selfish wanker I'd been dealing with for the last two years, the one who didn't care about anyone except himself.

Christ! I wanted the *old Dylan* back, and I hoped Mum was right about my real brother still being inside this seemingly empty shell I was talking to right now.

"I'm sorry about Mum seeing that photo," he said flatly, his eyes glazed as he glared at me. "But as far as Lancaster International goes, I couldn't care less. Is that all you care about, Damian? Is everything about business for you now? You didn't used to be that way."

I clenched a fist, so damn tempted, for the first time in my life, to literally beat some sense into Dylan. "Like I have any choice?" I completely lost it. "Lancaster is *our* legacy. I was supposed to have your help managing our empire. Instead of dividing and conquering,

I've just been trying to keep my head above water, doing both your work and mine because you abandoned me two years ago. I'm also picking up the slack by trying to keep your personal life private, as well as covering our business interests alone. Do you have any idea how damn difficult it is to erase an entire history from the internet? Or how hard it is to maintain it, especially when you're out there pulling some gossip-worthy stunts on a regular basis?"

His green eyes went dark. "You know why I drink," he ground out angrily. "What do you think I'm going to do, Damian? Just get over it? We made a deal."

"There was no damn *deal,* just my promise to help you disappear. We never set a time limit on just how long all of this was supposed to last. I've kept my word, Dylan, but you aren't exactly using this time to get your fucking head together. In fact, you seem determined to screw it up even more."

I took a deep breath. I wasn't furious because Dylan had just checked out for a while.

I probably would have done the same.

I'd been patient for *two fucking years.*

Giving him his space.

I'd been more than willing to wait until he was ready to slowly check back in and talk to me.

So I'd waited.

Hoping every damn day that he'd finally talk to me about what had happened, confide in me about his pain.

But Dylan had just become more withdrawn, more out of control, more self-destructive.

It was time for me to admit to myself that Dylan probably wasn't going to come back after he'd had some time to heal.

Like it or not, I was going to have to drag him back, kicking and screaming, if I wanted my brother back.

"Nobody expects you to just get over it," I told him in a calmer tone. "But what you've been doing isn't helping you heal, Dylan. You're spiraling down to where I can't reach you anymore, and I can't let that happen. If our positions were reversed, I know you wouldn't let me go."

My brother shot me a glare that would have made anyone else in the world back the hell off. "I would have kept my promise, Damian. You know I would if our circumstances were reversed."

I tried not to let myself be manipulated. "Do you think I've ever betrayed you, Dylan? I haven't. Not once. Now, all I want is my twin brother back."

Dylan stood, and walked unsteadily to the bar to grab himself another beer. "Did it ever occur to you that maybe I don't *want* to be saved, Damian? That I don't deserve to heal?"

I tossed back the last of my whiskey and slammed the tumbler on the side table before I got to my feet.

"Why in the world would you feel *that way*?" I said, irritated. "Talk to me, Dylan. I've never really understood—"

"I don't *want* to talk about it," he snarled as he tore the top off the bottle. "Take Lancaster International, Damian. Give me enough money to live on and you can have the whole damn empire. It's not what I want anymore. I don't want to live in a fishbowl. I don't want to be one of the richest guys in the world. I just want to be left alone."

Oh, hell no! Left to his own devices, Dylan would continue to spiral downward until he hit rock bottom, and there was no telling whether he'd survive that fall or not.

I snatched the beer from his hand, and started to pour it down the sink as I answered, "Not happening, brother. No more alcohol for you tonight."

I'd keep my word because Dylan was nowhere near ready to step back into his old life. In fact, doing so might completely destroy him right now.

But I'd be damned if I was going to let him go down without fighting for him.

Dylan had just given me a ray of hope. He was *angry*, and I hadn't seen that emotion from him in a long time.

Before, all I'd seen was apathy.

I'd take his outrage over his indifference any time.

In fact, I welcomed it, and I'd be more than happy to do everything in my power to irritate the hell out of him in the future if that's what it took to see some kind of emotion from him.

Maybe my biggest mistake had been leaving him alone in the first place.

I didn't regret giving him his space and privacy from other people. He *did* need that right now. But maybe I shouldn't have backed off, even though he'd requested that, too.

I'd empathized from a distance for two very long years.

I'd probably given him *too much* space from *me* to screw up his life when he hadn't been thinking straight.

I tossed the bottle I'd emptied into the trash can. "From now on, no more drunken orgies, setup or not. No more alcohol until you can handle it. No more hanging out with people who just want to party and don't give a damn about you. You don't need another beer; you need help. It's time to get your head on straight, Dylan, and start acting like an adult instead of a spoiled adolescent."

It wasn't easy for me to say that because I knew what my brother had been through, or at least, I knew the basics. But he wasn't helping himself at all, and most likely wouldn't if somebody didn't step in.

And I *was* that somebody. It would be better to gain his hatred than to see him end up dead somewhere.

"Who in the fuck made *you* my boss, Damian? You can't tell me what to do. I'll live my life exactly the way I want." His voice was dripping with acrimony as he fisted my linen shirt like he meant to threaten me.

Again, his irritated tone did nothing except encourage me. "I'd be interested to see how *that* all works out for you since you gave me power of attorney to handle *everything*, so you'll need *my* approval to transfer funds into your bank account. Judging by the amount I last deposited for you, I'd say you're going to be running low very shortly. Which is really too bad because I've just decided you're cut off until you get yourself sober and at least presentable again."

I almost hated myself for threatening the brother who should be my partner with poverty, especially when he was entitled to half of Lancaster International's wealth.

I let the considerable guilt I felt cover me, but not break me.

Dylan gripped my shirt harder and tried to shake me, but he didn't have the strength to move me very far in his intoxicated state. "You can't do that, Damian. I'm a Lancaster, too. You can't just take everything."

Remorse continued to claw at me, but I shrugged it off. "I can. You gave me that right when you wanted to disappear from the public eye. You signed over all of your responsibilities to me two years ago. Pull yourself together, and we'll talk. You look like shit."

Dylan's eyes lit with fury, his usual icy stare completely gone as he pulled his arm back in what I knew was going to be the first punch ever thrown between the two of us.

Not today, brother. Not today.

He was shirtless, dressed only in swim trunks, so I gripped his shoulders and heaved before he could land a single hit on me, sending him hurtling into the swimming pool.

I folded my arms over my chest as I watched him come to the surface, making sure the idiot wasn't drunk enough to drown. "Meet me for breakfast in the morning, and make sure you're sober," I instructed.

Dylan sputtered. "I swear, I'll beat the crap out of you for this, Damian."

I grinned back at him as I said, "Try it, tosser." If he ever got sober and balanced enough to throw a real punch, I'd probably be fucking ecstatic.

I turned and left the pool area.

Maybe I couldn't *make* Dylan pull himself together, but I could certainly make him uncomfortable enough to try.

CHAPTER 10

Nicole

"I PICKED UP YOUR usual," Kylie said as she breezed through the door of my office with a couple of food bags in her arms.

My eyes raised to the clock. "Wow! It *is* lunchtime already." I was surprised at how fast the morning had flown by.

I'd had a lot of work back up while I'd been in London, so I hadn't even paused to look at the clock after I'd gotten into the office this morning.

"You've been pretty quiet in here." Kylie pulled the soup and sandwiches from the bags. "You're not still upset over the whole Damian Lancaster thing, right? I mean, he's a jerk, and it was just a kiss."

I looked up at her and frowned. *Okay. Yeah.* It *was* just a kiss, and I couldn't think of a way to explain just how *intimate* that embrace had been. "I'm good. I was just trying to get my email caught up and some proposals done."

Kylie shot me a puzzled gaze. "You know you don't *have* to do any proposals, right? You own the business. You can leave that to the rest of us."

"Mom did some of her own proposals," I argued. "And I feel like I need to know every part of this business to be able to lead everyone else."

How could I be in control of a business I knew nothing about?

Kylie dropped my lunch in front of me, grabbed her own soup, and plopped down in a chair in front of my desk.

Even though she'd just made a food run outside in the heat, my best friend still looked as fresh as she'd appeared first thing this morning.

Her makeup was perfect, covering every freckle she'd abhorred since childhood. Kylie had gotten teased in grade school about her endless freckles, bright-red braids, and her willingness to take on anything a boy could do.

That tough girl had blossomed into a beautiful redheaded woman with more confidence in her little finger than I had in my entire body.

"Your mother *loved* doing proposals, which is why she did some herself," Kylie pointed out. "She didn't *need* to be that hands-on, either. And since you don't exactly enjoy doing proposals, neither do you. Nic, you're allowed to be who you are. You don't need to be your mother. You're the boss, which means you don't have to do anything you don't want to do. Just because you're keeping your Mom's business, it doesn't mean you can't put your own spin on it, and do things *your* way."

I pulled the lid off what I already knew was minestrone soup. I'd caught the mouthwatering aroma before Kylie had pulled the food out of the bag. "I've been doing this for a year, and I still feel lost," I confessed.

Kylie lifted a brow. "Did you really expect to be perfect in just a year? You were a corporate attorney, not a PR expert."

"I don't think I knew what to expect. I just wanted to keep Mom's company alive." I'd been thinking with a broken, grieving heart when I'd impulsively packed my stuff and moved back to Newport Beach.

"And you've done that, quite successfully I might add," Kylie answered. "Give yourself a break, Nic. The company is still thriving, and it has so much potential for future growth."

I shot her a doubtful look. ACM was flourishing as a result of my employees like Kylie, not because of my leadership. "Sometimes I wonder if I should have sold and stayed in my corporate law job." I'd never actually said those words out loud, but I'd thought about it plenty of times over the last few months.

"I think Estelle would have been perfectly okay with that," Kylie answered gently. "In fact, she *expected* it. She was proud of you, Nicole, and she'd want you to be happy with whatever you choose to do with your life. If I could, I would have been the first one in line to buy ACM, but I'm not in the position to do that right now. I don't have that kind of cash."

I stopped eating, and looked at Kylie. "I didn't know you'd be interested."

Never once had my best friend mentioned that she'd like to actually *own* an agency herself. In fact, she never stopped talking about how much she loved her job as director of ACM, and how it allowed her to pursue her personal interests outside work.

She shrugged. "I would like to have my own business someday, but it wouldn't have mattered. I couldn't have bought ACM, anyway."

That wasn't *entirely* true. I owned the business, and Kylie and I could have worked something out. We *still* could. Nobody was more qualified to step into my mother's role than Kylie. After her short marriage, my best friend had come back to Orange County to work for my mother. Kylie had fallen in love with the PR business, and had worked to complete her college degree while she'd worked beside Mom.

ACM was probably never going to make me outrageously wealthy unless we expanded significantly, but it was a profitable company that made me a good living right now. Realistically, Kylie probably couldn't afford to buy the entire company right now, but we could have come to some kind of understanding.

Because of my mother's hard work, and the scholarships I'd been awarded, I'd gotten all the way through law school without a single student loan. I'd been making a good living as a corporate attorney. The last thing I'd needed was income from ACM.

Granted, I hadn't wanted to see ACM go to a *stranger*, but I could have let it go to *Kylie*. My mother had adored her, treated her like a second daughter.

"I'm sorry, Kylie," I said sincerely. "I should have thought of a way to bring you into ownership. I had no idea that you wanted that, or I would have done it."

Her eyes widened. "What? No! Why would you do that?"

I sighed. "Because you loved her, too, and you belong here more than I do."

She shook her head. "Don't be silly, Nicole. You were her daughter."

"She loved you, too," I said softly.

She smiled. "I know that. Your mom was always there for me, even when we were kids. But she sure as hell didn't expect me to take the business away from her only child. I'm happy in my job, Nic. I make a great salary plus bonuses. I'm saving. I have plenty of time to seek out my own company when I'm ready. I'm perfectly content exactly where I am right now."

I eyed her skeptically one last time before I started eating again, thinking about how we could revisit the idea of her taking over ACM in the future.

"I wasn't exactly levelheaded when Mom died," I told Kylie ruefully. Normally, I was far from impulsive, but I'd nearly lost my mind when my only parent had died.

Honestly, I was still grieving Mom, and probably would for the rest of my life. Her death had left a big, dark hole in my world that nobody could ever fill up again. Yeah, the excruciating pain of losing her had dulled, but there wasn't a single day that went by that I didn't miss her.

Kylie nodded. "That's to be expected, Nic. You were her only child, and she was your only parent. You guys were really tight."

"We were," I agreed. If I'd only known what was going to happen in the future, I would have spent more time in Southern California as an adult.

I could have practiced corporate law in Los Angeles, but my mother had encouraged me to apply to one of the most prestigious law firms in New York. She'd fought her battle with cancer alone so I wouldn't feel like I *had* to come back to California, not telling me about her diagnosis until she knew she was going to lose that fight.

I sighed. I couldn't have a do-over. Regrets wouldn't bring her back. And if I'd done everything differently, I wouldn't have the memories of all the times Mom had come to the East Coast to see me.

We'd traveled from New York to Maine. Every time she came to the East Coast, we found a new place to visit, a new adventure. Those road trips had been some of the happiest times of my entire life.

"I know time is supposed to make her death easier, but it hasn't taken away how much I miss her," I admitted to Kylie.

Maybe the acute pain was gone, but the ache and emptiness were almost as bad.

Kylie shot me an empathetic look. "It hasn't been that long, Nic. She was your mom, and your only immediate family. It's going to take time."

I nodded. "I know."

"How about we grab Macy and do a girl's weekend soon?" Kylie suggested.

Okay, maybe it wouldn't exactly be a road trip, but spending time with my two best friends was always an adventure, too.

I smiled at her. "I'm game. As long as we stay away from the clubs, and you promise *not* to drink tequila. Last time we all went out, you were dancing on the bar."

Macy and I had slowly talked Kylie down from the bartop, and gotten her home to her bed.

None of us had ever suggested going to a nightclub again.

Honestly, it wasn't like I didn't know that Kylie was way beyond that kind of behavior *now*. That incident had happened soon after she'd become single again, and she hadn't been in a good place back then.

Kylie scoffed. "*One time.* I got on the bar one single time, and you're never going to let me forget it. That was a decade ago, Nic."

"Nope. I *won't* stop talking about it," I agreed. "If *I'd* done that, you'd be reminding me of it on a daily basis for the rest of my life. Admit it. You'd love to have something like that to tease me about forever."

Kylie smirked. "You're probably right. It kind of sucks that you've never done anything even remotely inappropriate. Well, except for kissing a stranger on an airplane," she reminded me. "Believe me, I'll never stop giving you a hard time about that one since it's the *only* dirt I have on you."

"I know," I said with a chuckle. "But I *was* under the influence at the time, just like you were a decade ago."

She rolled up the empty wrapper from her sandwich. "So are you *really* feeling better about kissing Mr. Orgasm? I know you, Nic. Are you telling me the truth when you're insisting that you've just blown the whole thing off?"

"No," I said immediately. *Dammit!* Kylie did know me way too well. "You're right about the kiss just being a kiss, but I feel like an idiot when I think about the way he was trying to console *me* about bombing a presentation with *his* damn company. What kind of guy does that sort of thing?"

"Let's see," Kylie pondered. "I'd say he's either really twisted or really desperate. He's either a psycho who enjoys sick little mind games, OR…he liked you and didn't want you to know it was his company that gave you the we'll-call-you-later brush-off."

I preferred the second explanation. "Are you certain the guy you saw getting into that car at the airport was Damian Lancaster?"

She raised her brows. "Nicole Ashworth, don't try to tell me that you didn't look that picture up for yourself last night."

I had, and she knew it. "Maybe the guy has a doppelganger?"

Hell, maybe I was grasping at straws, but I didn't want the man I'd shared an intimate kiss with to be the owner of Lancaster International. For me, that kiss had been real…

"Right. And that *doppelganger* just happens to be named Damian, too?" Kylie asked wryly.

"Okay. It *was* him," I conceded. I *had* found the scandalous picture of him, and the more serious picture of him on the Lancaster International website. "But why in the hell would he be taking a flight in business class on his own airline, for God's sake? He must have a private jet or two."

"It's definitely weird," Kylie agreed. "But what if he really did like you, and then *couldn't* reveal who he really was? It would completely explain why he never asked for your number. The truth would have come out eventually."

I rolled my eyes. For a woman who had experienced her share of heartache, Kylie could still be the eternal optimist. I let out a groan of mortification before I said, "I wouldn't have kissed him if I'd known his true identity."

Damian had made me feel special, and it did hurt to know that the entire encounter had been nothing more than a game to him.

"Exactly!" Kylie exclaimed as she wriggled her eyebrows. "He didn't fess up because he *wanted* to kiss you. Maybe he wasn't messing with you, Nic. Maybe he isn't a complete narcissistic asshole. I can tell you from experience that things aren't always how they seem. When someone is out of their mind from alcohol, sometimes shit just...happens."

I tossed the trash from my lunch into the garbage can, and crossed my arms as I watched my best friend try to make something out of...nothing. "He wasn't intoxicated on that flight."

"But he definitely was in that naughty picture," she said. "Sometimes, people do things when they're drunk that they'd never do sober. Honestly, he was so glassy-eyed in that picture that I'm not even sure if he was capable of getting it up. I'm not saying that you should forget all about the whole orgy thing, but maybe you need to hear his side of that story."

Really, I loved Kylie dearly for not wanting me to feel like a fool, but there was no saving Damian Lancaster.

He was a liar.

He *had* to be twisted to play that stupid game with me on our flight.

He *was* the type of guy who indulged in orgies and multiple female partners.

Lastly, Damian was *exactly* the type of man I'd run from like my ass was on fire if I'd known who he really was *before* I'd kissed him. Maybe I had been tipsy, but I couldn't blame *that damn kiss* completely on the alcohol. Even after the alcohol had worn off the next morning, I'd *still* been just as attracted to him as I'd been the night before.

"Give it up, Kylie," I urged. "You just can't save Damian Lancaster. Nothing you say is going to convince me that he isn't a complete jerk."

A deep baritone voice suddenly sounded from the doorway. "I'm *definitely* a wanker, but I'm hoping I can change your opinion of me, eventually, Nicole."

I didn't have to shift my eyes to my open office door to know *exactly* who was standing there.

I could *feel* his presence, and even if I couldn't, that damn voice with that sexy British accent was unmistakable.

What in the world was Damian Lancaster doing at my office?

CHAPTER 11

Nicole

KYLIE SQUEAKED AS she jumped to her feet, her eyes as wide as saucers. "Mr. Lancaster?"

Damian gave my best friend a smile that was so charming I wanted to punch him as he said, "Kylie, I presume. Nicole mentioned you during some of our conversations." He held out his hand in greeting.

Kylie nodded as she shook it, her expression still a little stunned. "What are you doing here?" she questioned suspiciously.

"I wanted to have a word with Nicole," he answered amiably.

I stood. "I don't think we have a single thing to talk about, *Mr. Lancaster.*"

I hated the fact that I couldn't control my reaction to seeing Damian again. My heart tripped, and my *body* instantly responded to his raw sensuality, while all my *brain* wanted me to do was kick him in the balls.

Damian moved past Kylie once he'd dropped her hand, and stopped right in front of me. "Give me five minutes to explain, Nicole."

Ha! That request had sounded more like a demand to me, and I wasn't about to give Damian Lancaster anything he commanded. He sure as hell wasn't *my* boss. *Thank God!*

I shook my head, trying not to let him know that his actions on our flight had gotten to me. "You had over twelve hours to tell me the truth."

"It's...complicated," he said.

Kylie interrupted in a cheerful voice that I knew was completely faked. "Well, I'll be right next door in my office if you need me." She walked to the door before pausing. "I mean, *right next door*," she added in a warning voice. "Like...my office *shares a wall with this one, if you know what I mean*."

Damian nodded. "Message understood. Nicole is safe with me, Kylie. I just want to talk."

"She'd better be," Kylie barked at Damian as she left and closed the door behind her.

An oppressive silence filled the room the second she was gone, and the tension was so thick between Damian and me that it was almost unbearable.

I glared at him, but there was a stubborn determination in his gorgeous eyes that made me aware that he wasn't leaving until he'd said what he wanted to say.

"Just say your piece and leave, Damian," I said, resigned. Listening to him was apparently the fastest way to get this man out of my office, and I really, really needed him to go. I looked up at the clock. "Your five minutes is ticking down as of right now."

His sexy green-eyed gaze met mine as he said, "I should have told you the truth, but as soon as I found out that Lancaster International was the source of your unhappiness, the last thing I wanted to do was admit that I was the head of the company. I doubt you ever would have uttered another word to me, and rightfully so. I should have been at that meeting, Nicole, but something happened—"

"Something *happened*?" I interrupted indignantly. "I *know* what *happened*. A front-page article and a naked orgy picture were more than enough to tell the story of what you'd been up to until the wee hours of the morning. I doubt you were in any condition to attend a morning meeting."

His expression was grim. "Yes. That's why I wasn't there." Damian didn't attempt to explain any further.

I crossed my arms over my chest defensively, doing my best to act like I didn't give a damn what he did. "Why were you taking a flight in the business section of your own airline?"

He shrugged his massive shoulders. "What better way to get a passenger experience? I like to know how my customers feel when they're taking Transatlantic, and what changes we need to make to be better than the competition."

I wasn't about to tell him that I found that...refreshing. There probably weren't very many billionaires who gave a shit about how their companies were run, as long as the bottom line was in the black. "Why bother talking to me at all? Why bother to kiss me? Are you twisted? Was that entire flight just a game for you to play to pass the time?"

"Of course not. I usually mind my own business when I'm doing a test flight, but I wanted to talk to you, Nicole. And yes, I wanted *that damn kiss*. I'm not going to lie."

I lifted an eyebrow. "Why?"

Damian raked a hand through his perfect hair like he was frustrated. "Because you're the most captivating woman I've ever met. You're beautiful. You're intelligent. Easy to talk to. You were the one woman I couldn't possibly ignore, Nicole, and to be completely honest, I have no fucking idea *why*." His voice sounded sincere.

But I knew better. I didn't believe a single word that was coming out of his mouth. If I did, I'd probably have to admit that I'd felt the same weird attraction he had, and I *didn't* want to go there.

His eyes were intense, a dark, swirling pool of emotions.

I had to give it to Damian—he *was* an excellent actor. I *almost* believed that a little of his chagrin might be…real.

I forced my gaze away from him and looked up at the clock.

Shit! He still had a little more time.

I turned my eyes back in his direction. Damian was dressed more casually today in a pair of black jeans and a green polo shirt that matched his eyes. I didn't want to admit that the casual style made him seem more…approachable. "Why are you here?" I asked bluntly.

"I had to see you, Nicole. At first, I thought it would be better to let it go, but I don't think that's true anymore. I wanted your number. I wanted to ask you out. I was just too cowardly to tell you the truth because I was pretty sure you'd end up hating me."

He reached out a hand, as though he wanted to touch me, but I stepped back before he could make contact. "Don't touch me," I said in a warning tone. "Look, you've said what you wanted to say. What else do you want? Your five minutes is almost up."

"Do you really want me to answer that question?" he asked in a husky tone.

"No!" I said hastily. "Forget it. Just get out of my office. God, did you really think you could just apologize, and I'd fall all over you just because you're Damian Lancaster?"

He shrugged. "Most women do."

Oh, I'm sure they did. Strangely, I didn't detect a hint of arrogance in his comment. He sounded more like having women fall all over him because he was one of the richest guys in the world was just a…fact. "I'm not most women," I told him firmly. "I actually have to like a guy to go out with him. And I don't like you. Now just…go."

I hated the way my heart was racing, and how damn hard it was to keep up my indifferent façade.

"Not so fast," he said smoothly. "There's one other issue I'd like to discuss."

"I think I'm done here," I snapped, my hostility rising. I was thoroughly pissed off at myself because even though I *knew* he was a man-whore and a liar, my body *still* wanted him. My involuntary reactions to Damian were hard to control, and that was something my rational mind just didn't understand. How could I want this man to fuck me when I didn't even like him?

Damian ignored my curt dismissal. "You were right about everything you said about Lancaster International," he said in a more businesslike voice. "We *do* need a good crisis management agency right now. Social media is having a field day with the article and the photo, and that's something my marketing team has never had to deal with in the past. We're seeing more pushback from the public than I ever imagined. We do need a specialist."

I couldn't hold back on my sarcasm as I retorted, "Maybe you wouldn't need a crisis manager if you could keep your damn pants on when you're in front of a camera."

Damian's lips twitched like he wanted to smile. "You looked up the photo and the article, I assume."

Busted! "Strictly for business reasons," I explained hastily. "I wanted to see the scandal that screwed me on my presentation."

"The whole story was a setup," he said, frowning. "A trap to make Lancaster International look bad, probably by a competitor."

I scoffed. "Seriously? Do you really expect me to believe that?"

"No. Not now. But if we're working together, maybe you will someday."

"That would be impossible since I don't plan on taking on your company." Did he really think he could hire me, and it would make what he did all right?

His brow furrowed as he studied me. "Nicole, it would be a ridiculous business move to pass on Lancaster International. It would be a huge account, and it would definitely open the door for a lot more international clients for you in the future."

Dammit! I hated the fact that every single word he said was…true.

"I don't care about the money," I said defensively. "I have to be able to work with every client, and I can't work with you."

The guy was arrogant and presumptuous, not to mention the fact that he'd already lied to me, and I had no idea whether he'd do so again and again if we were working together.

"You *can* work with me," he told me, his voice persuasive. "Don't turn down this opportunity. You'll hate yourself for it later."

I was silent as I thought about what he'd just said. Would I hate myself later for making a big decision like this based on emotion instead of reason?

I'd desperately wanted to secure Lancaster International as a client, not only because they'd be a huge account, but also because of the doors it would open for ACM to branch out into the UK and European markets.

My employees had kept this business booming after my mother's death. I felt like I owed all of them a decision that was made with a clear mind and not emotion.

"I suppose I should take some time to consider it," I told him reluctantly. "Are you sure you'll be able to stifle the urge to throw another orgy while I think about it?"

He grinned at me. "I think I can contain myself."

His smile made me so breathless I couldn't say a word.

Dammit! I really hated the way I could still want this man, even though I knew what an asshole he really was.

I needed to get Damian Lancaster out of my office. "Then I'll consider it," I said with absolutely no enthusiasm. Thank God

I managed to resist the urge to get in another insult, though. I was showing my cards every single time I let him know he could irritate me.

Lancaster International was one of the largest and most successful corporations in the world, and Damian hadn't stayed in that position without being a master at manipulation and an excellent game player.

I refused to be one of his pawns, but how could I not take some time to think about something that could mean so much to the future of my mother's beloved company?

This opportunity wasn't just about *me*. If it was, I could have easily told him to go fuck himself. But I had employees, and a business that needed to grow in the future. My decisions directly affected the people who worked for ACM, and their job security.

What if I *could* use Damian Lancaster to further my business interests?

He reached into the back pocket of his jeans and pulled out a business card. "Don't take long to decide," he suggested. "The situation is out of control already."

My PR mind kicked in as I asked, "What kind of damage control are you doing right now?"

He shrugged. "The PR department is mostly punting questions at this point, hoping it will die down. We've never had something like this happen before."

I let go of a sigh. "I told you that you needed to get *in front* of it. If this has really blown up on social media, avoidance is only going to make it worse. Have you made a statement?"

"Not yet."

"Get on social media and make it clear that you were set up, but take total responsibility for putting yourself in a bad position in the first place. I'm assuming all this started in a bar or a nightclub?"

My heart ached when he nodded slowly.

Part of me still didn't want to believe that the Damian I'd gotten to know on the plane had been so out of his mind on alcohol that he'd allowed himself to end up in this situation.

My memory went to the single beer he'd consumed before he'd asked for tea.

Was he trying to reform?

"Stay away from the club scene in Los Angeles," I suggested tersely. "There are usually reporters around who are trying to catch celebrities misbehaving in some of the posher nightclubs."

He held up a hand. "I'm here on business only. I wasn't planning on setting Hollywood on fire."

Honestly, I couldn't see Damian partying at a swanky club. It just didn't seem like his style. But what did I know? He'd obviously gotten drunk enough to be set up, if this whole thing had ever really been a trap.

I took his card and tossed it on my desk. "I'll be in touch. I need to think about this. If you aren't sincere about wanting to fix this, then it could ruin *my* company's reputation."

I watched as he raked a hand through his hair again. "I do want to fix it. I hate the fact that my family is going to suffer. Reporters are already camping out at my mother's home in Surrey, trying to get some kind of statement. She doesn't need this."

"So most of what you told me on the plane is true? Your mom lives in Surrey at your childhood home?"

"Nothing I said was untrue," he said. "Although I'm definitely guilty of lying by omission."

For a moment, I felt bad about his obvious distress over his mother's treatment by the media. If I could trust nothing else about this man, I was pretty sure his agitation about the press hounding his mom was completely sincere. "They'll go away eventually," I said quietly. "There's always going to be another story more scandalous than yours. It's just really uncomfortable while you're in the hot seat."

He nodded sharply. "Don't get me wrong. My mum is a strong woman, but she's been through a lot, and our family reputation means a lot to her. Like I said, nothing I told you on the plane was a lie, really. My mother was born in Spain, and she met my father while he was in her country on business. She came from a humble background, and she turned herself inside out to be accepted by the social elite once she married my father. She said she never wanted him to regret that he'd married beneath himself."

I surveyed his expression as I asked, "Did he marry beneath himself?"

He shook his head. "Hell, no. My father never felt that way. Ever. He loved my mother, and he didn't care what the gossips said. It was Mum who always felt like she wasn't good enough to enter the Lancaster empire. She even cultivated a British accent, so nobody was reminded of her origins. My father thought it was ridiculous that she worried so much about appearances. But I think she was traumatized after her first meeting with the Queen."

I gaped at him. "She met the Queen?"

"Of course," he said nonchalantly. "Technically, my father was the Duke of Hollingsworth. It isn't a royal dukedom, but we're well acquainted with the peerage."

I moved to my desk and sat down in my chair, trying not to hyperventilate. Dear God! No wonder Damian's mother had felt like his father had married beneath himself. I could only imagine what her struggles had been in trying to find a place in such a powerful family.

I looked up at him as I said breathlessly, "So doesn't that make *you* the Duke of Hollingsworth now?"

He looked disgusted as he answered tersely, "Yes. But I rarely use the title unless I'm at a royal event. My father didn't put much importance on something he'd simply inherited, and I don't, either. I'd rather be known for my business acumen than for an aristocratic position I never earned. I was born to privilege, and I inherited a fortune. I'd like to work hard to prove that I'm worthy of *that*, not some antiquated title."

I nearly smiled because he was starting to sound like an American. While I didn't believe in advanced status just by a happy accident of birth, I also couldn't deny that the Lancaster family must carry a lot of weight in England's social circles. "I thought the British loved their titles."

He shrugged. "Some love their traditions."

I'd read enough English history to have a basic understanding of the peerage. "So nobody refers to you as *Your Grace*?"

He actually looked embarrassed as he admitted, "Occasionally. I don't encourage it."

It was strange that Damian seemed to be a lot more comfortable as the billionaire CEO of Lancaster International than he did with his position as the Duke of Hollingsworth.

"So your mother actually became a duchess when she married your father, and the wife of a billionaire, too. I get why she was intimidated. I'm American, and I'd find meeting the royals pretty daunting."

"She put more importance on our title than our father ever did," Damian scoffed.

Maybe so, but I could *still* empathize with her. I'd nearly buckled under the stress of having a conference room full of Lancaster executives staring at me. I could only imagine how his mother had felt when she'd been under the critical eye of England's aristocratic crowd. "I can totally understand why this entire situation upsets her."

He studied my face until it grew almost uncomfortable. "Can you, Nicole?"

I nodded. "Give me some time, Damian. I'd like to help, but please understand that I don't trust you. I doubt I ever will." I saw no reason to dance around the truth.

"I'm sorrier about that more than you'll ever know," he answered in a low, regretful tone.

I let out a shaky breath as I answered. "I'll call you tomorrow. Where are you staying?"

"Here in Newport Beach," he informed me. "I took some time to drive around the city. It's beautiful here. A friend of mine has a place here that he's not using at the moment, so he offered it to me for as long as I wanted to stay here. The press found me at my residence in Beverly Hills early this morning. So I'll be hiding out here in Newport Beach for a while. I doubt the press will find me since this place isn't affiliated with Lancaster."

If the US media had picked up on the story, the social media storm *must* be crazy right now. "Where exactly are you staying in Newport Beach?"

His brow furrowed. "The exact address is in the car, but it's on Seashore Drive. Do you know it?"

I let out a long sigh. *Know it?* I lusted after those multi-million dollar homes right on the sandy beach. But they'd always be way out of *my* price range. "Most of them are breathtaking," I informed him. "And directly on the beach."

"I'm on the way there to check out the house. Care to come with me?" His tone was casual, but persuasive.

I shook my head regretfully. "No. I'll call you tomorrow."

He smiled at me as he sauntered toward the door. "I'll look forward to it."

Damian departed without another word, and I sagged back into my chair, relieved that I could finally take a deep breath.

Damn him for letting me get to know more about his family, about his mother in particular.

I didn't really *need* another day to know I was going to help Damian Lancaster, but I was going to make him wait to find out my decision.

I just hoped I didn't end up regretting it.

CHAPTER 12

Damian

I SETTLED INTO MY loaner beachfront home later that afternoon.

I'd flung open all of the huge glass doors to the patio, grabbed my laptop, and planted my ass in a lounge chair with a bottle of American beer.

Strangely, a lot of my stress melted away with the sound of the waves hitting the shore, and the balmy temperatures that made the place feel like a getaway instead of a location where I was hiding out from the press.

I grinned as I watched a flock of birds circling over the water. I'd decided *not* to tell Nicole that this home was actually owned by a Mediterranean prince who used the Newport Beach house as a vacation home to occasionally escape the confines of his royal duties. I hadn't lied. The owner *was* actually a friend, but Nicole had already had more than enough surprises for one day.

The last thing I'd wanted was to push her away by mentioning all of my royal and aristocratic acquaintances. I'd seen her horrified expression when she'd discovered that I was a duke. It wasn't that I *sought out* that crowd, but it was hard *not* to know and be friends with some of them since we'd orbited in the same circles growing up.

What I'd told her about my title was true. I had no use for it, and I didn't encourage anyone to use it.

I heard my mobile *ping* with the sound of an incoming message. I grabbed it, hoping to hell it wasn't Dylan again, whining about being trapped inside the Beverly Hills residence because he was surrounded by the media.

As requested, Dylan *had* met me at breakfast this morning, before our home had been attacked by a mob of reporters.

He'd been sullen, but sober.

What choice did he have when I controlled the money?

He'd been born outrageously wealthy. It wasn't like he had any idea how to live on a budget.

One quick glance told me that it *wasn't* a text from Dylan, and I smirked after reading the message that was clearly from Nicole.

Nicole: *If I do this thing, I want you to know I'm doing it for your mother. Not for you.*

I chuckled. Now that she knew exactly who I was, Nicole still didn't have any problem giving me hell. She had no idea how fascinating that made her to me. Nicole treated me like any other guy who'd pissed her off, and she had no way of knowing just how... alive, how damn real I felt because of it.

Me: *I was under the impression that you'd do it for ACM.*

Nicole: *Yeah. That too. But I want you to know this is definitely not about you.*

Like I didn't get that already? Her gorgeous baby-blue eyes had been shooting daggers at me in her office. If those blades had been real, I'd be dead by now.

***Me:** I'll take you any way I can get you.*

Could I find another fixer, another company who could jump into the fray to salvage the Lancaster reputation?

Definitely.

But I didn't *want* another company. I wanted *her.* I wanted *Nicole.*

I was starting to feel like a damn stalker, but I hadn't been able to control my instincts to find her today, even though I'd known she'd probably hate me.

That whole I'll-forget-all-about-her-once-we-go-our-separate-ways bullshit wasn't working for me.

I was going to have to find a way to get Nicole Ashworth into my bed.

Maybe once I'd had her, once I'd buried myself inside her and felt her shudder into the massive orgasm she'd never had before, my desire to find her wherever she went would go the fuck away.

***Nicole:** You wouldn't have me. You'd have my job skills. Everything would have to stay strictly business.*

***Me:** Agreed.*

I *wasn't* consenting to keep my distance from her *forever.* Just until she could trust me, and we could renegotiate those terms.

***Nicole:** I'm not even going to pretend like I understand that damn kiss on the plane, but that can't happen again.*

***Me:** Is it really so hard to admit that there's some kind of dynamic attraction between the two of us, Nicole?*

***Nicole:** Yes. No. Oh God, I don't know. I really want to hate you. I feel like a complete idiot because I let you play me on that airplane.*

***Me:** I wasn't playing you. I think you know the attraction between us is genuine. And you could never hate me more than I hate myself for hurting you.*

***Nicole:** I wasn't hurt. Not really. How could I be? I hardly know you. I just feel silly.*

I *had* hurt her. I wasn't exactly sure how I knew that, but I knew it was true.

Me: *Don't. I thought we agreed not to regret it.*

Nicole: *That was before I knew you were Damian Lancaster and a man-whore.*

Me: *Which was worse, me being Damian Lancaster or me being a man-whore?*

I definitely couldn't change the fact that I was Damian Lancaster, but I might be able to eventually convince her that I *was not* a man-whore who got drunk until I was out of my mind and made having sex into one big party.

Nicole: *Being Damian Lancaster, I think.*

Okay, then I *was* well and truly fucked.

Me: *Why?*

Nicole: *Because I poured my heart out to you, Damian. I sat right there and told you about my presentation. And then I even told you about my sex life. I told you almost everything about myself, and you told me nothing except a few facts. Do you really think I go around sharing my entire life with everybody?*

Me: *No. I know you don't. But would you have told me all that if you'd known I was Damian Lancaster almost from the start?*

I didn't get an immediate answer.

Finally, she texted back.

Nicole: *I don't really know. Other than the whole creepy reading my texts behavior, and that bossy thing you do, I kind of liked you. I'm not sure how I would have felt if I'd known who you were from the start.*

Me: *I should have told you. Can we just start over? Hello, Nicole. I'm Damian Lancaster, CEO of Lancaster International. Yes, I realize that whole orgy situation doesn't look good, but do you think you could hold off making judgments until you actually get to know me? My cock has been painfully hard since I saw you sitting in the seat beside* *me, and I'd very much like to shag you until you're screaming my name in the throes of your first orgasm while having sex with a guy.*

Nicole: *Now you're just being nonsensical.*

Me: *Did it make you laugh?*

Nicole: *Yes.*

Me: *I would have said that if I could have. It's the absolute truth.*

Nicole: *You have to stop saying those things if we end up working together! You did say it would be business only.*

Me: *You haven't said yes to my offer yet, so we're not working together. Does that mean you've made up your mind to take on Lancaster International?*

Nicole: *No. I'll call you tomorrow morning.*

Fuck! I really didn't want to wait until tomorrow.

Me: *Let me call you. Are you still in your office? Maybe we could have dinner together. A business dinner, of course.*

Nicole: *I'm still in my office, but I'm getting ready to leave. I have plans for tonight.*

Me: *A date?*

It was Friday night, so it made sense that she might have a date. With another guy. A male who might actually…touch her, kiss her.

Oh, hell no!

Nicole: *I guess you could call it that. Look, I'll seriously think about taking on Lancaster International and call you tomorrow morning.*

Jesus Christ! Did she really think I was just going to go on with my night and not think about her out on a date with somebody who wasn't…*me?*

My voice of reason suddenly reared its ugly head:

Of course she thinks you'll go on with your night without thinking about her. She doesn't believe you're even attracted to her, and even if she did, the woman thinks you're a man-whore and a liar. Pull your ass together, Lancaster. You had one amazing kiss, and that could very well be all you'll ever get from her. It's none of your business if she's got a date. There's no reason it should ever bother you. It's not like she's yours. So get a damn grip, man.

I took a deep breath, and tried to listen to that rational voice, even though I hated that little bastard.

Me: *Nicole?*

Nicole: *Yes?*

Me: *Be careful, and call me early, okay?*

Nicole: *Around 8 am?*

I wanted to tell her to call me when she got home from her damn date because I knew I wouldn't be sleeping.

Me: *Fine.*

Nicole: *Have a good night.*

I tossed my mobile back on the table, closed my eyes, and beat my head against the back of the lounger several times.

What in the fuck am I doing? I've never had a single jealous, possessive, or envious thought in my entire life, even with the females I've dated and shagged. I'm Damian-Fucking-Lancaster, CEO and owner of one of the biggest, richest, and most powerful corporations in the world. I don't have time to sit around waiting for some female who makes my cock hard to call me. I'm a serious businessman who needs to concentrate on the work that's been piling up for the last two days while I've been trying to figure out how to get Nicole Ashworth into my bed.

I took a deep breath and let it out before I muttered, "I just need to get her into bed, and all this shit will go away. It has to. I want my goddamn brain back."

I didn't really need my voice of reason to know that I was being highly irrational.

I knew it.

But when it came to Nicole, some idiotic primitive instinct I never knew I had completely overrode my damn logic.

My obsession with Nicole Ashworth has to end.

I grabbed my laptop, opened it, and got to work, trying like hell to block out everything else from my mind.

CHAPTER 13

Nicole

"SO YOU'RE REALLY going to do it?" Kylie asked.

"I think you should," Macy chimed in.

I stretched out on my beach towel as I took an appreciative sip of the latte we'd stopped for on our way to the beach.

Kylie, Macy, and I spent almost every Friday night in the same way.

We stopped at our favorite coffee shop for a to-go latte right after work, and took it down to the beach.

We liked to call it a standing date for the three of us as long as nobody had other plans.

I smiled at the two women who had been my friends since grade school. All three of us were so different, but it hadn't stopped us from being sisters at heart.

"Is it really so hard to believe that I want to expand ACM to go international?" I asked.

Kylie shook her head as she stretched out on her own towel. "Noooo. But this isn't just any international account, and you know it. It's Lancaster International. You had an interlude with the man who heads the company. A guy who got himself into this mess by being photographed during one of his orgies."

"He swears it was a setup," I informed both of them.

Macy had been caught up on the Mr. Orgasm situation by Kylie on our way to the beach.

"Maybe it was," Macy considered. "He's incredibly rich. Obviously, he has competitors who want him to look bad."

"Or maybe it wasn't, and he really is an asshole," Kylie answered with an unusual amount of skepticism. "Yeah. Sure. I'd *like* to think he's on the up-and-up, but maybe he's just a skank. I don't think we can rule out that possibility."

I shot her a surprised glance. "What happened to your optimism about him? What happened to the Kylie who wanted me to give him the benefit of the doubt?"

"Oh, God," she moaned. "I'm torn. I *do* want you to give him a chance, but I don't want you to get hurt."

I shrugged. "It's not like it really matters," I said. "We aren't going into a romantic relationship. It's all business. Even if he *is* an asshole, my job is to make him look like a good guy."

Kylie huffed as she flopped onto her side and propped a hand under her head. "Come on, Nic. I saw the way he looked at you when he was in the office today."

"How did he look at her?" Macy asked curiously.

Kylie snorted. "Like he was starving, and she was the *only* item on the lunch menu that he wanted."

"Are you attracted to him, Nic?" Macy asked guilelessly.

"Yes," Kylie answered emphatically.

"Not really," I countered.

Both of them raised their brows as they looked at me.

I caved. These were the two people that I trusted completely. "Okay, I *am* attracted to him. How could I not be? The guy is physical perfection, and that British accent plays hell with my hormones, but I know when a man is out of my league. I *can't* get hurt. I'm going in with my eyes wide open this time, and it's strictly business."

Kylie rolled her eyes. "You're *not* out of his league. He's out of yours. He's a liar and possible man-whore, remember?"

"You're right," I said with a groan. "I guess the whole story about his mother and finding out that he's a duke really got to me today."

Macy's eyes popped open wide. "He's a duke?"

I spent the next few minutes explaining the conversation I'd had with Damian earlier in the day.

"So part of you is doing this for his mom?" Kylie asked.

I nodded. "It sounds like she's worked so hard to feel worthy of the Lancaster family, and she doesn't deserve this."

I sorely missed my own mother, so maybe I was a sucker for a mom in distress.

"I'm not saying that it wouldn't be advantageous, Nic," Kylie mused. "You want to go international. It would be good for ACM. But not if the bastard breaks your heart in the process."

I let out an exasperated breath. "Damian Lancaster is not going to break my heart."

I just had to make sure I reminded myself that his looks and charm meant nothing if his personality and morals sucked.

Kylie sighed. "I wish he could be the kind of guy who you could just have a fling with if he's really your Mr. Orgasm."

"Is he the one, Nic?" Macy asked.

As I thought about the way Damian made me feel, and *that damn kiss*, I answered honestly, "Maybe. I'm not saying he'd definitely make me fall to pieces sexually, but he made me feel... something I never have before."

Damian had made me feel beautiful.

Desirable.

Raw, powerful lust that I wanted to drown in.

"Could you have a fling with him?" Macy asked.

Was it possible that I could do a one-nighter with somebody like Damian Lancaster just to see what it felt like to have sex with a man who really seemed attracted to me?

It was a tempting thought, but I needed to keep my head on straight if I wanted to be his fixer. "Probably not. I don't want to mix business with pleasure. Doing this job right means too much to ACM."

"So what's your plan?" Kylie asked curiously.

"I already told him that he needs to make an official statement," I answered. "And stay away from any further orgies."

Kylie's expression shifted, and I could tell she was thinking about crisis management now. "I think the hoopla here in the US will die down fairly quickly. The only reason the press here got interested was because it's such a big deal in England at the moment. I'd say he'll have to do most of his reforming in the UK."

"I think you're right," I agreed. "We Americans can have a short attention span, especially when it's a story that isn't happening here. But I doubt that England is going to be quite as forgiving."

"He's going to need some very carefully crafted *good* publicity," Kylie pondered. "You're going to have to go with him to London."

My stomach clenched in protest, even though I already knew that I was going to *have* to go to London with Damian to fix the situation. "I know."

Kylie smiled slyly. "Maybe England needs a fairy-tale romance fit for a duke. Love can change a man, right?"

My heart protested that idea for a moment, but I knew it had to happen. "That was my plan. He needs to find a woman with an excellent reputation and no skeletons in her closet, and then be seen treating her like she's the only female in the world for him.

Eventually, people will put that whole thing behind them if he can put on a convincing performance."

"If this is all for show, what happens when it's over?" Macy asked, sounding confused. "It's not like he's going to marry someone just for good publicity."

Kylie sat up as she answered, "That's where it would come in handy if the woman was American. Eventually, she could just claim that she misses her own country, and disappear permanently back to the US. Damian could say it was an amicable parting, and he could even be the injured party."

"Fantastic idea," I said. "But where are we going to find this paragon? I don't know how many American women Damian knows, and I'm a little afraid of the ones he might suggest. And really, I don't think this should be an outside job. Even bound by a tight nondisclosure, it's going to be hard for any woman not to talk about this job, or try to make the whole scenario real. Kylie, who do we have at ACM who could pull this off? It has to be a woman who isn't married, and has a very clean background. And she has to be a believable love interest for Damian."

Macy and Kylie pinned me with a fixed stare.

"There's only one woman at ACM who isn't married, and who's *that* squeaky clean," Kylie said. "A female who has never had a single fling, or anything remotely questionable in her past. Nic, our staff isn't that big. You and I are about the only ones who are the right age and single, and I'm sure as hell not doing it. I have some dirt that could be dug up if reporters looked hard enough."

Horror flooded me as I realized what she and Macy were contemplating. "Oh, no, I'm not going to pose as Damian's love interest. Absolutely not. I own his PR agency. People would know it's bullshit."

Kylie shook her head. "They'd never have to know that he hired you. You haven't signed an official deal yet. You could wait until this whole thing is over to make it legal. Damian would never back out of the deal. The truth would actually be a good backstory. You and Damian met on a plane when he was flying on his own airline. You're a businesswoman from the United States who just happened to be sitting next to him. You chatted the entire flight, and fell for each other over morning tea or something."

"I don't really like tea," I said in a panicked voice. I really didn't like this idea at all.

"Coffee then," Macy answered. "Does it matter? You can make it a love story, whether you drank tea or coffee."

"You can do this, Nic," Kylie encouraged. "You're the ideal woman for him to fall for here. There's not a bad word that anybody could say about you. You graduated with high honors from college, and busted your ass to get through law school. You worked as a corporate attorney until you turned your attention toward the PR business."

"Do I look like the kind of woman Damian Lancaster would fall for?" I asked. "Really? I'm overweight—"

"Curvy," Macy insisted. "You're in great shape, Nic. We've been scuba diving together for years, remember? I know how physically taxing some of those dives were, so don't even go there with me. We're in the water every chance we get. You're shapely, and fit."

"I'm way too tall—"

"Models are tall," Kylie interrupted. "And Damian's a tall guy. You could rock some pretty high stilettos and still feel dainty next to him."

"I wouldn't have a chance in hell of catching Damian Lancaster's roving eye," I said adamantly. "You saw those naked women in his bed. I am *not* his type."

"I call bullshit," Macy said emphatically. "You're beautiful, Nic. You've just never seen yourself that way."

Kylie raised her hand. "I call bullshit, too. Macy is right. And it's pretty clear that Damian's *already* attracted to you. I hate it when you sell yourself short just because no man has ever made you feel as gorgeous as you are, Nic. In my opinion, you're way too good for somebody like Damian Lancaster, but you can always pretend that you're slumming it."

"She's absolutely right," Macy confirmed.

I looked at the two women who had been my greatest supporters for most of my life, and I knew they believed every word they were saying. How could I not adore both of them for seeing me way differently than I saw myself because they loved me?

"I love you both," I said as I broke into laughter. I had two very adamant defenders beside me, and had for most of my life. There was no way I couldn't find joy in that, and be pretty damn grateful that these two amazing women would always be my fiercest allies, just like I'd always be theirs.

I flopped onto my back, my heart still racing at the idea of playing Damian's love interest.

"I'm not sure I can do it," I admitted.

Really, I didn't have a whole lot of choice if I wanted to be completely certain the truth would never come out.

"Of course you can," Kylie argued. "You've never failed at anything in your life. This will be a piece of cake."

"I haven't completely decided that I'm the perfect woman to pull this off," I warned them. God, there had to be some way to get me out of this, right?

"If you don't believe your two best friends, ask Damian," Kylie insisted. "I doubt very much if he'd mind you playing the part of his love interest. Maybe I don't completely trust him, but the way he was looking at you in the office was no lie, Nic. I think he'll convince you that you're absolutely perfect."

I sighed as I remembered that he'd *already* told me that I was perfect, and I hadn't believed a word of it.

CHAPTER 14

Damian

"THIS PLACE IS amazing." Nicole's tone was filled with awe, and her big blue eyes sparkled as she admired the view from the patio of my borrowed beach house. "You're steps away from the ocean, and literally right on the sand."

All the glass doors were open, and it was a clear, balmy early summer morning in Newport Beach.

When Nicole had called me earlier, I'd asked her to meet me here at the house since her office was closed on the weekends.

I'd also wanted the advantage of having her in my territory in case she'd decided against taking on Lancaster International as a client. I'd have a better chance of changing her mind if she couldn't just slam her office door in my face.

"Can we sit here?" she asked, gesturing toward the lounge chairs on the patio. "Since I'll definitely never own one of these homes, I'd like to admire the view while I can."

"Make yourself at home," I insisted. "Can I get you some tea? I don't think I have any coffee."

She held up a supersized to-go coffee that she'd brought in with her. "I came prepared. I stopped for my own coffee. I'm not that big on tea. I've never really understood the British obsession with it."

I grasped my mug of Taylors of Harrogate black tea as I plopped down on a lounger beside her. "How can you not like tea? There's a blend for everybody."

She shrugged. "It's not that I *dislike* it. But how can it ever compare to a good latte?"

Obviously, the poor woman had never had a good cuppa. "Very easily. With tea, there's a blend for every occasion, and you never run out of new ones to try. Coffee is just…coffee, no matter what you put in it."

She rolled her eyes. "I'm not going to even try to argue with a tea-loving Brit."

I shot her a mock warning glance. "Best not. Never argue with an Englishman about his tea."

"Do you ever drink coffee?" she asked curiously.

I shook my head firmly. "No. Nasty stuff."

She laughed at the look of disgust on my face, and for some damn reason, all I wanted was to keep her laughing. It might sound a little dramatic, but the sound was like music to my soul.

Fuck! When in the hell had I gotten the least bit poetic about… anything?

Not until…*her.*

I studied Nicole, still trying to figure out why she made me so fucking crazy.

Her blonde hair was tied back in a ponytail, and her attire was casual—jeans, a lightweight red summer top, and a pair of sandals.

Nothing different there. It was the way most people dressed in this coastal city.

She had a serene smile on her face as she gazed out at the water, and when she turned her head to look at me, that expression turned into a full-fledged grin.

My dick was completely hard in seconds, and for some damn reason, there wasn't a single thing I could do but smile widely right back at her.

Nicole had some kind of inner radiance that spilled out when she was unguarded, and damned if that shit wasn't contagious.

Maybe I was drawn to the way she could find so much humor in a single comment. Or the way she'd made me feel alive—again—since the second she'd walked through my door this morning.

I cleared my throat. "How was the date last night?"

Okay, so maybe I hadn't *quite* been able to forget about *that.* And dammit! I'd certainly tried. Hard. Nothing had worked. Not even my voice of reason.

She smiled. "It was good. Kylie, Macy, and I always have a good time at the beach on our standing date nights."

I frowned at her. "You had a date with…Kylie and Macy?"

She nodded. "Every Friday night. Going to the beach is a standing date for all three of us unless one of us has a real date or something. We've been doing it since I moved back to California."

Okay. I have to admit that I grinned like a damn idiot. Maybe I should be annoyed with myself for jumping to conclusions, but the only thing I could feel was a profound sense of relief. "So that's why you turned down my dinner invitation?"

"I'd already told Macy and Kylie that I was going," she explained.

"No problem." I could be pretty magnanimous now that I knew that there wasn't a single male at their standing date. "So you like my loaner house?"

She let out a sigh that made my cock twitch. "I've always loved these houses. How could anyone not want to be right on the water?

The second I hear the waves, I relax. I can't imagine what it would be like to actually live here."

"I thought you did live here."

"In Newport Beach, yes. But I live in a city-view condo that I inherited from my mother. These homes are outrageously expensive. I make a good living, but not nearly enough for a waterfront of any kind in this city."

"I guess I've never thought about my income not being enough for...anything," I told her.

She chuckled. "That's probably *not* something a Lancaster has to think about, but most of us normal folks have to stick to a budget."

I considered her comment as I took a swig of my tea. I'd been a billionaire since the day I was born. There was never much that was off-limits to me because I lacked the funds. Most of my friends were rich, too, so I had no idea what it was like to stay on any particular budget. I signed my name; I got what I wanted. Period. End of story. "I guess that makes me abnormal," I said.

She shook her head, and for a moment, I was distracted by the way her blonde ponytail bounced with that particular action.

"Not abnormal," she corrected. "Being rich and powerful is *your* normal. It just isn't natural for most of the population."

I loved the way she could just accept the fact that I was obscenely wealthy without being enamored by that lifestyle.

"So you're happy with your own normal?" I asked.

She thought for a moment before she answered. "For the most part, yes. I consider myself lucky. I'm well-educated, and I make a good living. I think it's human nature to want to keep doing better, but money isn't everything. I have great friends, and I get to spend time doing all the things I love to do."

"Such as?" I wanted to know more about her, find out what made *her* happy.

"I spend as much time in and on the water as possible," she shared. "I'm certified in scuba, so I spend a lot of time under the water. I get out for dives a couple of times a week when I'm not slammed at the agency."

I hadn't expected her to say *that*. "So there's a daredevil beneath your gorgeous exterior?"

"There's something really magical about spending time with aquatic animals in their own habitat, and it's not that dangerous."

I nodded. "My brother Leo says the same thing. He's a diver. Instructor level. He's always trying to talk me into trying it."

"You should take him up on it. Life should never be all about work. Where does he dive?"

I shrugged. "Everywhere. He's away far more than he's home. Sometimes I envy that. He's a wildlife biologist who searches for extremely rare or probable extinct species across the globe. Leo has a large sanctuary and breeding program in England to help save animals that are near extinction. He's never had any interest in Lancaster International. He was bought out when the estate was settled, but I don't think he really cares about the money. Well, other than the fact that it helps him do what he's always wanted to do."

I surprised myself with the casual observation that I sometimes coveted Leo's lifestyle, but it was probably true.

"I'm sure his life has *some* downfalls," Nicole observed. "I couldn't imagine being away from home all the time, and living out of a backpack or a suitcase. You travel, too, right?"

"Yes. But not like Leo does," I confessed. "Sometimes I'd like to travel simply for pleasure and not for business, but my life doesn't work that way right now."

"I can understand that. My one and only trip to London was my first time outside the United States, and I didn't get much of a chance to see anything because I was working. I was too worried about my presentation."

"Then I guess you'll just have to come back," I said hopefully. "You didn't do any sightseeing?"

"I tried. I got lost on the Tube. I thought I was going the right direction to get to the Tower of London, but it turned out that I was headed the wrong way. By the time I straightened it all out and got to the Tower, I didn't have much time. I couldn't see the whole thing."

She sounded so forlorn that it made my damn chest ache. "Take a taxi or an Uber next time," I advised. "Everyone gets lost on the Tube unless they take it all the time."

"Well, I *might* get another chance," she said, her tone nervous.

I shaded my eyes from the sun and looked at her face. "You think so?"

Fuck! I really hated the way I found myself anxiously waiting to hear what she had to say.

"Maybe," she said carefully. "If you agree with my proposal."

Okay, she sounded twice as apprehensive now. "What's wrong, Nicole? You sound worried. Talk to me. What's so bad about coming back to England? You'll never have to do a pitch for my executives again. I swear."

"It's not that." She fidgeted in her lounge chair. "Look, I really *do* want a chance to help you fix your current situation."

"And I want you to do that," I said eagerly. "I took your advice already, and made a public statement. So why is working with me a problem?"

She took a deep breath. "I think I'll need to go back to England with you."

"Excellent," I agreed. "That definitely won't be an issue. We'll fly together. Take my jet. It's a hell of a lot more comfortable than business class."

I *wanted* Nicole to go back to England with me, so her plan was the same as mine so far.

"You need to find yourself a girlfriend," she said in a rush, like she was having a problem forcing the words out of her mouth. "A woman who has a good reputation and background. Preferably American so she can go away quietly when the good publicity is over. The media needs to tell another story about you, Damian. Something positive."

I frowned at her. This definitely didn't suit my plan. "I don't know any American women, and I've never had a long-term love interest. I told you that, Nicole. I don't have the time."

Nicole glared back at me. "Then it's time for a change."

"Even if I *was* on board with your idea, which I'm *not,* where do you suggest I find this woman?" I was irritated. I had no desire to cozy up to some suitable woman just for the pictures and the positive press. Especially considering that my plan was to seduce Nicole.

I'd just wait it out, let the whole damn thing blow over, and keep Dylan out of the country until that happened. There was no way I was going to pretend to be a pathetic, lovelorn idiot. Yeah, I'd do a lot for my mother and for the Lancaster name, but not *that.* Anything but *that.* I had no fucking idea how to romance a woman.

"Maybe you *already* have found her," Nicole suddenly squeaked.

"I'm not following you." I was getting annoyed, and all I wanted her to do was tell me her plan so I could simply refuse to cooperate.

I wanted her in London, but we'd just have to come up with *another* plan. I wasn't good at being charming or pretending, so the public would *never* buy my false affection for a woman I didn't know.

Dylan could have pulled this whole idea off, but I couldn't.

Nicole sounded anxious as hell when she started to speak. "I'm educated, and I haven't had any scandals in my past. I don't have skeletons in my closet. And I know exactly what has to be done. There's no paper trail of you hiring me, so we can wait to sign an agreement until *after* this is all over. *I'm* willing to go play your temporary girlfriend if *you'll* give it your best effort," she said stiffly.

"Believe me, I don't like this plan any better than you do, but I don't want any of this to go outside of ACM, even with a nondisclosure. The less people who know, the better, and I'm really the only person at ACM who can do it."

A large, glaring lightbulb finally switched on in my sluggish brain, and my lips curved up in a smile as I looked at Nicole's flustered expression.

Oh, hell, yes!

I *completely* changed my mind about her proposed plan. It was absolutely brilliant, and it was going to mesh with my strategy perfectly.

She was going to be the one to play the adoring girlfriend.

She was going to be my love interest.

She was going to go back to England to drum up some positive publicity about what a great guy I could be when I *wasn't* participating in orgies.

Now didn't that just change…*everything*?

I wouldn't have to *pretend* that I was fucking obsessed with Nicole, *and only Nicole,* because that was actually my reality right now. No acting necessary. With her, my annoying fixation was very, very real.

"I'm in," I agreed, no questions asked. "But you do understand that we're going to have to be up close and personal, right?"

"Of course," she snapped.

"You'll have to let me kiss you again, fondle you whenever we're together." I was completely warming up to this whole scenario.

"No…fondling," she said uneasily.

I shook my head. "There will definitely have to be fondling to show how much I adore you," I argued. "You want me to be your Prince Charming, don't you?"

She snorted. "You're already charming enough as a duke, Your Grace. You can touch me, but no…groping."

Typically, I hated the ducal address, but Nicole said it so playfully that it was *almost* an endearment. So I wasn't about to complain if *she* used it.

I *was* incredibly tempted to tell her that there would be a whole lot of groping, which would inevitably lead to getting her into my bed, but I held that thought.

She looked uncomfortable enough, so the last thing I wanted to do was dissuade her, not when I wholeheartedly endorsed this particular plan.

"I'll be on my best behavior. I promise," I told her.

Which *really* meant that I'd do everything I possibly could to coax her into my bed so the woman could experience her first orgasm…or two…or three.

There was no possible way that I'd screw up this opportunity to seduce Nicole Ashworth, and *finally* get my sanity back again.

In return, I'd make damn sure she was satisfied, and teach her how important it was for *her* to get to the finish line, too.

It seemed like a fair deal to me.

Nicole, however, might need some convincing.

"One hint of an orgy and I'm gone," she mumbled.

I grinned at her. "Absolutely."

Since the only female I wanted to get naked with was *her,* that particular term would be no problem at all.

CHAPTER 15

Nicole

"IF YOU DON'T have a fling with that man, I swear that I'm going to offer *myself* up for one," Kylie said the following week.

She kept her voice hushed as we gathered up more snacks and drinks from the kitchen of my condo.

It was a wise choice for her to modulate her voice since Damian and Macy were still sitting in my living room.

My two best friends had decided that they *needed* to have a going-away party for me tonight, and Damian had boldly invited himself to the festivities.

He was cutting his US visit short because the social media nightmare wasn't getting any calmer, so we were departing for London tomorrow to get this plan into motion.

"The man is dangerous," I mumbled in a quiet voice to Kylie as I opened my cupboard to find more chips. "He hasn't even *looked* at another woman while he's been here. The only one he pays any attention to is…me."

Damian had been adamant about…practicing to be my boyfriend. He'd taken me out to dinner on Monday night, and played the adoring male love interest so well that it was almost…uncomfortable.

As his PR agent, maybe I should be ecstatic that his acting ability was Oscar-worthy. I probably would be if it didn't make me so damn…nervous.

Tuesday, he'd shown up at the office with lunch for my entire crew, and had proceeded to charm Kylie to the point where she'd seemed to forget that he was a man-whore.

When he'd found out that the girls were doing an impromptu bon voyage this evening, he'd shown up with an armful of food, and started swaying Macy to his side.

Was it ridiculous that I felt like my two best friends were traitors?

"He's not what I expected," Kylie said with a sigh. "I really wanted to hate him, but he does look at you like you're the only woman he could ever want. And he's so…nice."

I went to the fridge and pulled out the bottle of wine Damian had brought, and a beer for him.

"Have you forgotten he's a man-whore?" I said in a loud, frustrated whisper.

Kylie shrugged as she took the wine and beer. "Maybe I have. He's charming, and the way he treats you is making me forget. Nic, you're right. The only female he sees is you. It's so obvious. It's hard to believe that it was Damian in that naked picture. The whole thing just doesn't make sense. Maybe it really *was* a setup, because the guy I see in your living room right now doesn't seem like the type to get drunk and throw a massive orgy."

I snorted. "You saw the picture. It was *definitely* him."

I couldn't quite blame my friend for her conclusion. I'd been having a hard time reconciling Damian and that scandal myself.

"But here's the thing..." Kylie said thoughtfully. "You and I spent all day today trying to dig for information on the Lancasters on the net. We did our research, and we pretty much came up empty-handed. Yeah, we ran into a few innocuous things about Leo and Damian's mother, but for the most part, I have to assume they live very private lives most of the time. And what kind of dirt did we dig up about Damian? Absolutely nothing except for that orgy picture and article, and some painfully dry business articles. Nic, doesn't it seem a little strange to you that if Damian really is a man-whore, that we didn't see a single thing about his past indiscretions on the internet? Doesn't that make you think that maybe this *was* all a setup?"

I nodded slowly. "It is strange." I'd thought the same damn thing after the two of us had spent so much time today chasing every single mention of the Lancaster family for the last two years on the net. I wouldn't be doing my job if I hadn't *really* looked for other possible scandals, things that might pop up while we were in London. Oh, there was plenty of information about Lancaster International, but very little personal stuff about the man who owned it, Leo, or Damian's mother. Strangely, I hadn't been all that surprised that nothing more had popped up. So maybe I *did* believe some of the things Damian had told me over the last several days.

It was probably true that his mother hadn't ventured out much, or attended events since his father had died.

And it could also be true that Leo was considered way too boring for the tabloids.

Okay *maybe*, just *maybe*, the whole orgy situation *was* a setup, and Damian generally lived a workaholic life that wasn't exactly newsworthy. I certainly hadn't found a single shred of evidence to the contrary today.

Although Damian could be charismatic, he never acted like a man-whore. It was obvious that he took his responsibilities to his business and his family seriously. In fact, Damian was...*too serious* most of the time.

Kylie shrugged. "I think it *was* some kind of setup, and Damian was in the wrong place at the wrong time. Has he made a move on you?"

"He hasn't even tried to kiss me again," I admitted. "He acts like he's trying to get me to trust him."

That damn kiss was always dancing around in my head every time I looked at Damian, no matter how much I tried to forget it.

Not that he hadn't gotten as close to me as possible when we'd had dinner together, but he'd settled for putting his arm around me, and inundating me with sexy innuendos that never saw follow-through.

I wasn't sure if I was relieved or disappointed that he'd been all talk and no action.

Kylie smiled. "He probably is trying to gain your trust."

"Ha! Or he could be a serial killer trying to lull me into a sense of security before he pounces," I countered.

I *had* to keep reminding myself that there was a side of Damian I *hadn't* seen. Even if the whole scandal was a setup, he wasn't completely innocent. He'd obviously made himself a target by getting drunk enough to allow somebody to spike his drink.

But is that really fair, though? I got shitfaced myself on an airplane with a complete stranger.

The only difference was that Damian Lancaster was a billionaire duke who was in the public eye, and I wasn't. If I wanted to believe he'd been tricked, I really couldn't blame him for something that could happen to almost anyone.

Kylie refused to give up. "He's really attracted to you, Nic. And I think you're equally attracted to him. Why not give the guy a chance? We all do stupid things sometimes. God knows I have."

"He's a client, Kylie," I reminded her sternly.

She raised a brow. "Not technically. You could have a fling *before* you sign that contract."

I shook my head and blinked back the tears that were beginning to blur my vision. "I can't. I think I'm actually starting to *like* him."

I was discovering that there were too many things to actually admire about Damian, and some of those things really touched me.

As much as he reminded me that he was born to privilege, and had no idea what a normal life was like, I was starting to think that his wealth and power weren't *always* good for him.

Damian took his responsibilities to heart, and even though he *had* all that money, I didn't think he took much time to really enjoy it.

During his unguarded moments, I could tell that he was stressed, exhausted, and worried more about his family and his company than he did about his own self-interests.

It was really hard *not* to like a guy who put everyone else's needs before his own.

"I'm starting to like him, too," Kylie confessed. "But not the same way you do. He seems genuinely interested in getting to know me and Macy. When he asks questions, he actually *listens* to what we have to say. I can recognize another fixer when I see one, and I think Damian *is* a fixer. He seems to want to solve everyone's problems except his own. I think he's probably an amazing older brother, and a good son. He seems...loyal to everyone he cares about, Nic. Did you know he donated an obscene amount of money to Macy's animal charity?"

I'd started to rummage through the fridge to find some dip, but I stopped what I was doing, and pulled my head out to gape at Kylie. "That's weird. He didn't mention it."

"See. *That's* what's confusing," she said as her brow furrowed. "I don't think he *wants* to talk about *any* of the nice things he does. He slipped Macy a check earlier. One with a hell of a lot of zeros.

He was discreet, but I saw it. I don't think he wants the recognition for helping."

"I wonder if he does a lot of charity stuff in England," I mused. "We could use some charity events to our advantage."

She nodded. "I can guarantee that he gives generously, but probably doesn't make a big deal about it. I wouldn't put it past him to somehow donate anonymously if he can. The guy seems to have a huge sense of duty, and I'm willing to bet he sees it as his responsibility to right everything that's wrong in the world."

"Believe it or not, I can see that," I agreed.

There were times when I got the feeling that Damian carried the weight of the world on his very broad shoulders.

"Do you think that you can at least consider that he might not be the man you assume he is?" Kylie asked me. "I have great spidey-senses, and he's not alarming a single one of them. I'm not sure what's going on, but I don't think Damian is the type who sleeps around with every woman he sees. I think he's completely enamored with *you*, and has no idea what to do about it."

My heart skittered. "He's the kind of man who could hurt me, Kylie."

"Or give you multiple orgasms," she added. "He's scorching hot. I admit it. And it would be easy to blow him off as a womanizer because of one mistake. I don't want to see you get hurt, but I also don't want to see you miss an opportunity with a man who really seems to see...you. And loves *everything* he sees. Aren't you the least bit tempted to throw caution to the wind and see what it's like to drown in his adoration?"

"Very tempted," I admitted, dropping all sense of pretense with my best friend. "But what happens if I can't handle a simple affair?"

I felt panicked at the thought of getting that close to a man like Damian, and making myself vulnerable.

"It's definitely a risk," Kylie said. "And only you can decide if he's worth it."

I brushed a tear from my cheek. "I'm scared, Kylie."

She ran a soothing hand over my back. "I know. I get that. Believe me. Being that attracted to someone is hard. You're afraid that your infatuation will blind you to the truth. And God knows we have reason to doubt Damian Lancaster. Follow your instincts, Nic. If I'd followed mine before and during my marriage, I could have avoided a whole lot of heartache."

I pulled my best friend into a big hug. I could hear the pain still vibrating through her voice when she talked about one of the most painful parts of her past.

We held on to each other silently for a few moments. When I finally pulled back, I asked her in shaky whisper, "Did you know, Kylie?"

She pointed at her temple. "I knew it here." She moved her finger to her heart. "I just didn't want to believe it here. I wish I'd listened to that little nagging gut instinct that told me I was making a mistake."

I nodded and pulled her in for another brief hug to comfort her. "I guess I'll just have to see how it goes. The problem with me is that I just don't hear *anything* telling me that trusting Damian would be a mistake. My instinct says to trust him, but I keep making up excuses why I shouldn't."

Her face was completely serious as she warned, "Don't let fear make your decisions for you, Nic. It will suck every ounce of joy out of your life. Do you really want to wonder what it would have been like if you'd given Damian a chance, even if it *doesn't* turn into something you want forever? Do you want to carry those questions along with you for the rest of your life?"

"No," I told her. "I'm just not sure he's the best guy in the world to trust with my *first fling*."

A mischievous glint sparked in Kylie's eyes. "The really orgasmic, beautiful ones rarely are. They're a huge risk. I guess that's what makes them so damn exciting. Live a little, Nic. When have you ever been so attracted to any man?"

I swallowed hard. "Never. Which makes this really scary."

"If things go bad, you know Macy and I will be here for you when it's over," she said solemnly. "But I think not taking a chance at all would haunt you far worse than the melancholy you'll experience for a while if it ends badly. At least you'd know that Damian *wasn't* your Mr. Orgasm."

My heart clenched as I wiped any sign of my tears from my face.

When I was old and gray, I didn't want Damian Lancaster to be my one regret. For once, I wanted to live dangerously, and maybe a little bit recklessly. I was thirty-two years old, and I'd never put myself out there to find anything more than an okay-for-now boyfriend.

I *did* want more, and Damian was the first man who had ever tempted me to take a risk to experience that elusive *something more.*

"I'll think about it," I promised. "I'm not as brave as you are when it comes to taking chances. I wish I was."

She smirked. "Sometimes I wish I could be as cautious as you are, so that makes us even."

I wanted to tell her that being guarded, and wanting to always make my mother proud, wasn't exactly a great way to live, either.

My mom had busted her ass as a single parent to make sure I'd gotten everything I needed as a kid, and as an adult. In return, I'd second-guessed every step that I took to make sure it was the right one. I hadn't rushed into anything that might disappoint her, or hamper my ability to be successful.

Maybe that was why I'd always played it safe with the men in my life.

If they didn't distract me from my career goals, maybe I'd thought that was a good thing.

I'd been Mom's entire world, and she'd become mine, too.

Not that she would have wanted me to sacrifice anything for her, but I'd been her only child, so I think subconsciously, I'd wanted to do all I could to make her sacrifices worth it.

I shot my best friend a dubious look. "Being squeaky clean can be incredibly boring. Didn't Mom ever warn you about jumping in headfirst without checking to see how deep the water was first?"

Kylie shook her head. "Never. She wanted everyone around her to be happy. Just like you do. You got that from her, you know."

"I wish I was *more* like her," I said with a sigh. "I wish I was petite, charming, and adorable."

"She wouldn't have changed a single hair on your head, Nic. She loved that you were tall, blonde, curvy and absolutely gorgeous. She always talked about how beautiful you were, and how much you took after your dad."

"She did?" I was astounded. Mom had never mentioned my father all that much to *me*.

"She talked about how much you were like him all the time," Kylie responded. "She wouldn't have changed that, Nic. Your father was a brilliant engineer, and she never let anyone forget that her daughter was as scholastically gifted as her father was."

I smiled at her weakly. "My father was really tall, too. Maybe being a giant isn't all that bad if you're standing next to a really tall guy who doesn't make you feel like an Amazon woman."

"Hmmm…maybe somebody like Damian Lancaster?"

I took a deep breath, and it came out in a tremulous exhale as I gathered up all the things I'd gotten out of my fridge and pantry.

"He's too damn physically perfect," I mumbled.

Too tall.

Too muscular.

Too bossy.

Too…much of everything.

"He's…overwhelming." I handed a bag of chips to Kylie.

She winked at me as she took it. "Which is exactly what could lead to one of the best orgasms you'll ever have."

"I'm not sure I want that," I grumbled. "I'm not quite sure I'd live through it."

Kylie laughed as she jerked her head toward the living room. "Let's go, Safety Girl. Danger awaits."

She led the way out of the kitchen, while I trailed behind her, wondering if I could *ever* really offer myself up for a wild fling with someone like Damian Lancaster.

CHAPTER 16

Nicole

"I LIKE YOUR FRIENDS," Damian informed me after I closed the door on the flurry of goodbyes from Macy and Kylie. "Although both of them did warn me that if I were to break your heart, they'd cut my balls off. I think Macy said something about feeding them to a hungry pack of wolves."

I let out a startled laugh. "She actually said that?"

He nodded solemnly, and followed me back into the living room. "Not that I blame them. If I were your friend, my first instinct would be to protect you from me, too."

My body shuddered as I turned and saw the covetous look in his ever-changing green eyes.

He moved toward me with an expression so intense that I almost backed away as he kept talking. "I can't imagine that anyone who knows you *wouldn't* want to shield you from a tosser like me, beautiful."

I wasn't surprised by his comment, or the endearment. Damian had a habit of mocking himself sometimes, and I'd almost gotten used to him throwing out outrageous compliments to me.

I inhaled deeply as he stepped right in front of me, and I wallowed in his scent. "Are you such a bad man, then?" I asked as I looked up at him.

Damian was a complicated guy, but I *wanted* to understand him.

"When it comes to *you*, I think that answer would probably be *yes*. You're way too good for a man like me, Nicole, but I can't stop chasing you."

I inhaled sharply as his hands landed on my shoulders.

One simple touch from this man was all it took to unnerve me.

He'd made it a point to have his hands on me at every opportunity, calling it practice for the big event.

Every female hormone in my body rose up and demanded satisfaction the second he got close enough to touch. Or smell. Or taste.

Get a grip, Nicole. If you're going to meet him as an equal, and eventually offer yourself up for a crazy affair, you can't run away from the way he makes you feel.

I lifted my chin and held his gaze. "I'm not a child, Damian. I don't think I need protection."

He wrapped a powerful arm around my waist. "Famous last words, sweetheart. You'd be better off to run, but that wouldn't work. I'd probably catch you."

I followed my instincts and let my arms creep around his neck.

God, he smelled good.

He felt good.

I let my fingers play in the short, coarse locks at the back of his head, delighted when I found that his hair had some wayward curl at the very ends. No doubt Damian powered them down ruthlessly to achieve his well-put-together appearance. But that tiny human irregularity made him seem a little more approachable.

"What if I don't really want to run away?" I asked breathlessly.

He smoothed his thumb over my lips. "Then I'd say you're in serious danger of being thoroughly kissed, and then seduced," he replied coarsely.

Memories of *that damn kiss* shot through my mind like a runaway train.

The heat.

The desire.

The loss of any semblance of control.

Drowning in a passion so intense that all I could think about was finding a way to get closer to him.

As my body trembled with need, I had to wonder what it would feel like to experience *that damn kiss* completely sober.

Would it be the same, or would all of those sensations lose their potency if there was no alcohol to intensify their strength?

When he put his hands on my jean-clad hips and jerked me forward until I could *feel* the hard length of him, I knew I needed answers to my questions.

I had to know what it would be like to kiss him when I wasn't drunk.

"Then I guess you'll have to kiss me," I murmured softly.

"Do you have any idea how hard it's been not to kiss you, Nicole? Tonight? At your office? When we were alone on Monday? It's like fucking torture to touch you and *not* pull you into my arms and kiss you senseless." His voice sounded tormented.

"It's been hard for me, too." The confession tumbled out of me without a second thought, and Damian's mouth slowly descended until I could feel the warmth of his breath on my lips.

"Not nearly as *hard* as it's been for me," he groaned, right before his mouth crushed over mine.

Then, I couldn't say another word, even if I wanted to speak.

All I could do was feel.

The longing was much sharper this time, and it was instantaneous, starting from the second his lips touched mine. I tightened my arms around his neck and let the raw hunger throbbing through my body try to find satisfaction by just surrendering to the fierce embrace.

He tightened his grip on my body, one arm tightly around my waist, and the other behind my head.

I moaned against his mouth as he devoured mine.

If anything, this kiss was more intense than the one before it.

Hotter.

More sensual.

More overwhelming.

"Damian," I whispered when he finally pulled back to nibble on my bottom lip.

I needed more.

So much more.

The liquid heat flooding between my thighs scorched me, and every part of me was taut with an unsatisfied craving that was pulling me apart, piece by piece.

"Relax, sweetheart," he crooned beside my ear right before his mouth skimmed over the tender skin of my neck.

Relax? Oh, hell, no. *That* wasn't going to happen.

I moaned as his heated breath wafted over my ear, leaving me shaking with desperation.

I melted.

I sighed.

I moved into every single touch.

Maybe I was terrified by the unchecked passion flowing between the two of us, but not enough to make me want to stop it.

I couldn't bear to make this kind of pleasure come to an end too soon.

I could feel Damian's chest heaving as his forehead rested on mine. "Bloody hell, Nicole!" he rasped. "I can't do this without wanting to get you naked."

I panted for a second before I answered. "I guess I'm finding out that I can't, either."

My heart was racing, and my body was forcefully protesting the fact that Damian had mellowed his sensual assault.

As my rational mind started to function, I realized that I had my hands fisted in his hair; I'd been holding on for dear life.

"Sorry," I mumbled as I relaxed my hands. "Did that hurt?"

"Oh, fuck, no," he said huskily. "You could yank every hair from my head, and I wouldn't complain as long as I could touch you. The way your body responds to me is hotter than hell, Nicole. I can't kiss you without wanting to fuck you. It's just not possible."

"I lose control when you kiss me," I said, my voice slightly wary now that I was more coherent.

This damn kiss had been even more powerful than the one on the plane.

So yeah, I had my answers.

The alcohol hadn't done a damn thing to strengthen my desire.

Every sensation, every emotion, every single thing I'd felt had been...real.

He plastered our bodies together like he couldn't bear to let me go. "I want you to lose control, Nicole. I want you to trust that I'll be there to take care of you when you come apart."

I buried my face in his shoulder as my body quaked with unsatisfied desire. "I need—"

He interrupted. "I know what you need, Nicole. Let me give it to you."

I shook my head in confusion. "I'm not sure that I can."

Every cell in my body craved Damian Lancaster, but my brain couldn't forget that sex was nothing to him. He'd told me he was capable of getting up, getting dressed, and leaving behind a woman he'd just fucked.

I wasn't sure I could deal with that kind of reaction from him. I felt too damn exposed with Damian.

I didn't expect him to promise me everything, or even give me some kind of commitment, but I did need to trust him.

How would I feel if he wasn't as shaken as I would be after a night of intense physical pleasure in his bed?

Damian pulled back and kissed my forehead. "You're thinking too much, Nicole. Tell me what's in that beautiful head of yours."

I want you.

I need you.

And it's scaring the hell out of me.

"I-I—don't have casual affairs, Damian. And I have a job to do."

He put his hands on my shoulders, and pinned me with a dark, brooding stare. "You want this, Nicole. Do you think I can't feel that? Your body craves *this.* Just like I do."

I met his gaze firmly. I wasn't going to tiptoe around the attraction between us anymore. "I do. I have no doubt that the sex would be earth-shattering. Maybe I just don't entirely trust that you'll be there with me *after* that happens."

My heart ached when I saw the disappointment in his eyes, and I instantly knew he wasn't just feeling defeated over the fact that we weren't going to rock each other's world tonight.

"I'm sorry," I whispered.

He shook his head. "No. I've given you a reason to feel that way. Don't be sorry. The timing is just so fucked up. But I'll make it right. Maybe I am a tosser sometimes, but I'm not quite the man you think I am, Nicole. We have time. We'll figure this out. This kind of attraction is new for me, too, you know."

I nearly caved in when I saw the turbulence in his gaze, the uncertainty that he couldn't quite hide.

Should I tell him that I *wanted* to trust him, that maybe we could go slow and explore the madness of this undeniable chemistry together?

Unfortunately, I never got that chance.

Damian slowly released me with a throaty growl. "I'll wait until you trust me. You deserve that." He took my hand. "Walk me to the door and kick me out of here, woman, before I change my mind," he demanded.

I went with him, and he gave me a brief kiss on the forehead before he left.

When he was gone, I closed the door and sagged against it, feeling relieved and disappointed at the same time.

I closed my eyes and forced myself to breathe slowly, trying to calm my body and mind.

Eventually, I *was* going to give in to Damian Lancaster. He did something every single day that brought me closer to trusting him.

I very much doubted that he knew what tonight's early departure had said about him, and what those actions had proven to me just now.

He had to have known that it wouldn't have taken much to get me to fall into bed with him. God, I'd nearly been there when he'd let me go.

Yet, he'd still wanted to gain my trust more than he wanted to fuck me into oblivion. He could have pushed me over the edge. Instead, he'd backed off because I didn't completely trust him.

"Oh, Damian," I said in an awed whisper as I hefted myself off the door and walked toward the kitchen. "You really don't have any idea how sweet you can be."

CHAPTER 17

Damian

"NO, MUM, I *can't* tell her the truth right now," I said as I talked to my mother on the phone the next morning.

I'd explained Nicole's entire plan for improving my reputation with the people of England.

She'd been entirely on board except for the part about not telling Nicole that Dylan had been the source of the scandal, not me.

"It's not right, Damian. She should know the whole truth if she's trying this hard to help you. She doesn't know you have brothers?" my mother questioned.

I let out an exasperated breath as I fastened my favorite Patek Philippe watch onto my wrist. I couldn't say I was a collector of wristwatches, but I had a lot of them since I lived my life within a very tight schedule of obligations. "She knows about Leo," I said in a clipped tone. "She doesn't know I have a twin. Obviously, the enormous check I wrote to make Dylan's existence disappear from the internet was well spent. Nicole has never said a word about him, and I sure as hell didn't mention him."

"Your loyalty to your brother is going to get you into trouble," she warned stiffly. "And how am I going to explain the family pictures?"

"Take them down?" I suggested. I'd already made damn sure that any evidence of his existence was eliminated from my home in London.

"I don't understand why you can't just tell her the truth," she said firmly. "Certainly, someone will mention him here. You can't erase his past entirely. He had a life here, Damian."

"I don't want to erase his whole damn life," I grumbled. "And nobody mentions Dylan to me. Ever. I think since most people have no idea where he is or what he's doing, they assume he still can't cope with his grief. So nobody says a word about him to me. They probably consider his absence a sensitive subject, which is just fine with me."

"You'll still be taking a risk," she warned me.

"It's a risk I'm willing to take," I answered. "I can steer Nicole around the people who might be bold enough to ask, and introduce her to the ones who won't. She's not officially working for me, Mum, so she hasn't signed any kind of nondisclosure."

Her voice was softer as she asked, "Do you really think you need it, Damian?"

"I can't risk it," I replied. "This isn't just about me—"

"I know, I know," she interrupted. "You gave Dylan your promise. I just keep wondering when you're going to see that your brother has used that promise to manipulate you, Damian."

"Do you really think I don't know that?" I asked. "He's taken advantage of the fact that I gave him my word, but I still can't throw him to the damn wolves. Dylan is my twin. If our positions were reversed, he'd have my damn back. I know he would."

Mum sighed. "He probably would. And I'd be telling him the same things I'm telling you right now."

"Dylan seems like he's starting to come around, Mum. He's stayed put in Beverly Hills, and out of trouble." I'd talked to Dylan every day, and I was starting to sense some remorse. "If I level with Nicole, I'm almost certain she'd insist that I put the blame where it belongs. She's a straight shooter. I think she'd back out of the whole plan, and want to clear my name."

"Then she's a sensible woman," my mother replied.

I smiled as I moved to the kitchen to drink the tea I'd brewed earlier. "Very. You'll like her."

"I have a feeling *you* already like her," Mum guessed.

"Guilty," I confessed readily. "She's probably one of the most remarkable women I've ever met."

I wasn't even going to pretend that I didn't care about Nicole. Mum would spot that lie before it ever came out of my mouth.

"Why do I get the feeling that bringing her here isn't all about recovering your reputation?" she asked suspiciously.

I grinned as I picked up my cup of tea. "She's beautiful. Outspoken. Brilliant and educated. Can you blame me if I *want* to spend some time with her?"

"It's not normal for you, Damian. When have you ever cared about anything except your family and Lancaster International? I think you *really* care about this woman."

How did a son tell his mother that he wanted to shag a woman so badly that he felt like his balls were going to fall off if he didn't?

I had no idea how to explain *that* to the woman who had lovingly raised me, so I replied, "I already admitted that I like her."

"And does she feel the same way?" Mum asked.

I leaned a hip on the kitchen counter. "I hope so."

I heard my mother expel a deep breath. "So maybe she'll forgive you when she finds just how much you've hidden from her."

"I'm hoping she'll *never* find out," I explained. "She'll have to return home to the States when this is over, and I'm hoping Dylan will shape up and come back to London after that, so there won't be any need for Nicole's agency to put out any major fires again. Ashworth Crisis Management can just do regular brand improvement for us in the future."

"And what happens to your relationship with Nicole?" she asked softly.

"We stay friends, I hope." Even as I said those words, my whole being protested, but I tried to shove those feelings aside.

"And you'll be okay with that?"

I raked a hand through my hair in frustration. "Do I have a choice?"

At the moment, I felt like my back was against the wall. I wanted Nicole, but if I told her the truth now, she was inevitably going to hate me for lying to her about Dylan.

Honestly, I wasn't sure if I was more afraid of Nicole's reaction, or the fact that we had absolutely no nondisclosure signed to keep her from outing Dylan.

Bloody hell! Maybe I'd always tried to never tell her a direct lie, but wasn't all the shit that I didn't tell her just as bad?

I wanted the woman's trust more than I'd wanted anything for a very long time, yet I didn't deserve it.

How fucked up was that?

The line was silent for a moment before Mum finally answered. "You *do* have a choice, Damian. If you could put your damn duty and obligations to your brother and Lancaster International aside long enough to see your options. Don't sacrifice your entire life for your brother, Damian. In his right mind, you know he wouldn't want that, and the choice to come back into the family has to be his, not yours. I've talked to him on the phone. I think you could be right. He might be coming around, finally. He apologized for putting me into this media storm. I think you may have gotten through to him when you tossed him into the swimming pool, and forced his hand. I'm proud of you because you're finally putting your foot down. But that has to come with letting him take responsibility for his own mistakes, too."

I rubbed a hand over the muscles in my neck in an effort to stop my damn head from hurting. "I don't know if he's ready for that yet."

I might be disgusted with Dylan, but my desire to protect him was still way too strong. What if he just needed a little more time…

"You're never going to know that until you let go," Mum said sternly. "You're a good brother and a good son, Damian. You always have been. You've always been driven by your sense of responsibility to everything and everyone—except yourself. If you like this woman, give her a chance to get to know the real you. Don't screw this up by making her believe Dylan's actions are yours. How can she ever trust you?"

"Don't you think I've asked myself that a million times?" I rasped. "It's not like I *want* her to think that I don't take anything seriously. But Dylan is my brother, my twin, and until a couple of years ago, my best mate. I can't just turn my back on him."

"Of course not. We'll be there for him, Damian. All of us will support him. But is it so wrong for me to want my eldest son to find his own happiness, too?"

I wanted to tell her that I wasn't all that sure what happiness looked like anymore, and probably hadn't experienced it since my father had died.

"I'll be happy when Dylan gets his ass back into his real life and his head on straight again," I told her.

"When he does, I think you're going to regret not being honest with Nicole," she mused.

"*If* he does, Mum, not *when*."

"Oh, Damian," she said, sounding disturbed. "It's always been a matter of *when*, not *if*. Regardless of everything he's been through,

Dylan is strong. I've never had a single doubt that my wayward son would find his way back home. He's stubborn, and it's taking him a long time to pull himself together again, but the situation has *never* been hopeless. Even though the two of you are identical twins, your personalities are very different. Don't you remember how long one of Dylan's pouts could last when you were children?"

My brow furrowed as I thought about my childhood. "Like the time that you and Father didn't let him have a scooter because he was way too young to drive one?"

My mum chuckled. "That, and so many other occasions when Dylan didn't get his way. I think he punished everyone with his sour attitude for an entire year over that scooter. But that was never your way, son. You took *no* for an answer and carried on."

I frowned. "I never saw the sense in wasting time. Once you and Father said no, you weren't known to change your mind."

"Exactly. But it took your brother a long time to realize that being sullen wasn't going to change a single thing. That boy was always obstinate, but he wasn't disrespectful, so your father and I simply waited him out. So right now, I'm doing what I always did with Dylan. I'm waiting him out. But I've never thought for a single moment that he's *lost*. He's too intelligent not to eventually pull himself out of his own head."

"But he's not a kid anymore, Mum."

"However, he's just as stubborn," she said calmly. "This isn't the first time he's walked away from Lancaster International."

She was right. I took a gulp of my tea as I thought about the two years that Dylan had gone to work for our competition right out of university.

He'd been insistent about getting into riskier businesses because he could see the potential for huge income.

My father had refused.

Dylan had bucked the constraint and went to work for our biggest competitor for a couple of years before he decided that his family loyalty was stronger than his desire to be right.

"So you think this is one big sulk?" I asked her, unable to believe he'd put all of us in hell just to make some kind of point.

"No," she answered sadly. "I think we all know how much Dylan has suffered. I hurt for him, Damian. He's my son. But I also know how long he can be hardheaded, so I knew he was going to need time to deal with this kind of pain. We talk when he wants somebody to listen. He doesn't say much. But he will when he's good and ready. In the meantime, I wouldn't be a good mother if I didn't hate the way you've had to shoulder all the responsibility."

"I don't mind," I said hoarsely. "I just want Dylan back."

"You've never lost him," she reassured me. "Wait and see."

"You really do think he'll pull out of this?" I asked desperately.

"I know he will. So stop putting your whole life on hold waiting for him, Damian. And for God's sake, don't throw away your chances with a decent woman. I'm not getting any younger," she said adamantly.

I smirked. "Please don't start counting your grandchildren before they're made. How many times do I have to tell you that I'm not marriage material?"

"Nonsense," she argued. "You'd make any woman a wonderful husband. And I wish you'd get the deed done so I could start pestering your wife for my grandchildren."

"I'm not thinking about getting married, Mum. Why don't you give up and badger Leo for a while?"

She made an inelegant sound that I rarely heard from her. "That boy will never settle down," she complained. "I can barely keep him in England for more than a week or two. He's coming home tomorrow, but I doubt he'll stay long."

"I'm going to have to call him—"

"Never mind," my mother interrupted. "I'll fill him in if you're hell-bent on following through with this ridiculous plan. I'll ask the staff not to mention Dylan, too, but I won't tell them why."

I tossed back the last of my tea and put the cup in the sink. "Thanks, Mum. I have to run. Don't forget to take down those pictures."

She paused before she said reluctantly, "I'll do it, but I hope you know what you're doing, Damian. It's going to be hard to dig yourself out of this one."

"You're a peach, Mum. Have I told you that lately? I'll bring Nicole around so you can meet her."

"Don't try to flatter me into submission, Damian Lancaster," she said in an ominous tone. "And you won't just bring that girl around. You bring her to me. She can't stay at your house if you're trying to sell some kind of sweet love story. Besides, she'd be bored there with you if you're keeping the same work schedule. I think it's time for me to arrange my first social event since your father passed away. And I'll accept some of your charity event invitations in your name. The press will already be at all the large, important functions, hoping some well-known family will do something newsworthy."

I swallowed hard as my head started to hurt again. Dad was gone, so there was no reason for my mother to be forced to entertain anymore. "There's no reason for you to do that—"

"There's every reason. I'm still the Duchess of Hollingsworth, and my son has a love interest. I think there's been enough sorrow around this monstrous estate. Leo will be here to attend. Please don't think I can't play the delighted mother in this whole plan. I fulfilled the role of duchess quite well all these years."

I certainly couldn't argue with her about anything she'd just said. At one time, our Surrey estate had hosted enormous social events, and most of the time it had been filled with laughter, music, and parties.

I'd grown up surrounded by family and friends.

I guess I'd just forgotten what it was like to be happy during the last five years.

My mother had stopped hosting the social scene, and the entire estate had gone silent when we'd lost my father.

Just when the pain of losing my father had started to dull, *Dylan's* problems had begun, so there had never been any attempt or desire to actually leave that empty solitude of mourning.

"You actually *want* to host an event?" I asked, astonished.

"If it will get you married faster, I'll do one every single night," she said amiably. "I can't avoid hosting some of the snobs, but not everyone in our social circle is a nasty backstabber."

"You're absolutely relentless," I said, letting out a bark of laughter.

"Bring that girl to me, and you'll see just how persistent I can be," she teased.

"I think I'll be staying at the estate as well," I said, a little nervous about leaving Nicole entirely in her hands.

"Perfect. I'll see you both soon."

Mum disconnected, but it took me a few seconds to do the same.

By the time I finally dropped my mobile into my pocket, I wasn't quite sure if I was happy that my mum was finally coming out of her solemn retirement, or completely terrified.

CHAPTER 18

Damian

"I CAN'T BELIEVE I'M actually flying to London on a private jet! It feels so weird that we're the only passengers. This plane is amazing, Damian. It feels like a luxury home!" Nicole exclaimed, looking like she was about to bounce out of her seat as we prepared for takeoff.

Her blonde ponytail hopped up and down in her excitement, and her beautiful face was flushed as she turned her head toward me with a look of complete astonishment.

My chest started to ache as badly as my damn head as I watched her.

She was smiling, and fuck! That smile got to me. Every. Single. Time.

Nicole's enthusiasm about life in general was probably one of the many things that drew me to her.

Other than the first time I'd seen her, she was always...excited about life. Even when she was arguing with me, she was passionate, and so full of emotion that I wanted to reach out and grab her, hold her close to me so some of that vibrant personality would rub off on *me.*

For me, life was all about work, duty, and obligation. I didn't have time for anything else, but that didn't mean I didn't *wish* I could feel happiness like I had before my father's death.

I'd never even thought twice about the privilege of flying private. I did it all the time. But I could almost feel *her* enthusiasm as I watched Nicole, and possibly share it, even though the experience was second nature to me.

"Transatlantic Airlines isn't good enough for you anymore?" I joked.

"I love to fly," she answered brightly. "And going business class was kind of a splurge because the flight was so long. Honestly, before I took over Mom's business, I hardly got to fly at all. Will we have to stop to refuel?"

I was relieved that she'd splurged on a business class ticket from London. If she hadn't, we never would have met. "No. We'll go directly to Heathrow."

I didn't want to mention that my custom jet had taken very specialized engineers a couple of years to design, or that it was one of the fastest, and most costly, planes flying right now.

It didn't matter.

The joy on her face was a hell of a lot more important than the specs of the aircraft.

Eventually, she'd figure out that there was a theater room, a huge master suite, and any convenience she could ask for built into the custom airliner.

For now, all she seemed to care about was the roomy, luxurious cabin that could easily sit both of us, and probably forty or so of her closest friends.

I reached over and fastened her seat belt before she sprang right out of her tan leather recliner. "We're rolling," I informed her.

Once she was buckled in, I leaned back in the seat next to hers and fastened my own seat belt.

She settled down with a sigh. "I can't believe I'm headed back to London. I'd really like to do some sightseeing this time."

I smiled as I closed my eyes. "I'll make sure you see anything you want to see. No Tube this time."

She was quiet as we took off, but once we were in the air, she asked, "Are you okay? You don't look like you slept well."

I actually hadn't slept for more than a few hours at a time since Dylan had dropped off the radar. "I have a bit of a headache."

A bit of a headache was putting it mildly. But it wasn't like the stress headaches were anything new. I'd learned to live with them most of the time, but today's pain was the worst I'd ever experienced.

After I'd spoken with Mum, the discomfort had increasingly become a torturous agony. It was so bad that I could barely function.

I felt her hand on my arm. "Is it a migraine?"

"Nah. Just a tension headache, I think. I'll be fine. I took a couple of aspirin. I just need a few minutes." My explanation was much too forced, even to my own ears.

Nicole's warm palm gently stroked my jaw as she said, "You look kind of pale, Damian. Hang on."

The captain had reached altitude, so Nicole wasn't confined to her seat. I heard her unbuckle her belt, and get to her feet.

"Where are you going?" I inquired weakly in protest. It wasn't like she could go far, but I felt like I should get my ass up and show her around.

"Don't move," she instructed from a distance.

I opened one eye, and saw her chatting with the attendant assigned to the flight, a very sweet, efficient, middle-aged woman named Claire who I'd stolen away from Transatlantic because she'd been thinking about retiring from the rigorous schedule she had to maintain on commercial flights.

Claire had worked for my airline for almost thirty years, so I'd convinced her that she'd have it far easier working *part-time* for me.

I closed my eye again, hoping to Christ the aspirin I'd taken before the flight would kick in soon.

Nicole eventually came back to her seat, and laid a gentle hand on my shoulder. "Here, Damian. Take these."

I lifted my head and took the water and pills from her hand. "I already took some aspirin."

She shook her head. "Ibuprofen will work better. It's an anti-inflammatory. Just take them."

I didn't argue. I popped the pills in my mouth and chased them with a slug of water.

Nicole took the cup from me. "My mother used to have headaches like this," she said. "It was miserable for her. Do you have a shower in this floating hotel? Never mind. I'll check it out myself. Just rest for a while."

"Nicole, I'll be fine," I told her.

When she didn't reply, I knew she'd already gone exploring.

Five minutes later, I felt her take her seat gingerly. Her voice was soft as she spoke. "Oh, my God. It's like a five-star hotel back there."

Apparently, she'd found the master suite, master bath, and probably the theater room, too. "I like to be comfortable when I fly, which is pretty often."

"Do you log any time on that enormous bed back there?" she asked dryly.

I wanted to crack a bawdy joke about her comment, but I couldn't muster the energy to do it. "I occasionally sleep there, yes."

"You need to do more than take a nap," she scolded. "You need a hot shower to relax you, and a good night's sleep. It will make a world of difference. Let's get you into the shower."

I felt her tug on my hand, and my cock suddenly became *very interested* in her intentions. Apparently, even excruciating misery couldn't keep my dick from responding to Nicole.

I opened my eyes. "Are you planning on getting me naked?"

She frowned at me, which I decided I didn't like at all. "I'll help you. Come with me."

The innuendo had obviously flown right over her head because her focus was on curing my nasty headache.

What the hell? I was more than willing to follow her if she was going to help me take off my clothes.

Not that I wasn't capable of doing that myself, but I was beyond curious to see how far Nicole would actually go to ease my pain.

I quickly disengaged the clip on the seat belt, got up and followed her to the back of the plane.

I sure as hell wasn't used to anybody trying to help *me*, but I couldn't deny that I was touched by her tender concern. How long had it been since a woman other than my mum had worried about me for any reason?

My brain was a little foggy from pain, but I was fairly certain no female had *ever* really cared about my physical wellbeing since I'd always been very capable of performing sexually.

But this…this whole tender affection thing was brand-new, and I wasn't quite sure how to deal with it. Okay, it wasn't that I didn't *like* getting it from Nicole, but I had no idea how to respond.

She closed the door to the master suite behind me. "Let's get you undressed."

There was absolutely no artifice in her tone. Her gentle voice was that of a woman who simply wanted to…help me.

Suddenly, I felt like a complete wanker for playing along just to see how far she'd go.

Granted, my head was pounding, and I was feeling a little nauseous because my lack of sleep was catching up with me, but I wasn't exactly an *invalid*.

"Maybe I'll just lay down for a while," I sputtered. Guilt was starting to play hell with my conscience.

She shot me a displeased look. "Absolutely not. You need a hot shower, and *then* you can get some good sleep, not just a nap. You need to relax those muscles before you pass out. You'll sleep better and longer. When you wake up, the headache should be completely gone. You're not invincible, Damian, even if you think you are."

I nearly cringed because I avoided hot showers like the plague. I stepped into *cool* water every single morning to get my brain to function after a couple hours of sleep.

I watched, helpless to stop my gorgeous package of TNT as she started to dislodge the buttons of my white button-down shirt.

Holy hell! She *was* going to get me naked without a second thought about doing it.

She pushed the open shirt over my shoulders, and caught it before it hit the ground. She folded it quickly and dropped it on a nearby dresser.

"Come with me," she said like a general commanding her troops as she grabbed my hand again.

I didn't launch a single complaint as I followed her into the bathroom, watched her turn on the shower, and then observed the rosy glow of her cheeks as she faced me again and grabbed the top button on my jeans.

Fascinated, I didn't move a muscle as she yanked every button free, which was probably considerably more difficult right now since my cock was excitedly welcoming the touch of her fingers on my fly.

"Nicole," I said with a strangled groan. "I can finish."

She was fucking killing me. Even though my head felt like it was caught in a vise, it wasn't like I could exactly ignore the fact that she had her hands exactly where I wanted them to be. Well, almost, anyway.

"Let me help you, Damian. Don't be stubborn," she chastised as she pushed the jeans down my legs.

I knew there was no damn way she could have missed my enormous erection, but she'd obviously decided to ignore it.

Which, I had to admit, rankled just a little, no matter how painful my headache was at the moment.

I looked down at her kneeling at my feet, and it wasn't difficult to imagine her being there for a far different reason than just assisting me to undress.

Hell, yes, my mind was going to go *there.* I was a red-blooded male, for fuck's sake, and Nicole was the star of every single one of my sexual fantasies.

How could I *not* go there?

I held back a frustrated groan as she rose to test the shower water.

"It's nice and hot," she announced as she turned back to me. "Do you want me to stay with you?"

For the first time, she sounded a little bit anxious.

"No," I answered in a strangled tone. "I got it."

No matter how much I wanted her to jerk down my boxer briefs and greet my painfully erect cock, I knew I was in no position to perform, and the last thing I wanted to give her was a lackluster shag.

She deserved my complete and undivided attention when I drove her into her first screaming orgasm, and every time I touched her after that as well.

Nicole was a woman a guy took his time with, so he could savor every strangled cry that he could drag from those plump, succulent lips of hers.

Okay, not *some guy. Me. Just…me.* I never wanted to imagine her with anybody else but *me.*

Ever.

"I'll just wait right outside," she said hesitantly. "Just call if you need me."

I reached for her hand as she started to go. “Nicole,” I said huskily as I wrapped my hand around hers. “Thanks.”

I didn’t want her to feel awkward because she’d been trying to help my sorry ass.

I lifted her hand and kissed it gratefully before I let go.

“Take your time,” she insisted. “Try to relax those muscles.”

I nodded, and she turned and left.

I shucked my boxer briefs and stepped into the steamy shower. I’d just been completely humbled by a woman who’d been driven by the desire to do nothing more than help me ease the pain of a horrible headache.

CHAPTER 19

Nicole

ONCE DAMIAN WAS asleep, I made use of the ridiculously-large-for-being-on-an-airplane shower, and changed into a pair of sleep shorts and a lightweight cotton T-shirt.

I was going to stay with him in case he needed anything, and truthfully, I was pretty tired myself.

I hadn't slept much the night before. After I'd gotten everything packed, I'd still been restless when I'd finally hit my bed.

I left a dim nightlight on in the bathroom in case he needed to get up, and then opened the bathroom door, careful not to make enough noise to rouse Damian.

The bedroom was completely dark, but my heart skittered as I remembered exactly what Damian had looked like right before he'd hit that king-sized mattress.

Had I really stripped him down to a pair of boxer briefs without thinking about the wisdom of getting a man like Damian naked?

Yes, I had, and I'd do it all over again if necessary.

My heart had ached at the vulnerability I'd glimpsed in his eyes before he'd closed them in the cabin.

For once, he hadn't been issuing orders, or hiding behind a haughty billionaire façade.

He'd simply been a guy in pain, one who obviously suffered horribly from debilitating stress headaches, and tried to carry on like nothing was wrong.

I'd recognized the signs immediately because my mother had been plagued by the same symptoms when all of her responsibilities of being a single mother and the only breadwinner had overwhelmed her.

Damian's normally warm, naturally tanned skin had been so ashen that it was a little bit scary, and lines of tension and pain had marred his strong facial features.

I'd followed the gut-wrenching instinct to help him, no matter what it took to achieve that.

So, yeah, after I'd gotten him something to take that would help him a lot more than aspirin, I *had* dragged him into the bathroom for a hot shower.

When he'd finally emerged from the master bath, his color had come back, but his exhaustion had still been completely evident, so I'd insisted he sleep.

Honestly, it kind of pissed me off that Damian had been willing to suffer in silence.

A bit of a headache, my ass!

The stubborn man looked like he hadn't slept in days. Damian Lancaster had reached his breaking point, whether he wanted to admit it or not.

He was apparently there for everyone in his family, and for all of his employees, but I had to wonder: who in the world was there for Damian Lancaster?

I straightened my spine. *Me. I'll be there to make sure he takes care of himself.*

If no one else was going to look after the obstinate man, *I would.* If no one else could see that he wasn't a robot, and that he occasionally needed to sleep, eat, and take care of himself like any other human, *I'd* remind him that he wasn't completely invincible.

I let out a soft sigh as I replayed what I'd uncovered as I'd stripped the clothes from his massive, drool-worthy body.

I'd tried not to think about *that.* I really had. But vulnerable or not, Damian Lancaster nearly naked had been a sight to behold.

I'd been completely right about the man harboring six-pack abs underneath all of those custom shirts. If my main goal hadn't been relieving his pain, I'm pretty sure I would have been gobsmacked and salivating like a ravenous animal.

Damian was simply...beautiful, and there was nothing I'd wanted more than to unwrap the considerably large, hard package that I'd felt beneath my fingers as I'd divested him of his jeans.

The only thing that had held me back was the fact that he *didn't* need me in a sexual way right now.

He needed peace.

He needed a defender for what I knew was an exceptionally rare glimpse of the *real* Damian.

But, dear God, I had eyes, and there was no way I could see him in all his male hotness, and *not* have my body react to *that.*

Half-naked, Damian Lancaster was the embodiment of any woman's red-hot fantasies.

"Nicole," Damian mumbled, sounding like he was only half awake.

His voice startled me out of my lurid thoughts. *Put your tongue back in your mouth, Nicole.*

Concerned, I quietly approached the bed. "Sleep, Damian," I said in a hushed voice.

"So this is what you look like when you let your hair down. Literally. You look like a sexy angel," he grumbled.

I suddenly realized that I was standing in the ray of light coming from the bathroom as I reached up to touch my still-damp hair. The blonde curls were spilling over my shoulders.

I lifted the covers and slipped into the far side of the bed. "You're hallucinating if you're comparing me to an angel," I informed him lightly. "Get some sleep."

"You're too damn far away," he said hoarsely as he stretched out a powerful arm and pulled me to his side of the bed so easily that I almost forgot that I weighed more than the average female.

I let out a sigh of contentment as his warmth enveloped me like a heated blanket.

He wrapped two muscular arms around me as he spooned me, and I snuggled my back against his front.

God, he smelled so damn amazing, even though I knew that the shower had washed away any remnants of the expensive cologne he might have been wearing.

His scent was musky, raw, and uniquely Damian.

My body shivered as I felt the heat of his breath against my neck.

My core clenched viciously with the primal need to get so much closer to Damian than I was right now, but I let that bodily instinct pass.

His hands roamed lazily over my body—my belly, my hips, the side of my thighs—and then settled beneath my breasts.

I wanted to arch back against him like a cat savoring a warm caress, but I forced myself to stay put since I knew Damian was half asleep.

"This is where you belong, Nicole," he murmured huskily near my ear. "With me. I think I've known that since the moment I saw you. *Fuck!* You feel so damn good. Smell so damn good. I have you exactly where I want you, and there isn't a single fucking thing I can do about it right now."

I wrapped my arms over his, like I wanted to prevent him from letting me go. "Go to sleep, you silly man," I scolded. "The only thing I want right now is for you to finally get rested."

It wasn't that Damian wasn't dangerous, but the threat was temporarily leashed. Rich or not, powerful or not, titled or not… Damian was simply a man. Granted, he was one hell of a male specimen, but he *was* fallible, which, for me, was unfortunate, because it made him all the more desirable.

Damian let out a low groan. "Do you really think I can go to sleep with your shapely ass plastered against my painfully hard cock? It's like hellish torture."

I made a halfhearted attempt to escape his hold. "I can move."

"Don't you dare," he answered in a low growl. "I'll come find you."

"So you're fond of torture, then?" I teased softly as I settled back against him.

Damian made me feel like the most desirable female in the world, and it seemed to be bringing out the inner goddess inside me.

Who knew that I actually *had* an inner goddess?

"Apparently, I've only recognized that proclivity since I met you," he rumbled unhappily. "Now, I seem to revel in it."

I smiled into the darkness of the room. "You'll live. Go to sleep."

"You're becoming rather bossy," he observed.

"Do you have a problem with that?" I asked lightly. I loved the fact that I was becoming a whole lot bolder about sparring with Damian. Honestly, I was starting to enjoy that kind of freedom with him.

"Not at all," he replied. "I rather think I'm starting to like your sassiness."

"Were you really attracted to me from the very beginning?" I queried, unable to stop myself from asking.

I could feel him nod slightly against my hair. "So much so that I wasn't quite sure what to do with that kind of instant attraction, beautiful. I'm generally not the kind of guy who strikes up conversations with a woman I don't know. I normally work through a commercial flight. I *was* there to observe what kind of experience my customers were having, after all."

How could I really believe that a guy who possibly sought out multiple women for an indulgent orgy was hesitant to talk to a single woman? Yet, I *was* somehow starting to believe that Damian was normally a no-nonsense businessman who didn't make his sexual pleasure a priority. At all.

"So reading my text messages was out of the ordinary for you?"

"Appalling behavior for me," he explained. "But I couldn't stop myself. I had to know why you looked so troubled, sweetheart."

"I was a total stranger," I reminded him.

"You were no stranger to me," he replied. "I can't quite put a finger on why I felt that way, but there it is. You captivated a man who isn't used to being led around by his balls."

"You didn't seem like a stranger, either," I confessed. "There was something about you that was familiar, but not. I guess it was my instinct to trust you on the flight. I don't normally overindulge in alcohol, or spill my life story to anyone I don't know well. But you were right. I *did* want someone to talk to when I was all alone on the long plane ride. But if it hadn't been you sitting next to me, I would have kept my mouth shut. You listened to me, gave me your total attention. I've never had a guy who truly listened to me, like what I had to say was important."

"Never settle for a man who doesn't recognize how damn lucky he is to be with you, Nicole," he demanded.

"I don't think any of them ever felt lucky," I mused, thinking about all the halfhearted men I'd had in my life.

"Idiots. All of them," he said irritably.

I smiled wider. "Because none of them ever gave me a screaming orgasm?"

"No," he answered roughly. "Because they *had* you, and never appreciated what an extraordinary woman you are."

My heart ached at his words. "I'm not quite sure how to handle you sometimes," I admitted. "You see things in me that nobody else ever has, and it's a little bit scary. I'm not exactly a femme fatale, Damian. I'm not putting myself down, but men like you just aren't attracted to a woman like me. They date supermodels, A-list actresses, or other wealthy, gorgeous socialites. Not an ordinary woman who owns a small business, and is perfectly happy on a beach somewhere, swilling lattes with her friends."

"I've dated supermodels," he said with a masculine sigh. "They can't enjoy a meal without thinking about every single calorie they put into their mouth. They're painfully boring, and perpetually unhappy most of the time. Same thing with A-list actresses and the social elite. Appearances matter to most of them, and they don't really matter to me."

"Please, don't tell me that you don't care about how people perceive you. If you didn't, I wouldn't be here right now."

"Maybe I just *seem* to care," he suggested. "So I can spend more time with you and get you into my bed."

My body let go of a small shudder. "I'm already in your bed."

"Don't remind me," he said with a grunt. "And I'm in no position to give you a good shag."

For a moment, I let myself bask in the warmth of Damian's unexplainable desire to fuck me senseless. "I like the way you want me."

"I'm glad you like it, because it's driving *me* fucking insane," he replied grumpily.

I actually giggled at his self-deprecating tone, and I was a woman who *never* giggled. "I'm starting to believe you," I told him, and it was the truth.

If I took Damian at face value, and assessed everything I knew about him personally, I'd say he was a stuffy, workaholic suit who *rarely* made time for a woman, and when he did, it was brief, and in between his other obligations.

Not a single thing I knew about him painted him as some kind of womanizer.

Damian was finally completely still, and within moments, I could feel his breathing even out, telling me that he'd allowed the sleep he so desperately needed to take him away.

I was careful as I snuggled back against him, but he seemed to sense the motion, and tightened his hold on me.

I relaxed my body, and let myself wallow in the pleasure of having my body plastered against his rock-hard chest, stomach, and powerful thighs.

My *body* might still need him with a fierceness I could barely contain, but as I drifted off to sleep, my *heart* was completely content exactly where I rested.

CHAPTER 20

Damian

"ARE YOU READY?" I asked Nicole as we pulled up in the long, circular drive of my mum's home.

We'd left the gaggle of reporters at the end of the driveway. They weren't allowed inside the gate.

Nicole's eyes widened. "*This* is where you live? It looks more like a castle than a home."

I lifted my gaze to the impressive stonework of the Lancaster country home, Hollingsworth House.

To me, it was nothing more than the home I'd grown up in, but I supposed I could understand Nicole's look of total astonishment.

For one, the property was enormous, especially by English standards, and probably a bit imposing. Some of the stonework on the front of the home was original, but the entire estate had been added to, fastidiously remodeled and updated over time.

"It's been in my family since the seventeenth century," I explained. "Every generation has put their stamp on it, changed it, or added something, so it's a hodgepodge of tastes, I'm afraid."

"It's...extraordinary," she sputtered.

I grinned as I noticed that Nicole was still gawking out the car window at the house.

I jumped out of the leather seat of the Phantom, and jogged to Nicole's side of the car. "Let's go then," I said as I took her hand and blocked her view of the large estate.

If I didn't get her body in motion, she was likely to spend the entire day staring at my childhood home.

She nervously smoothed down the red dress she was wearing after she clambered out of the vehicle. "Are you sure that your mother completely understands this plan?"

Nicole wasn't the type of woman to shrink from a challenge, and I didn't like seeing her unsure of herself. "Absolutely. She's even agreed to host an event. Don't be nervous. You two will get along fine."

She stiffened her spine. "I'm sorry. It wasn't like I didn't *know* that you were ridiculously wealthy. I guess I just wasn't quite ready to see you in your own environment."

"Was I that different in the United States then?" I looked at her curiously as I took her hand. "You look absolutely gorgeous, by the way. Have I told you that?"

She shot me a small smirk. "You've told me *at least* a dozen times since we got off your jet, but thank you...again."

It was a beautiful early afternoon in Surrey, and the sun was glinting off Nicole's beautiful blonde hair.

For once, she'd left it unconfined, and it was sexy as hell on her.

I took a deep breath, incredulous at how much better I felt after a very long, restorative sleep.

My headache was completely gone for the first time in two years, which I certainly didn't regret. However, I couldn't quite seem to forget how damn good Nicole had felt plastered against my body *before* I'd passed out.

Unfortunately, I'd slept so long that Nicole had already been awake and dressed before I woke.

"Are you okay?" she asked as we strolled toward the house. "Is your headache still gone? Your color is so much better than it was yesterday."

Never in a million years would I have considered myself the kind of guy who wanted a woman to fuss over him, but bloody hell, Nicole's concern warmed my heart. "I feel fantastic," I answered honestly.

She shot me a genuine smile. "Good. I'm glad your swagger is back."

"I don't swagger, woman."

"Oh, you do," she argued. "I think it's probably imbedded in your Lancaster DNA, but it's pretty hot."

Well, all right then. If Nicole liked my so-called swagger, then maybe I did have one.

We climbed the stone steps, and the door opened before I could even ring the bell.

"Welcome home, Your Grace," my mother's elderly steward said in a jovial tone.

I ignored the accusatory look that Nicole shot at me. I'd never said that *nobody* used my title. I'd given up on reminding Barnaby that I'd prefer he didn't use a formal address with me. The older man was in love with tradition, and his family had worked with the Lancasters for generations.

"Hello, Barnaby." I led Nicole into the house. "Haven't you retired yet?"

When he was going to retire had become an ongoing joke between me and the elderly steward.

"No, Your Grace. I'll retire when your mother does," he retorted smartly.

Mum didn't actually have an occupation, but she worked tirelessly for her charities. I grinned at him. "Then be prepared to work until you die," I advised.

"Most happily, Your Grace," the old man shot back.

I clapped him on the shoulder. "Barnaby, meet Nicole Ashworth. She'll be staying here at the estate with me while I'm in residence. We're going to do some sightseeing, and attend some of the social events."

I already knew that none of the household employees had been advised that any of this was a ruse, so I had to be convincing.

"It's a pleasure, Miss Ashworth," Barnaby said with a genuine smile.

Nicole reached out her hand in greeting, and Barnaby shook it in a typical American greeting.

Smart man.

"Please call me Nicole," she said smoothly. "I'm really excited to be here. From what I could see from the car window, Surrey is absolutely beautiful."

Barnaby beamed at her.

Bravo, Nicole. There isn't a single other statement you could have uttered to please an elderly gentleman whose roots are firmly entrenched in the Surrey soil.

"You're early, Damian," Mum exclaimed as she sprinted down the stairway in a manner that shouldn't be possible for a woman her age.

I caught her petite figure up in my arms and kissed her cheek. "No, Mum. You're fashionably late, as usual."

My father had once said that my mother was always running behind because she cared far too much about her appearance. Her attention to how she looked was much more about anxiety than vanity, and her desire to fit into my father's world.

It had never escaped my attention that my father had always happily waited for Mum indulgently, without a word of complaint. Evidently, he'd known why my mother fussed, too, and he hadn't minded waiting until *she* was comfortable.

I was fairly certain that he would have kept his ass planted in that chair by the door until he collected dust if necessary, as long as my mother eventually descended the stairs and took his hand.

"You must be Nicole," my mother said as she pulled out of my embrace. "Damian was right. You're absolutely beautiful."

Nicole blushed as my mother came forward and hugged her, and then shot *me* a dirty look over Mum's shoulder as the older woman greeted her enthusiastically.

Like it was my fault that she was a stunner? It wasn't like I'd told Mum something that wasn't true.

Nicole greeted my mother with the same warmth she'd been shown, although she stopped short when my mother tried to drag us into the sitting room for tea.

"Shouldn't we grab our luggage?" she asked hesitantly.

Mum looped her arm through Nicole's. "Barnaby will make sure it gets up to your rooms," she assured Nicole.

I watched as Nicole tried to cover up her puzzled expression. Yeah, it was obviously going to take her a while to figure out that here at Hollingsworth House, there was someone to do almost any mundane task that she was used to doing herself. She recovered well as she followed along with Mum. "Of course," Nicole said breezily. "Thank you, Your Grace."

My mother tapped her arm lightly. "No formalities. Please call me Bella."

I nearly choked on my tongue. My mother rarely invited *anyone* to call her *Bella* since it had been the nickname my father had chosen to use throughout their very long marriage.

Certainly, no one outside of the family used that name, so I was already suspect about my mother's motivations.

Tea was casual at our house, and I noticed that everything had been set out on the side table as we entered the living room.

"Please help yourself," Mum said with a wave toward the table.

I snatched a cup from the sideboard, and started to fill it from the teapot. "Silver Tips Imperial," I said as I caught the aroma of the brew.

"Of course," Mum said. "One of your many favorites. Just because I don't touch the stuff is no reason not to serve something you enjoy."

Nicole raised a brow. "You don't like tea, Bella?"

Mum made a face. "Can't stand the stuff. I tried for years to force myself to drink it. I'm too old to do that anymore. The other pot is filled with café con leche."

"Coffee with milk," I informed her quietly.

"Thank God," Nicole said fervently as she grasped the handle of the coffee pot. "I was afraid I was going to have to suffer until I got back to the US."

"I could never abandon all of my Spanish roots," my mum informed Nicole as she took the pot from her. "We Spaniards love our coffee."

I stacked some sandwiches and scones on a plate for Nicole, and then piled food on another one for myself.

My mother was already happily seated in her highbacked chair when Nicole and I sat across from her on the sofa.

"Is there a right way and wrong way to eat this thing?" Nicole asked in a whisper as she gently lifted her scone.

Grateful that my parents had never stood on formality, I told her, "No. If you like jam and cream, pile it on top and eat it. Eat it plain. Dunk it in your coffee. Whatever makes you happy."

She proceeded to slather the scone with jam, and then plopped a healthy portion of cream on the top.

She appeared to stifle a small moan as she closed her eyes and savored the taste of the freshly baked scone.

Her orgasmic expression nearly killed me, but I suffered through every moment of it, and would willingly bring her more if she liked them that much.

I held back a groan as she delicately licked some cream off her finger once every morsel was gone. "I think that's one of the most amazing things I've ever tasted."

"So is it possible that you've found one good thing about British tea?" I asked her with a wink.

"If it comes with scones and coffee, then I've definitely changed my mind."

I sat back and devoured everything on my plate, washing it down with one of my favorite blends.

As long as Nicole was here, tea would *always* be served with an endless number of scones.

Call me a masochist, but a man had to take his pleasure where he could find it, and seeing Nicole happy was far more gratifying for me than I was willing to admit.

CHAPTER 21

Nicole

IN LESS THAN a week, I was completely exhausted by the sheer volume of appearances I'd made with Damian, a large number of them requiring that we travel back and forth to London.

I'd forgotten most of the names of the people I'd met. It was impossible to keep track of them all, but I *had* noticed that I'd seen a lot of the same faces at a variety of engagements.

Bella had helped me by accepting some invitations that involved the multitude of charities that Damian donated to faithfully. The press was usually present because of the large number of prestigious people who attended.

To give him credit, Damian never strayed from my side when we were out together, and he played the perfect, storybook boyfriend.

In fact, he did it *so well* that I often forgot it was only a game that we were playing.

"I think it's time to take time off," Damian said as he entered the large sitting room of the east wing.

We were occupying most of what was considered the east wing, which consisted of an enormous living area, with several bedrooms on each side of the space. There were also two enormous master suites. Damian was occupying one, and I'd taken the other on the opposite side.

During the last week, I'd gotten comfortable with my surroundings. At first, I'd been terrified I'd break one of the many priceless heirlooms that decorated Hollingsworth House, but I'd eventually loosened up. I adored Damian's mother and his brother, Leo. So the residence was warm, even though it was almost impossible not to share space with some very expensive antiques.

I wasn't particularly fond of some of Damian's acquaintances who I met during the round of endless parties, but then, Damian didn't seem to enjoy their company much, either. People might claim that the class system was gone in England, but as an outsider, I didn't quite see it that way. Some of the charity events had been filled with downright snobby or titled individuals who obviously looked down on anyone who didn't orbit in their sphere.

Nobody had overtly snubbed me as an American of no importance. I didn't think they'd dare with Damian standing next to me, but I had no doubt that they would, if I wasn't the guest of a powerful billionaire duke with an elite pedigree.

Now I understood exactly what Bella had been facing when she'd married Damian's father. I couldn't imagine trying to *really* fit in and be accepted by people who were incredibly eager to find the smallest fault in a newcomer. No wonder she'd twisted herself into knots about being accepted. I was playacting, but *she* hadn't been.

I looked up from my position on the sofa. I was barely awake, still chugging coffee, and scanning through social media. Most of the negative talk about Damian was gone. "So there's nothing scheduled for today?" My voice was probably way too hopeful, but

I was sick of attending charity events where I had to watch every single thing I said or did. Luckily, Damian had kept my interactions with guests at those events brief. Yeah, it was my job to mingle, but it was starting to wear me down.

Damian strode across the room, his hair still wet from the shower, and casually dressed in a pair of dark jeans and a button-down shirt.

"I think we're already a success," he said in a mischievous tone as he handed me a paper.

I glanced at the title.

DAMIAN LANCASTER LEAVES HIS ORGY DAYS BEHIND HIM!

I smiled as I dropped the scandal sheet on my lap. "Congratulations. You're a changed man."

"I'm the same guy I was on the day that scandal broke. It's them who see me differently," he informed me.

"So we can take a day off from the endless social rounds? God, I don't know how you do it."

He shrugged. "I don't, normally. I hope you're not under the misunderstanding that *this* is how I usually fill my days. I don't like these ridiculous gatherings, either."

"But you know so many people—"

"I don't really *know* them. I tolerate a lot of them when I have to be at the same location they are. I'm selective about the ones I actually call friends. There are some genuinely nice people in the wealthy crowd, but most of them don't attend these events, either. They donate without needing the damn accolades."

I was secretly happy that Damian didn't like most of his elite crowd. "So tell me about how much time we can afford to take off."

"As much as you'd like. I think we should start your sightseeing, and stay at my place in London to make things easier on ourselves. We can come back for Mum's event on Saturday night."

I nodded eagerly. "I'd love that, but won't your mother need help?"

"Seriously?" he said. "Do you really think Mum can't plan this gala without us? In fact, I guarantee she wouldn't want us messing with her plans. She's an expert party planner. She just hasn't done it since my father died. It's nice to see her back in action again."

"I think she loved your father very much," I told him. Bella never stopped talking about her deceased husband.

"As much as he loved her," Damian confirmed. "They were incredibly happy, no matter how mismatched they may have appeared to be. Now go get ready for breakfast. We can be on our way to London right after we eat."

Bella had mentioned her humble beginnings in Spain, and how hard it had been for her to get used to living a far different life than she'd had growing up. "I have a sneaking suspicion that Bella is responsible for keeping you and Leo well-grounded."

I moved my laptop to the sofa and stood. I needed to shower and dress before I went downstairs.

"Kept us from being snobs, you mean?"

I nodded. Damian and Leo both seemed so normal in comparison with the lofty upper-class people I'd encountered this week.

"She did, actually," Damian readily agreed. "We were indulged, not spoiled, and she made sure we spent time with our family in Spain as often as possible, so we weren't constantly surrounded by other ultra-rich children. My father was a good role model as well. He worked harder than any of his employees. He wasn't the type to simply live off the family inheritance. I'm grateful for everything he taught me. I'd be bored to death if all I had to do was attend various social events and gossip about my peers." He paused before he added, "Now go get showered, woman. I need my breakfast."

I smiled as I scurried into my room, gathered up some casual clothing, and got myself ready to go downstairs within fifteen minutes.

When I reappeared, Damian seemed to be patiently waiting for me on the sofa.

He was working on his laptop, just like he'd done every single morning for the last week. I stopped at the entrance to the enormous sitting room and just...watched him.

Damian was the most focused man I'd ever met. He was an early riser, so I didn't know exactly what time he got up to work every morning while we'd been here, but I was willing to bet that it was well before sunrise.

Maybe not too early, because he still looks well-rested.

I hadn't seen a single sign of sleep deprivation, and Damian swore his headaches were gone. He seemed relaxed, even at all of the ridiculous parties we'd attended.

"Working again?" I said lightly as I entered the room.

He looked up from whatever he was doing and grinned. "Only until you graced me with your presence, beautiful."

God, he killed me with the way he looked at me.

Like I was a goddess.

Like I really was beautiful.

Like I was the most important person in his life.

Like...I was worth waiting for, no matter how long it took for me to arrive.

"Did you get caught up on your work?" I asked.

He put his laptop aside and stood. "Well enough. I turned some of my duties over to a few of my top executives for a while so I could put my full attention where it belongs."

"On attending parties full of uptight people?" I teased.

"No." Damian stalked toward me until he was right in front of me. "I'd much rather spend my time watching you right now, Nicole."

My heart did a somersault inside my chest.

Maybe Damian and I *were* playing a game, but the intimacy between us was becoming all too real.

We were starting to recognize the funny quirks each of us had, like lovers did, after they'd spent enough time in each other's company.

Damian was incredibly curious about my present and my past, so he asked a seemingly endless amount of questions, some that I had to think about before I answered.

I was grateful that he'd stopped being guarded about answering my questions about him. There were no more short answers. Instead, he not only told me about himself, but how he felt about his place in the world, too.

The two of us couldn't be more different, but we connected on a much deeper level than the superficial.

Both of us had high expectations of ourselves: me because I was an only child, and him because he was the eldest in his family.

At times, watching him try to be everything to everybody, and feeling like he often came up short, was like observing…myself.

I got Damian in a way that perhaps other people didn't, and through my eyes, the man was pretty incredible.

I was now completely convinced that whatever had happened the night that he'd been caught on camera, it wasn't exactly the way it had seemed.

Damian claimed that he didn't recall what had occurred that evening, and it was hard for me *not* to buy that.

I'd seen too much, learned too much about Damian over the past week to doubt his explanation.

When all evidence was contrary to his behavior on that particular day, I couldn't deny that he'd been set up.

"Watching me would probably be incredibly boring," I said lightly.

He toyed with the small tendrils of my hair that had escaped confinement when I'd clipped it at the back of my head. "Not at all. It's become my favorite occupation, I'm afraid. I've become completely addicted."

God, I was starting to become dependent on seeing Damian every single day, and on his nearly obsessive desire to make sure I was happy.

His concern wasn't something he turned on and off simply for a performance.

His "attentive boyfriend" switch seemed to be permanently in the *On* position, even when we were alone like this, and it was making me absolutely crazy.

I thrived on his attention, his affection, and the way that he looked at me like I'd made his entire day just by walking into the room.

Honest truth: I was falling in love with Damian Lancaster, and I couldn't seem to stop the progress of that dangerous plunge.

I pulled away from him defensively, and then mourned the loss of the crazy, topsy-turvy way he was conquering my heart with every touch. "I'm starving," I said in an overly bright tone.

Instantly, his expression filled with remorse, like he was deeply sorry that he'd kept me from eating.

Really? Like I can't afford to miss a meal or two?

"Let's go feed you then," Damian said as he took my hand.

My heart melted until it was a puddle on the expensive marble floor.

Truly, this man needed a woman who was as eager to meet *his* needs as he was *hers.*

I definitely didn't want to think about who that woman might be in the future as I let Damian take me down to breakfast.

CHAPTER 22

Damian

SOMETIMES I WISHED I could be a hearts and flowers kind of guy for Nicole.

She deserved a slow and steady seduction, filled with romance and whatever else a woman wanted from a lover.

Unfortunately, my patience was gone, and all I could think about was getting her naked and shagging her until my body and brain got back to normal.

Since I really needed more privacy to do that, I knew I had to get her to London.

Soon.

Now.

Today.

In the next hour or so.

"I'll have to head out after your gala, Mum," Leo informed my mother as we all sat around the breakfast table.

"So soon?" Nicole asked. She looked seriously disappointed as she gazed at my youngest brother.

Leo smiled at her, and I suddenly felt the intense desire to make him go away *right now.*

I was under no illusion that Leo was up to anything with Nicole when he piled on the charm. No, the bastard was simply trying to get a rise out of *me.*

And damn him, it was working.

"I want to see if I can work with Colombian officials to get a breeding pair of Rio Apaporis caiman that were recently discovered in the Amazon. They were thought to be extinct, but an American team recently found a population there. I'd like to put them in my conservation breeding program," Leo explained, still aiming that one-thousand-watt grin at Nicole from across the table.

"So I guess we'll be saying goodbye," Nicole answered, sounding highly disappointed.

Leo shook his head. "Never goodbye. I'm negotiating on some land near Palm Desert in California. I want to start another sanctuary and breeding program in the United States. We can meet up there. I'll get your number before I go."

I hated the way Nicole's eyes lit up as she said, "I'd love that. I know the one here is very successful."

Over my dead body are the two of them going to meet up...alone.

Brother or not, I'd have to kill the little shit.

I shot Leo my that's-never-happening-not-even-in-your-fucking-wildest-dreams frown.

He completely ignored it. "It has been really successful so far."

I ground my teeth as Leo proceeded to inform Nicole all about his breeding facility up north, close to the Welsh border, that had turned into one of the foremost sanctuaries in the world for saving very endangered species. Because Leo wanted his legacy to go on, well after he was gone, he'd turned it into a teaching zoo of sorts, so it could sustain itself in the future with visitors' fees and donations.

Even though it was a long trip for some people, those exclusive tickets to see such an array of endangered species were highly coveted.

"Wow," Nicole said with awe dripping from her voice. "You must be incredibly proud of everything you've accomplished, Leo. Will I be able to get tickets once you launch your facility in the US?"

He shot her a mischievous grin that I was dying to punch off his pretty face. "You won't need tickets," he said adamantly. "You'll come when I'm there, and I'll personally show you around."

"I'd love to bring my friend, Macy," Nicole mused. "She's an exotic and large animal vet. Conservation is in her blood. She'd love to tour a place like that."

"Bring all of your friends," Leo said magnanimously. "Any friend of yours will be a friend of mine."

I rolled my eyes. Leo wasn't exactly social. Yeah, he could talk to donors when he needed to do it, but he liked socializing about as much as I did. Most of the time, he got along much better with animals than humans.

"So how long will you be gone?" Nicole questioned as she spread marmalade on her toast.

Leo shrugged. "As long as it takes. We thought we'd lost that species, so it will be worth every bit of red tape we need to cut through to try to recover that population."

"Be careful," Nicole warned. "Isn't that kind of a dangerous area?"

Jesus Christ! If I had to live through one more second of Nicole turning her gentle concern toward my little brother, I was going to lose it.

Leo looked at me with a covert glance, and grinned like a damn idiot.

The tosser was enjoying my discomfort *way too much.*

How he knew that flirting with Nicole would make me into a raving maniac I didn't know, but *he knew.*

"It's not the safest place to be," he confessed. "But I've been through worse. Of course, if you're going to worry, I'll make sure to check in with you."

"Not. Necessary." I pushed out those two words through clenched teeth. "Nicole and I will be in touch. I'll keep her posted."

Wanker!

Leo shrugged. "I thought all this cuddling up to each other was all show. Certainly, Nicole is going to want to get back to her own life in the States, find herself a nice guy."

We were always given our privacy during our meal, so Leo had dropped all pretense of pretending that Nicole and I were really an item.

"Like hell she will," I growled.

Fuck! I was done pretending that my life would *ever* be normal again if Nicole wasn't in it.

I was done pretending that I didn't want to shag the woman until we were both panting and spent.

I was done pretending that if Nicole and I spent a week together in sexual bliss, that it would change the obsessive way I cared about her and restore my ass to normal again.

And I was *completely done* pretending she wasn't mine.

Nicole Ashworth *was* irrevocably mine. She'd sealed the deal on that soon after we'd met. She just didn't know it yet.

Maybe I'd always subconsciously known that, too, but I hadn't really admitted it to my conscious mind until she'd so tenderly and selflessly taken care of my sorry ass on my jet last week.

Nicole had decided her fate when she'd decided to care about the man—not the billionaire or duke—when I'd had a very rare moment of vulnerability.

"What was that?" Leo inquired politely. *Too politely.*

"Boys," my mum said in a warning tone, shooting us both a speaking glance as she said it. "We're enjoying a meal here."

I looked back at her with a frown.

Leo had been deliberately antagonizing me, but she obviously didn't want to acknowledge that. In fact, I was *highly suspicious* of the small smile she had on her lips.

I was only able to relax again once Mum had drawn Nicole into a conversation about what she wanted to see while she was in London.

"Everything," Nicole said with a sigh.

My mother smiled fondly at Nicole. "Do you like the theater, dear?"

Nicole's eyes sparkled like precious gems. "I love it. Especially musicals. I get to Los Angeles as often as possible to see the latest shows. I saw that *The Phantom of the Opera* is playing at Her Majesty's Theatre, but I'm here to work, and I doubt I can get a ticket at the last minute."

Dammit! Why hadn't I ever asked if she'd like to see something in London? "I'll get tickets for Friday night," I said, before my mother could offer to procure them. "You're done working, Nicole. We've accomplished our mission, and it certainly won't hurt to be spotted around town with me."

She turned her head and made me the sole recipient of her gorgeous, joy-filled smile.

I went from rage-filled savage beast to feeling like the luckiest bastard on earth in less than two seconds.

Being responsible for making this woman smile just felt like complete euphoria. I couldn't explain *that* if I wanted to, and I really didn't want to.

I felt like her damn hero for offering her something as simple as bloody theater tickets.

At some point, Nicole Ashworth had decided to move me from wanker to the good guy category. Maybe I didn't deserve it, but I was going to try my best to be worthy of it.

"Thank you, Damian," Nicole responded breathlessly. "I've always wanted to see that show."

Of course she did. It was a romantic tragedy. There hadn't been a dry-eyed female in the theater when I'd seen it years ago. I'd never quite understood *why* since Christine was rescued from the Phantom, and all was well in the end when she sailed away with Raoul.

Good guy wins.

Bad guy loses.

The end.

What in the hell was there to cry about?

Thank God there had been a lot of decent music in between the beginning and the end.

"It's really short notice," Nicole said anxiously. "Do you think we can still get tickets?"

"I have some connections."

She rolled her eyes. "Of course you do. If everyone will excuse me, I'd better go make sure everything is packed." She looked at Leo. "I won't give you a goodbye hug right now since I'll be seeing you at Bella's gala."

"I'll take one anyway," Leo teased.

"Ignore him. Go on," I encouraged Nicole as I stood.

Nicole flitted out of the dining room, apparently eager to start her London adventure.

I sat back down. "What in the hell was that all about?" I asked my little brother in a furious tone once I knew Nicole was out of hearing range.

He lifted his brows. "I have no idea what you're talking about."

"Flirting with Nicole. It's not...normal for you." At the age of thirty-one, I highly doubted that Leo was a virgin, but I'd never seen him personally take much interest in any particular female. He'd been much too busy trying to save the world.

He shrugged. "I like her. Is that a problem for you? It's not like the two of you are in a real relationship."

"It's a problem," I answered. "If you touch her with anything less than brotherly intentions, I'll have to kill you, Leo. You won't be around to save a single threatened species in the future. Think about that before you do it."

My little brother's fist slammed down on the table. "I knew it! You're crazy about her. I could see it, even if you don't really want anybody to know. Why in the hell don't you just tell her? It's pretty obvious she adores you, too. Tell her the truth, Damian. Tell her about Dylan. If you do it yourself, and come clean, it will go over a lot better than her finding out from somebody else."

My gaze shot to my brother's smiling face. He *had* been needling me just to get me to admit how much I wanted this show with Nicole to be real.

My indignation and anger flowed out of my body. No matter how misguided Leo's actions might be, he *had* been trying to find out how I really felt. "Don't do that again," I advised him. "I'm likely to lay you out on the ground, with that pretty face of yours completely rearranged."

Unlike Dylan and me, Leo was a blond-haired, blue-eyed male with perfect features. His muscular build was all from physical labor, not from grueling workouts in a gym. Women stopped and stared when Leo walked by them, but to give him credit, my brother never seemed to notice. He'd always lacked the vanity that usually came with a perfect genetic makeup like his.

"She obviously makes you happy, Damian. You don't know how glad I am to see you a little lighter. Nicole's an amazing woman. Why don't you make this real?"

My expression was grim as I asked, "How do you propose I do that? She thinks I'm a workaholic man-whore."

"She's got the workaholic part of it right," Leo agreed. "But you seem to be managing that well right now by actually utilizing all those executives you have. Just tell her about Dylan."

Leo had no way of knowing that I'd actually considered telling Nicole the truth. Maybe she didn't completely trust me, but I fucking trusted her, whether I had her signature on a nondisclosure...or not. The woman didn't have a vengeful bone in her body, and she'd never intentionally hurt anyone.

Maybe she'd be angry that I evaded the truth about a lot of things, but I was ready to admit that I'd rather have her mad than hurt. She might even forgive me if I groveled enough, and we could get on with the business of indulging in the earth-shattering sex that was going to occur the moment I could get her naked.

I finally spoke. "I'd have to trust that she'd keep the secret. The last thing we need, after all the work we've done to make people forget about that story, is to have Dylan's involvement come out now. Everything is just dying down."

I still touched base with Dylan every single day. The black cloud over his head wasn't gone, but he sounded sober. He was actually going to counseling, which I'd insisted on before I'd released a small fortune to his bank account.

Mum joined the conversation. "Dylan will be fine. And I think, by now, you're very much aware that Nicole would never betray your trust."

"Fuck Dylan," Leo spat out before he quickly said, "Sorry, Mum, but I'm sick and tired of watching Damian pay emotionally for every single stupid thing Dylan does."

"I completely agree, Leo, and I've said as much, but Damian has to make his own decision to stop covering for Dylan."

"He's my twin, and I gave him my word. That actually means something to me," I snapped.

"He's also a wanker," Leo added. "Look, I sympathize with him. I love him. Dylan is my brother, too. He's been through a lot. Every time I talk to him, I try to get him to talk about it so we can help him work through everything, but he closes himself off like a clam. He's not even trying, which is exactly what infuriates me. And it's been two years. Way too long to leave his older brother in charge of his life while he runs away in a drunken fog. If I thought I could help, I would, Damian. I'd stay here in England and work beside you to take some of the load off your shoulders. But I know almost nothing about running Lancaster International."

My damn chest ached as I listened to Leo's outburst. It meant a lot that he was willing to put his own career on hold to help me. "I've never wanted that, Leo. I'm proud of everything you've accomplished. Lancaster International will be fine."

"I don't care about Lancaster, Damian. I care about you. Which is why I'm happy to see you with somebody like Nicole. Don't screw this up over Dylan. She's real, Damian, and in our world, that's a rarity. You're going to have to decide what means more to you: Nicole, or continuing to protect Dylan from the real world, and the consequences of his actions."

"She's not the type of woman to reveal your secrets, even if she's angry," Mum added. "I don't trust a lot of people, but my instinct says you can trust *her*."

I already *knew* I could trust Nicole. She wasn't the vindictive type.

"I was planning on telling her after the gala. She deserves to know everything," I confessed. "If it sends her running back to the US, I don't want that to happen until she's done everything she wants to do in London."

Honestly, I wasn't planning on letting her go very far, even if she wanted to get away from me. No matter how long it took, I'd follow her until she could trust me.

"Then go and show her a good time," Leo suggested jovially. "If you run out of things to do, you could always fly her to Lundy Island. Nicole would love diving with the seals there. The currents are a little tricky on the deeper dives, but she's an experienced diver."

"Is it dangerous?" I asked hoarsely. I wasn't about to send her into dangerous waters in the middle of the Bristol Channel.

Leo shook his head. "Not really. Not for somebody like Nicole. She does tough, deep dives on a regular basis."

I shook my head. I'd probably die of a heart attack while I was waiting for her to surface. "Maybe later. After I get myself certified so I can go with her."

"I'm at your service," Leo said amiably.

"We'll set something up," I told him. "In the meantime, I want to get on the road to London."

I stood up and dropped my napkin onto my plate.

"I doubt it will take much to make her fall in love with you," my mother called after my departing figure. "I think she's already halfway there."

Mum's words didn't exactly comfort me, even if her presumption *was* correct.

Halfway still left a lot of ground to cover, and I was finally ready to admit that *I'd* crossed *that* finish line a long time ago.

Not only had I completed that race, but I'd kept driving myself directly into insanity long after I'd seen that checkered flag.

CHAPTER 23

Nicole

DAMIAN'S "PLACE IN London" turned out to be a Mayfair mansion that was almost too crazy to be believable.

If I wasn't currently standing on the second subterranean level of his home, which housed his indoor pool and spa, I probably wouldn't have been able to grasp the concept of three levels underground, and two above.

However, some talented engineer *had* made it happen, and I was standing right in the middle of the three underground levels, so I knew a home like this existed.

I just wasn't quite sure how I'd managed to become a guest here.

Beneath us was an entertainment space with a home theater, and above was Damian's gigantic home gym.

Above ground, there were two master suites on the first level, and several more upstairs.

After we'd arrived in London yesterday, I hadn't had much time to explore his extraordinary home. Damian had taken his duties of tour guide seriously, and he'd covered a lot of ground.

We'd gone to the Tower of London, since I hadn't seen much of it the first time I'd visited, and then strolled on to the Tower Bridge. Damian had taken me to see Big Ben before we'd had dinner, and then we'd finally returned to his mansion, exhausted and ready to fall into bed.

We'd moved at a slower pace this morning. Most of our day had been spent at Buckingham Palace. Since it was a little too early to hit the ten or so weeks when the Queen wasn't in residence in the summer, when the palace was open to the public, Damian had arranged to tour most of the residence and grounds with the assistance of his *connections.*

To my relief, and for the sake of my tired feet, I was glad we'd come back to Damian's home early.

We'd decided on a swim, and then we planned on devouring the meal his housekeeper had prepared before she'd left for the day.

"Are you just going to stand there, or are you planning on getting into the water sometime in the near future?" Damian teased after he broke the water, and slicked back his wet hair. "It's heated."

Nope. It wasn't exactly the temperature of the water I was worried about. The pool had to be warmer than the ocean temperature in California.

I was having a moment of uncertainty about yanking off the coverup I was wearing, and exposing my less-than-perfect body to a guy who was built like a Greek god.

Ridiculous. I swim all the time in California, and I've never had a moment of embarrassment about running around in a swimsuit.

It wasn't like I was a bikini wearer. I was sporting a modest, one-piece suit beneath my black-and-white flowered coverup that ended at my knees.

I just wished that it didn't hug every single curve on my body.

"What's wrong?" Damian questioned as he swam to the edge of the pool to talk to me.

"I don't think that *my* body will be similar to the bikini-clad women who usually use this pool," I said doubtfully.

"Are you saying that you're nervous about stripping down to your suit?" he asked, sounding confused.

"Bingo," I said sarcastically. "You win the prize."

He grinned as he looked up at me. "I'll get *my prize* when you take off that ridiculous thing you're wearing and get into the pool."

Okay. My coverup *was* kind of silly, but I liked flowers. "Easy for you to say since you have a perfect damn body," I grumbled.

"Yours is perfect, too," he replied. "Or are you just shy because your entire body is covered in bad dragon tattoos?"

I felt my lips start to curve up in a small smile. I knew what he was up to, and it was working. A little. Damian was trying to make me laugh, and realize that I had no reason to feel self-conscious.

"Of course it isn't," I shot back, playing along. "I've always much preferred unicorn tattoos."

"Now you've got me dying to see them, beautiful. Take it off."

He knew damn well that I wasn't sporting any kind of ink on my body, but his casual badgering *was* making me relax.

"Just for the record," he added. "You'll be the first female to ever swim in this pool. There's been no women, bikini-clad or otherwise, in this house at all."

I melted.

It was a home made to impress, yet Damian had never welcomed a female guest?

"Don't say you weren't warned," I muttered as I started to lift the only article of clothing standing between me and embarrassment.

I flipped it over my head determinedly, and tossed the garment onto a nearby lounger.

"Don't get in," Damian said hoarsely. "Not yet."

My entire body flushed bright pink as his eyes roamed over every tightly hugged curve, from the top of my head to my toes.

Finally, he met my eyes, and his covetous, hungry look told me everything I needed to know.

For some strange, unknown reason, Damian liked what he saw.

"How in the world could you see yourself as anything other than gorgeous?" he asked in a husky tone.

Frustrated, I did a twirl around slowly. "There's not a single thing that's gorgeous about me."

It wasn't like I *enjoyed* being self-conscious, but when I was beside a man like Damian, it was hard not to find every single flaw I had.

Granted, I was fit from swimming, diving, and all of the other physical exercise I did in the pursuit of fun in California, but the extra pounds I carried still stuck to my ass and hips like glue.

"Come here," Damian demanded in his panty-dropping baritone.

He held his arms up, and I leapt, already knowing he'd catch me.

Even though the pool was heated, I still gasped from the shock of my body hitting the water. Damian kept me from submerging very far, but my hair was wet when he tightened his grasp and hauled my body against his.

"Don't ever doubt yourself, Nicole," he rasped. "I hate it. You're gorgeously tall and curvy. You should be flaunting it. Or wait… maybe not, because seeing another man look at you like I do would make me fucking insane. But you should know that a lot of guys are going to salivate over a woman like you. And I happen to be one of them."

I let go of a sigh as I put my hands on his shoulders to steady myself. "I've never met one who did. Even my high school prom date backed out of our date at the last minute because I towered over him, even in low-heeled shoes. I guess he'd never bothered to actually stand right next to me before. I was heartbroken. We were supposed to hang out with Kylie, Macy, and their dates. Instead, I stayed home and watched TV with Mom, and my date found a last-minute fill-in who was shorter than he was. After that first humiliation, I guess I just learned to settle. Somewhere along the way, I lost my confidence in how I looked, and I never quite got it back."

Damian stroked the wet hair from my face. "You've had my dick rock-hard since the moment we met. Your prom date was an insecure idiot. And you should never have to settle for whatever affection a guy is willing to give you. You should demand whatever you want, Nicole, and if some guy won't give it to you, crush him with a high-heeled shoe, and move on. No…scratch that, because you've already met a man who salivates over you. You don't need another one."

My heart tripped as I saw the longing glint in his gorgeous eyes. I wasn't sure why I had such a hard time believing that Damian found me irresistibly sexy, but God, I really *wanted* to revel in it.

He made me *feel* beautiful.

Couldn't I just accept that, unlikely or not, I *was* his type?

"Where in the hell have you been all my life, Damian Lancaster?" I asked softly as I wrapped my arms around his neck.

"Right here, waiting to be the first guy to give you a screaming orgasm, gorgeous," he said playfully. "I think I've always been waiting for you."

My heart ached with yearning, because, jokes aside, I felt like I'd always been waiting for *him*, too.

Every other relationship I'd ever had in my life paled next to how I felt about Damian Lancaster.

And there was no way in hell I wasn't going to take this just as far as it could possibly go.

I wanted to be with him, and I was going to claim his gorgeous body as mine until it had to be otherwise.

Kylie had been right.

I'd regret it forever if I *didn't.*

I wanted to see how it felt to be really desired, and the perfect man to tutor me was right in front of me.

"Then show me, Damian," I requested softly. "Teach me what it's like to experience real physical satisfaction."

"Not yet," he said with a desperate rasp. "I want you to trust me, Nicole. I want you to know what kind of man I am first."

I smiled. "I already know. You're the kind of man who slips a veterinarian you barely know an outrageous check to help her animal rescue without really wanting any recognition for doing it. You're the kind of man who offers an older flight attendant a job on your private jet because it would make *her* life easier. You're the kind of man who worries more about his family than he does himself. You're the kind of man who would do anything to save your mother from a single moment of unhappiness. You're the kind of man who would play tour guide to a woman who wants to see London, even though you've been to every location a million times. You're a good man, Damian. I've known that for a while now."

"I want you to trust me," he said fiercely.

"I already do," I murmured as my lips touched the corner of his mouth.

"Then God help you, gorgeous, because now that you trust me, I can't wait another fucking moment to touch you."

My body could only tremble in answer as his mouth slammed down on mine.

CHAPTER 24

Nicole

I WASN'T SURE HOW it happened, but one moment he was greedily feasting on my mouth in the pool, and the next, he had me back to the ground level, and was striding toward his bedroom with me in his arms.

Of course, I *had* been highly distracted by the way he was kissing me like he couldn't possibly stop.

When he did cease his assault on my lips, Damian was lowering me back to my feet before I could mention that I was far too heavy to carry around his house.

That protest died before it could be uttered when my feet touched the ground, and I was caught in a sensual green-eyed gaze that I couldn't escape.

Damian didn't look the least bit winded.

He looked ravenous, hungry, and determined to devour me whole.

"W-we're wet," I stammered.

"My goal is to get you as wet as possible," he answered. "So I don't give a damn if I've already started the process."

I shuddered from the intensity of his gaze, and suddenly, I didn't really give a damn if we were dripping all over the expensive hardwood floor, either.

Honestly, I wasn't nervous anymore. All I really wanted was to be as close to Damian as I could possibly get. It didn't matter if I didn't think my body was perfect.

He thought it was, and that was good enough for me.

His master suite was similar to the one I was occupying, but other than a brief glance, I couldn't bring myself to care much about anything except the enormous bed right beside me.

Pushing the swimsuit off my shoulders, I shimmied out of it eagerly as Damian shucked off his swim trunks.

They dropped to the floor in a small puddle of water neither one of us acknowledged right before Damian backed me up to the bed, and let me fall gracelessly onto the mattress.

I scrambled up to the head of the bed, and allowed my wet head to land on a pillow.

I caught Damian's scent, and pulled the pillow against my nose, drowning in the heady, familiar, gut-wrenchingly sexy male smell of sensuality. I watched as the owner of that arousing fragrance stalked me.

His eyes never left mine as he crawled up the bed after me. "I knew you were beautiful, Nicole, but you've never looked more so than you do right now," he said in a voice that pulsated with lustful intentions. "Seeing you here like this was worth every painful fucking moment I had to wait."

I opened my legs as Damian covered my body with his, put a hand behind my head, and kissed me like he was trying to make sure I wasn't some kind of mind trick or mirage.

My entire body trembled in relief as we met skin-to-skin. How long had I waited to feel Damian's hot, gorgeous body fused against mine?

God, how I loved this confusing, stubborn, mouthwateringly beautiful man. I speared my hands into his damp hair, and savored the sensation as I rubbed against him. I'd probably never get my fill of having Damian this close to me, but I was going to relish every second of it.

Any sense of time slid away as he kissed me over and over, every embrace feeling like a covetous sense of ownership, a claiming that I couldn't deny that I wanted and needed from him.

"Damian," I murmured as he explored the sensitive skin of my neck, and then my ear.

My body was restless beneath his, desperate for some kind of release from the incendiary, blistering heat this man had been stoking inside me since the moment we'd met.

I'd bottled up every painful ache until *not* getting my satisfaction just wasn't an option anymore.

Sex had never been like this for me, like some kind of intense pleasure that was nearly painful. "Please," I whimpered as I fisted his damp hair.

"Be patient, sweetheart," he groaned against my breasts as he moved down to lave that wicked tongue over one of my agonized nipples.

I panted, holding his head against my breasts as he moved from one to the other in an effort that I swore he was doing just to torment me.

"You have the most amazing breasts," he said in a low, naughty bedroom voice that did nothing except ramp up my desire.

I tensed up as his tongue trailed down my belly.

Surely he wasn't going to...

Dear God, I wasn't sure if...

No man had ever...

"Damian, I don't…I can't…

"Oh, God…" My words came out of my mouth in an erotic moan that I couldn't contain when he spread my legs wider and buried his head between them with an enthusiasm that had my hands clenching the bedspread beneath me, so I didn't shoot straight off the bed.

He ran his tongue from the bottom of the pink, quivering flesh between my thighs to the top, where he found my clit, and proceeded to torment the sensitive, small bundle of nerves until I was squirming beneath his talented mouth.

"Damian, I never…" My babbled words seemed to infuse some kind of urgency into his successful efforts to make me completely insane.

Every sensation was unfamiliar because I'd never been with a man who had any desire to go down on me.

Except him.

Except Damian.

And he did it with a greediness that told me he thoroughly enjoyed it.

I let go of my past, and embraced every single raw emotion coursing through my body.

There was *only* him.

There was *only* this.

And the overwhelming pleasure *only* Damian could provide.

"Please-oh-please," I moaned breathlessly, not even recognizing my own voice anymore.

I grabbed his head, and ground up against his sexy mouth.

I wanted…

I needed…

I had to have…

When I felt a blinding climax creep tantalizingly closer, my head thrashed from side to side, and I wasn't at all sure I could handle the sheer force of it.

"Damian!" I screamed with abandonment, both fearing and welcoming sweet release. "Yes-please-make-me-come."

He thrust his fingers deep inside me without releasing the swirling pressure on my clit, and curled them in to a g-spot I never realized I had.

"I-can't-take-any-more-it's-way-too-much! Please, Damian," I yelped, even as I shattered, my entire body splitting into tiny shards as the most forceful orgasm I'd ever experienced tore me apart.

I gasped for breath as the giant climax turned into rhythmic spasms, and I tried to just take air into my lungs as the intensity slowly waned.

Breathe...just breathe, Nicole. You didn't die. You're still alive.

In.

Out.

In.

Out.

Holy shit!

Holy shit!

I was a mess by the time Damian climbed back up my body with a shit-eating grin on his gorgeous face.

"Please don't try to tell me you faked that one," he said as he stretched out beside me, and held my spent body against him. "And how in the hell is it that you've never had a man bury his face into that delicious pussy of yours?"

He kissed my forehead and stroked a comforting hand up and down my back. I felt so damn vulnerable, so completely destroyed that I *needed* his reassurance.

"You know damn well I could never fake *that*," I said, my pulse still racing, my breathing short and shallow. "And no man has ever *wanted* to bury his face between my legs. They like their blowjobs, but aren't eager to reciprocate."

He sent me a devilish smile that nearly curled my toes. "There's fantastic pleasure in making a woman come," he answered. "I get off on it. But this was better than any of those fantasies. You have no idea what it feels like for me to hear you screaming my name when you're about to come. Nothing like it. I'd happily stay planted there any time you let me."

Let him?

Like I was going to stop him?

"I felt like I was coming apart," I shared with him. "It was kind of...scary."

He toyed with a lock of my still-somewhat-wet hair. "I promised I'd be right there to catch you when you fell. I'm here. I'm not going anywhere."

His tone was earnest, and my heart ached because he wasn't afraid to make himself vulnerable to make *me* feel better. Damian wanted me to know that he was experiencing the same raw defenselessness that I was going through right now.

When I'd dropped *all* of my defenses, I'd felt it, and I still wasn't completely comfortable in my unprotected state.

We were probably both scared of this kind of intimacy.

It was too powerful.

Yet, neither one of us could shy away from it anymore.

My sense that Damian belonged to me, with me, was so natural that I couldn't possibly ignore it.

I wasn't going anywhere, either, because this man was worth the discomfort it was going to take to get used to the way he wanted me.

"Did you really get off to fantasies of giving me oral sex?" I asked curiously as my heart rate started to return to normal.

He frowned. "All the fucking time, sweetheart, but it didn't really take the edge off. And I have a pretty good imagination. I wanted it to be real way too much."

I stroked over the stubble of whiskers on his jawline, my mind trying to drum up an image of Damian leaning against the wall of a shower, his body wet and tight, his hand stroking up and down that gloriously aroused cock I'd barely seen before he'd gone down on me. The vision was so erotic that I had to block it out before it really began. "You're such an amazing man," I whispered.

He grinned. "What? Because I do what any other guy would do to expel unrequited lust?"

I shook my head. "No, although that is a tantalizing visual. And you know the lust was never unrequited."

There were dozens of reasons why Damian was so special, but he obviously didn't see them.

"I've thought about you getting yourself off, too," he said huskily. "But it didn't work. A woman like you should never, ever have to come alone, so I keep sending myself into *that* particular fantasy."

I finally smiled. "Touching myself was the only way I could ever have an orgasm, so it isn't all that bad. I guess I know what I want."

Strangely, I wasn't embarrassed in the least to discuss my masturbation habits with Damian. Maybe because he could talk about sex without an ounce of mortification himself.

Like it was natural, normal, a part of everyday life.

Thinking about it, sex *was* part of being a healthy adult.

I'd just never had a guy who could discuss it with so much… enthusiasm.

"Was I ever in your fantasies, Nicole?" he asked huskily.

I watched, fascinated as his light-green eyes darkened, changing shades in the blink of an eye. The ability of his irises to change from light to dark made it easier for me to know what he was thinking about.

When his emotions shifted, so did the shade of green in his eyes.

Right now, I'd say his thoughts had gone completely wild.

"You have," I told him in a sultry whisper. "Don't worry. You were an absolute stud. I felt a little uncomfortable stroking myself into an orgasm in your mother's house—"

"Fuck! You did it there, too? While I was in the suite across from you, trying to jerk myself off?" His eyes widened as he looked at me in question.

I let my eyelashes flutter like a seductress, feeling so damn powerful that I could easily arouse a man like Damian. "Apparently so."

"You're a very naughty girl, Nicole Ashworth," he said.

I sat up and pushed him onto his back. "Not nearly as misbehaved as I'd like to be," I answered as I ran my fingertips down his muscular chest. "I want to touch you, make you as crazy as you made me."

He locked his hands behind his head. "I'm all yours, sweetheart."

My heart tripped as I looked at the gloriously naked man spread out on top of the bedspread shamelessly.

The need to hear *his* hoarse cries of ecstasy overwhelmed me as I lowered my mouth to trace every one of his six-pack abs.

CHAPTER 25

Damian

THE FACT THAT Nicole was a hesitant seductress did absolutely nothing to cool my fucking rampant desire.

Her lack of experience in playing with a man in the bedroom only made her that much hotter.

She was so damn sweet that my base instincts were urging me to pin her gorgeous ass to the bed, and bury my long-suffering, achingly stiff cock inside Nicole until we couldn't decipher where one of us ended and the other began.

I'd fantasized about that, but I stifled that urge as I simply… watched her.

Christ! She was every wet dream I'd ever had come to life, but so much more vivid than a fantasy.

Her hair was starting to dry, and the blonde strands looked like white gold streaming down her shoulders and back in a messy fall of curls.

Her breasts were large and perfect.

I could have easily found my own release when I'd buried my head between those soft, silky thighs, and tasted her.

What man wouldn't feel like the luckiest bastard on earth to be the one who coaxed this woman into the best orgasm she'd ever had?

Certainly not me.

There was nothing in this world I wanted more than to be exactly where I was *right fucking now.*

With Nicole bent over me, her mouth ready to explore every inch of my eager flesh.

Don't get me wrong—I wanted to shag her until she begged for mercy, but I kept that desire on lockdown because I wanted to see what she had in store for me.

It was sweet torture as she leisurely made her way to my chest, and sucked on one of my nipples.

I tamped down a lusty groan because I'd never seen the male nipple as some kind of erogenous zone, for fuck's sake.

I nearly flinched as her luscious mouth connected with my heated skin, and her tongue darted out to swirl around, testing out the strength of every muscle in my abdomen.

I closed my eyes as I felt the brush of her soft, silky curls trailing over my skin.

Gritting my teeth in hellish frustration, I let her continue to explore, even though it was killing me.

Any other time, I knew I'd be savoring every touch of her curious tongue, but I'd wanted this woman for so long, and had been tormented by that desire for such a long time, that I felt like I was laid out on a torture rack instead of a comfortable king-sized bed.

"Nicole," I grunted. "Sweetheart."

If you don't let me fuck you very soon, I'm going to lose what's still left of my mind.

She stroked a soft palm down my abdomen. "I love your body, Damian. You're so strong."

This time, I couldn't hold back a groan of satisfaction.

"Oh, my, I wonder where this leads," she said.

I wasn't fooled by her innocent tone as her finger brushed over the trail of hair that started beneath my belly button, and ended where there was something better to feel than a paltry trail of hair.

My body shuddered when she reached the end of the line, and let her fingertip stroke up the shaft of my cock. "You're into the promised land now," I said in a strangled voice.

"I think I like it here," she said with a sexy sigh while she ran all of her fingers over the velvety skin that covered one very erect staff.

"Feel free to stay," I rasped.

"Thanks. I think I will," she answered amiably as she lowered her head.

Bloody hell!

Not that.

Not now.

I'd never fucking live through it.

In the end, I couldn't stop her, nor did I want to keep her from something she wanted.

I simply released a tortured groan as I felt her warm mouth suck my beleaguered cock inside of what I could only describe as complete and utter bliss.

"Nicole. Holy fuck! Don't. Oh yeah, just like that." The words tumbling out of my mouth didn't make sense, but it didn't matter.

Every bit of my attention was focused on how it felt to have those luscious lips wrapped around my cock. When she tightened her hold by sealing and sucking, the top of my head nearly blew right off.

"Fuck, yeah, sweetheart," I encouraged her as I buried a hand into the mass of blonde curls on her head.

I guided her mouth up and down on my cock. Not that she really *needed* any help. She'd been doing just fine on her own. Maybe it was *me* who needed to feel like I was helping *her.*

I let myself drown in the erotic pleasure for a couple of minutes, relish and record what it felt like to have Nicole go down on my cock like it was the most delicious thing she'd ever encountered.

I couldn't stop myself.

How fucking long had I waited?

Maybe it had only been a few weeks.

But it *felt like* a goddamn eternity.

"Nicole," I mumbled mindlessly, falling into a pleasurable abyss that I didn't really want to escape. "You feel so damn good."

My balls began to tighten, and I quickly closed my eyes.

I couldn't watch her greedily devouring me anymore.

The sight was too damn erotic.

I was way too close…

This isn't the way I want this to go!

I shook myself as I emerged from the veil of sexual euphoria that had kept me trapped inside it.

Even though it killed me, I tightened my hand in Nicole's curls and pulled gently. "No, baby," I protested huskily. "Not like this. Not this time."

No matter how much I wanted to let her finish what she'd started—and fuck, how I wanted her to finish—I had to end this a different way.

With *both of us* sweaty, panting, and completely satiated.

I *had* to be inside her to satisfy the rampant beast that demanded I find a way to make this woman mine.

"Did I do something wrong?" she asked, her tone confused.

"Not at all," I assured her. "It was way too right."

I stretched to open the drawer of my bedside table, because even though I'd never had a woman in my own bed, it just *seemed* like the right place to put condoms.

Her eyes grew wide. "Oh," she said in a hushed whisper as she realized I was beyond desperate to shag her. "You want…that."

Fuck yeah, I wanted *that*, and I wasn't stopping until I could feel her coming around my cock.

I fumbled like a damn teenage boy as I rolled on the condom because I could see the need in her eyes responding to my desperation.

"Ride me, Nicole," I said in a tone that didn't really make my words sound like a *request*. It was more like a gruff command.

She hesitated for a millisecond, and then slung one of those long legs over me until she was mounted to ride me like her favorite stallion.

"Thank fuck!" I let out the grateful expletive as I realized that, after a few weeks of near insanity, I was finally going to drive home to some kind of normality. Yeah, I knew this woman was always going to make me crazy, but certainly that madness would let up a little after this.

That was what I thought, anyway—until I fell into a pair of ocean-blue eyes that made me feel like I was never going to be rational again.

CHAPTER 26

Nicole

MY BREATH SEIZED in my lungs as Damian's eyes met mine, and I felt like they were capturing my soul.

At that instant, we were both vulnerable, wide open for the other to see.

I probably looked wild-eyed and brash, because that's exactly how I felt right now.

It didn't matter that I had no idea how to ride a man into oblivion, because I knew Damian would be there to show me how it was done.

I didn't care if I'd refused to get on top in the past.

I wanted this.

Damian wanted this.

And I was filled with a frenzied instinct to put both of us out of our misery.

Now.

Immediately.

I rose up, and guided his cock where I wanted it to be, and then sank down slowly.

I closed my eyes, trying to imprint the heady sensation of Damian filling me into my long-term memory, so I'd never forget the first time the two of us were fused together like we'd never come apart.

"You're so damn tight," Damian growled, his face a mask of barely leashed control.

It had been a while since I'd had sex, and it had never been like *this*.

He was a big man, but I was wet with need. Sweat was beading on both of our bodies when he was finally seated completely inside me, and I released a thoroughly satisfied sigh.

Our gazes were still locked, and I felt open in a way I never had before.

"Fuck, yes!" Damian's hands gripped my hips. "Take it all."

My body tightened as I started to move, losing myself in the rhythm of my body merging with Damian's.

His powerful hips surged up to meet every downward motion I made, the two of us perfectly synchronized with every satisfying thrust.

Every lunge moved me closer to freedom, and I relished that escape from the woman I used to be.

No more self-doubt.

No more self-consciousness.

No more worrying about not being a petite, adorable female.

I was wholly desired by this man, and that knowledge set me free.

"Take what you want, Nicole," Damian rasped.

I panted, my inner muscles deliciously stretched, my body on fire with the need for release.

"All I want is you," I cried out. My gaze tore away from Damian's as I closed my eyes. "Fuck me, Damian. Please."

I squeaked as he rolled us over and pinned me to the bed. He was still deeply embedded inside me as he asked urgently, "Like this? How do you want me, Nicole? Because I'll fucking give you whatever you want."

My heart was already racing, but it skipped a couple of beats as I opened my eyes and saw his fierce expression. "It really doesn't matter," I said breathlessly as tears formed in my eyes. "Any way you want it."

I just needed Damian, and I didn't give a damn how we accomplished that.

"I like it this way, too," he said, his heated breath caressing my face. "Wrap those fantastic legs around me, baby, and hold on. I want to watch you come for me."

I immediately complied, realizing that I liked it when Damian was in control of our pleasure.

"I trust you," I told him honestly as I wrapped my arms around his neck.

For some reason, in the middle of this madness, I needed him to know that.

I love you.

The words bubbled up inside me, but I closed my mouth.

I couldn't say *that*, but I desperately wanted him to know that, too.

I gasped as Damian began to move, and every forceful drive of his hips left me needier than the one before.

He moved, changed positions slightly until he dragged a hungry moan from my lips. "Please-oh-please-I-can't-take-any-more."

My fingernails dug into the skin of his back, and I kept clawing while my climax hurtled toward me.

In seconds, I was coming in deep, pulsating waves, different than the first one, but no less frightening.

"Damian!" I cried out, feeling a little like I was dying.

"You're mine, Nicole. Say it!" Damian demanded harshly.

"I am yours," I muttered. This man had my soul, and at the moment, I didn't really care what he did with it.

"I'll make damn sure you never want to be with anyone else."

His possessive promise was like an aphrodisiac to me, and my inner muscles clamped down and spasmed around his cock until I milked Damian to his own powerful orgasm.

"Fuck! Nicole!" he called out as he was coming, and I watched as the muscles in his throat and jaw clenched and released, every semblance of his control completely shattered.

His mouth crashed down on mine, and I returned the frenzied kiss.

His chest was still heaving as he rested his forehead on my shoulder.

Our bodies were damp with sweat, and neither one of us spoke as we tried to catch our breath.

Finally, he released a masculine sigh, and said, "You're going to kill me one day, woman."

Since he didn't seem all that worried about his demise, I said, "No I won't. I'll rescue you."

"You better," he grumbled good-naturedly. "Don't move. I'll be back."

Damian disappeared into his bathroom, most likely to trash the condom.

I stretched a little, like a cat enjoying the warmth of the sun, certain I was incapable of getting off the bed.

Damian was back in less than a minute, and I almost purred when he pulled my spent body into his arms.

"I think I'm ruined," I complained as I burrowed into his warmth.

"I didn't exactly steal your virginity," he said, his voice vibrating with wicked humor.

I punched his bicep playfully. "Not ruined in that way," I clarified. "You once told me that I'd miss having an orgasm when I was having sex if I ever had one. I think you were right. I'd miss it now. So I'm ruined."

"That won't ever be an issue if you stick with me," he answered.

I smiled against his shoulder. "Are you saying that it could be like that every single time?"

"Better," he replied playfully. "Now that we've gotten those first orgasms out of the way, I can work on multiple."

"I think that's a myth," I told him. "And I'm not sure I could handle any more."

"It's not a myth," he denied. "Just wait and see."

My slowly decreasing heart rate sped up again as I realized that he obviously didn't plan on this fling ending anytime soon.

Don't get your hopes up, Nicole. You knew going into this that it could never be more than a sublime experience that would eventually come to an end.

"You're a little arrogant about your skills," I teased.

"Not arrogant," he said gruffly. "Just willing to make your pleasure my priority."

His comment nearly brought me to tears.

Damian *was* always willing to do almost anything to make me happy, and that tendency he had to take care of me almost broke me sometimes.

Had I always been with selfish men, or was Damian truly a rare kind of guy?

Maybe he wasn't exactly a unicorn, but he *was* special.

"Hey, don't go to sleep," Damian said as he prodded me a little. "We need to eat."

I sighed. "I'm starving. And I stink. I need a shower."

"I think we both do. And you *don't* stink."

God, I adored him for saying that, but I knew it wasn't the truth. "Food, then shower? Or shower, then food?"

"We'll save time if we shower together," he suggested hopefully.

I giggled. I actually *giggled*. "You do have more than one shower in this enormous palace."

I'd never actually counted, but the bathrooms in this place had to outnumber the bedrooms.

"Ah, but the shower in this master bedroom is special."

"Is it?" I said doubtfully.

"Massage capability with a variety of shower heads."

I pulled back to look at him. "Same as my shower."

"There's a rain shower," he mentioned.

"There's one in the other master, too." I was pretty sure what he was getting at, and the ends of my lips started to kick up.

"There's one other difference."

My smile widened. "Do tell, Your Grace."

"My naked body will be in *mine,* not in *yours.*"

I struggled to sit up. "Okay, you win. That makes yours very special. Let's go."

He sent me a mischievous look that kicked up my heart rate again. "I knew you'd eventually see it my way."

I rolled my eyes, held out my hand, and let him lead the way to his shower.

By the time we came out for dinner much, much later, I had to give it to Damian.

It was the most incredible shower I'd ever had.

CHAPTER 27

Damian

"ARE YOU SERIOUS?" Nicole asked with an astonished look on her face. "You haven't been on this thing since it opened twenty years ago?"

I shrugged as we stepped into one of the large capsules on the London Eye. "I've never been particularly fond of heights," I told her. "Mum took all of us during the new millennium opening. I saw no reason to do it again."

She moved closer to me. "Are you going to be okay? I had no idea you were afraid of heights."

Nicole looked so concerned that it was like a swift kick in the gut to realize she was actually worried about…me. "Not afraid, really," I tried to assure her. "I'd just prefer to avoid them most of the time."

She snuggled against me and put her arms around my neck. "But you fly all the time."

"I don't sit by the window. Problem solved." Here, where the pod was made up of so much damn glass, I *couldn't* avoid noticing when we were climbing high over the river Thames, and the rest of the city.

Bloody hell! We were already starting to climb.

I'd been dreading this event since I'd noticed it was on Nicole's short list of things to do in London, but I wasn't about to send her on the attraction alone. If she was going to plummet to her death from one hundred thirty-five meters in the air, I was going with her.

Not that I could actually *do* anything about that if it happened, but at least I'd be there with her.

"How is it that we're all alone in this big capsule?" she questioned as we climbed.

It had been a simple matter, really. The *other thing* I really liked to avoid was large crowds of tourists, and I *had* been able to do something about that. "Aristocratic privilege?" I joked.

She sent me a look of pseudo displeasure. "Meaning you paid somebody off so we could go alone?"

"Something like that," I grumbled.

Actually, it had been *exactly* like that, and I wasn't about to regret having Nicole alone in the large pod.

She hopped over to the window. "Oh, my God. This is amazing. I'm starting to see the river."

I moved up behind her, and wrapped my arms around her waist. I pointed my finger. "You'll be able to see Big Ben shortly, and Buckingham Palace."

It took a very long thirty minutes to do a complete revolution, so there wasn't much in the city she *couldn't* see. It was a really clear day.

"If I had one of these close to me, I probably would have ridden it hundreds of times by now," she said with a sigh as she leaned back against me. "There's something about being able to see everything from the air that's totally surreal."

"I'm fine seeing it from terra firma," I replied dryly.

"It's the highest Ferris wheel in Europe," she said with a sigh, her eyes still searching for landmarks.

"Fun fact: there is no capsule number thirteen. We Brits are a bit superstitious."

"What?" she exclaimed with artificial outrage. "That's my lucky number. I was born on November thirteenth. Are *you* superstitious?"

"Not at all. I was born on December thirteenth, so I've never considered it an unlucky number, either. If you remember, we met on the *thirteenth* of June, so I could never associate the number thirteen with anything other than good luck. However, I'd say we're in the minority since there's no capsule number thirteen."

She laughed. "I don't care. I don't mind being unique."

She was special all right, and not just because she loved the number thirteen.

Nicole would be singular even if she didn't adore what was an unlucky number for many.

We took some time discovering and pointing out most of the things we'd seen during the week in London.

"There's the Tower Bridge," she called out, so excited that I felt like I needed to keep a tighter grip on her to keep her feet inside the capsule. "God, I feel like we're at the top of the world."

"I think you're a bit of an adrenaline junkie," I accused.

She turned and wrapped her arms around my neck. "Not really. Right now, I think I'm high on life."

I searched her face. I had to admit that there was something different about her. She'd always been a bright light in a sometimes-dark world, but she was positively glowing at the moment. "The result of multiple orgasms, maybe?" I asked hopefully.

Honestly, the woman should be barely able to walk after the number of times I'd inserted myself between her thighs over the last few days.

She swatted my arm playfully. "A real gentleman would never mention *that*."

"Sweetheart, I never *claimed* to be a gentleman."

She inspired every lurid thought that crossed my mind every minute or two.

"But you're a duke, Your Grace," she replied, her eyes dancing with mirth.

"I'm a *man*," I stressed. "A guy who never stops thinking about you naked and in the thrall of a good orgasm."

How in the bloody hell could I forget *that?*

Her head thrown back in ecstasy…

Her eyes closed as her release washed over her…

The way she screamed my name like a mantra when she was in the middle of said climax…

The way she looked at me *afterward,* like I was the only man who could satisfy her.

I was far from being some kind of savior to her.

I was still evading the unpleasant task of telling Nicole the truth, and I fucking hated that, even though I'd decided to tell her as soon as possible.

Which *was* going to be at my mother's gala.

Yeah, I'd considered coming clean earlier because the guilt of not telling Nicole was starting to eat me alive.

Every time I tried to tell her the truth about Dylan, I hadn't been able to get the words out of my mouth.

Truth was, I didn't want Nicole to stop seeing me as the one man she actually trusted.

I valued that trust more than I did my own life, so telling her that I'd been a major prick who had been bullshitting her all this time was going to be one of the hardest things I'd ever done.

Coward! The annoying voice in my head chimed in.

I answered. *I'll tell her after Mum's gala. She deserves this time to enjoy her visit to the UK.*

I shook my head as I realized I was arguing with…myself.

What in the hell was wrong with me?

"Maybe I'm glad you aren't a gentleman," Nicole murmured, and then blushed.

Jesus! How could the woman still turn pink after all the sexy times we'd spent together? Over the last several days, it had gotten to a point where there wasn't a room in my house that was still virgin territory. I'd even managed to bend her over in my gym, and shag her until neither one of us *needed* another workout.

"Damian? Are you okay? We're at the top," Nicole asked softly.

I took her face between my hands and tried to memorize the soft look of concern and affection she had turned in my direction. It might not last long. "Yeah, I'm fine." I fell into that glorious blue-eyed gaze of hers that told me how much she cared about me.

Me.

Damian Lancaster, the man.

Not the billionaire Duke of Hollingsworth.

She put a hand behind my head and pulled me close so she could kiss me. "Maybe you need a distraction," she whispered against my mouth.

I didn't.

I hadn't even thought about how high above the ground we were at the moment.

But I sure as hell wasn't going to turn down the opportunity to become entirely engulfed in this woman's warmth and tenderness.

I was honest enough with myself to admit that I was beginning to crave a hell of a lot more than just a shag from Nicole.

Maybe I always had.

Now, the very idea that I'd be cured of my obsession by just hopping into bed together once was a complete joke.

I took what she offered, but I savored it rather than swooping in like a wolf ready to feed.

I tasted her lips slowly and thoroughly, and tried to tell her how much I treasured her with a simple kiss.

Her surrender to me was so quick and instinctive that my dick was rock-hard within seconds.

I fucking loved the way she completely trusted me with her body, like she was certain she'd love every single thing I did to her.

I let my mouth trail over the silken skin of her neck and shoulders until she was purring with contentment.

"Damian." She said my name with a sigh so full of longing that it hit me like a sucker punch.

I lifted my head and pulled her soft, curvy body flush with mine. "I'd swear I'd fuck you right here if we weren't being watched by CCTV from all sides."

"Bummer," she answered, sounding disappointed. "But at least we aren't at the top anymore. Feeling better?"

"I hadn't even noticed," I said honestly. "I was way too distracted."

She laughed softly as she turned to admire the view going down. "I think this is one of the most amazing things I've ever done. Thank you for suffering through it with me."

"I wasn't exactly suffering, love." My arms tightened around her waist again.

If Nicole wanted to ride the London Eye over and over again, I'd be there right beside her without a single complaint just to see the jubilant look on her face.

It didn't take a lot to make Nicole happy, which was a rarity in my world.

A good meal.

A ride on a ridiculously high Ferris wheel.

My brother Leo offering to take her around his new sanctuary in the US.

A London theater production.

Seeing Buckingham Palace from the inside out.

Simple things that any woman in my social sphere would take for granted, or not be interested in doing in the first place.

Oddly, Nicole made me appreciate those things, too, when I was seeing them through her eyes.

"Almost down," she said with a contented sigh. "Thank you, Damian. The fact that you were willing to go with me and share this with me means a lot to me. Today has been really special."

There it was *again,* that murmur of appreciation for something so damn…small.

As we hopped out of the capsule, and I took her hand, Nicole gave me a kiss on the cheek in gratitude.

That was the moment I came to the realization that I thought it was a pretty special day, too.

CHAPTER 28

Nicole

I WAS STILL WIPING tears from my eyes as Damian and I exited Her Majesty's Theatre later that evening. After the intermission, he'd given me the fine linen handkerchief from the pocket of his tuxedo jacket, and muttered, "You might need it."

I'd scoffed at the time, but I was grateful to have it now.

He held my hand and walked slightly in front of me as he navigated through the crush of people, and tugged me into a room with only a few people occupying it.

Looking around, I saw a small bar, and assumed it was some kind of waiting room for VIPs.

"We'll wait a few minutes until the crowd clears," he said. "Please stop crying."

He strode over and snatched two glasses of champagne from the bar, and then handed me one when he came back. "You okay?"

Damian sounded so disconcerted that I smiled. He obviously had no idea what to do with a woman in tears. "Of course," I assured him. "The show was just...so sad. It broke my heart." I tested out the champagne. It wasn't too dry to consume, so I took a bigger sip.

His eyebrows drew together as he said, "See, I've never understood how anybody could consider the ending as a *bad* outcome. Personally, I think the poor girl had to choose between the lesser of two evils. Raoul ignores her distress, doesn't believe her when she tries to tell him about the Phantom, and pats her on the head like she's an idiot. But even worse, the Phantom is a homicidal stalker. So I suppose Raoul *was* a better choice. She really should have dumped them *both* and tried again. But she chose Raoul in the end, the guy who was condescending, but *not* a homicidal stalker, and the Phantom disappears. The heroine and hero get what they want. The end."

I rolled my eyes. He really didn't get it, but his hilarious summary did make me want to laugh. "Because I think there's a part of Christine that cares about the Phantom, and all of the pain he'd suffered."

His eyes widened. "The bastard was a murderer. And should we mention the fact that he manipulated her by pretending he was her father at first? Or the fact that he kidnapped her and forced her into his lair? More than once."

I shrugged. "He did all those things because he was so obsessed with Christine."

"Really? Does it matter *why* he offed people?"

"Yes," I answered, hiding my smile behind my champagne glass as I took another sip. "Couldn't you feel his pain, his sorrow, his longing to be a different man for Christine? He followed her everywhere."

He frowned. "Yeah. Just like a demented stalker who wanted to rape and murder the poor woman."

I laughed. "He didn't want to *kill* her. He wanted to be with her. Okay, so he was basically a crazed, tormented anti-hero, but I still felt sorry for him. I guess the silver lining is that at least Christine and Raoul lived happily ever after."

"If you want to keep thinking that, then I *highly* suggest you don't see the sequel," he said dryly. "Horrible music, and a very bad plot."

"I know there was a movie version, but I've never seen it. Was it really that bad?" I asked curiously.

He lifted a brow. "Would you like a brief summary?"

I nodded. I was enjoying his cynical reviews. "Yes."

He took a deep breath. "In short, ten years later, Christine's husband, Raoul, becomes a broke, abusive drunk. Christine once again runs into the Phantom, and we find out that her ten-year-old son is really the Phantom's love child. After she suffers through more torment and pain, she finally chooses the Phantom, and then gets shot by Meg. Her son runs away while she lies there dying because he doesn't want a homicidal stalker for a father. Christine declares her undying love for the Phantom—although God only knows how she found anything lovable about the creepy bastard—and she dies. The End. Seriously, the whole thing was another ridiculous tragedy without the incredible music to save it. Like most sequels, it never should have been written, in my opinion."

I burst out laughing. "Oh, my God. Now I have to see it. I'm completely intrigued."

"You're twisted," he accused jokingly.

"Maybe." I opened the small clutch I was carrying and dropped his handkerchief inside it. "Or maybe I'm just a sucker for really tragic love stories."

Damian tossed the last of his champagne back with a gulp. "I think it's a female thing," he observed as he put the empty glass down on a nearby table. "Hopefully, you enjoyed yourself—in between sobs."

I found his wry teasing so amusing that I grinned at him. "I did. Thank you. It's been an incredible evening."

My eyes roamed lovingly over the sight of Damian in a tux. He'd asked me what I was wearing, and had opted to go formal after I'd explained that I had an adorable black cocktail dress that I hadn't found the opportunity to wear yet.

Not that we'd needed to dress up quite so much for the theater. The attire had been anything from smart casual to dressy on the attendees tonight. But Damian had taken me to the most exclusive restaurant in the city prior to our arrival at Her Majesty's Theatre, so I wasn't about to don a pair of jeans or a sundress for that.

Now, I was grateful that I'd gotten the opportunity to see Damian Lancaster in formal wear before his mother's gala. I still couldn't say that he didn't take my breath away every time I looked at him, but at least I'd been able to gawk at him without a ballroom full of eyes watching the two of us.

There were very few men who could put on a tuxedo and wear it like they were entirely comfortable in the dressy attire.

Damian was one of those men.

The garments were obviously custom fitted, and Damian appeared to be at ease with what he was wearing. Not once had he fussed with his bow tie, or tried to adjust the cummerbund. The suit fit the man, not the other way around.

"Have I told you how gorgeous you look tonight?" he inquired as he leaned toward me.

I shot him an exasperated look that I didn't mean. He *had* told me. At least a dozen times since we'd left his house. But my skin still heated because he flustered me every single time he said it.

I'd put a lot of work into my appearance tonight. Along with the just-above-the-knee black cocktail dress I was wearing, I'd done a complete makeup job, and pulled back the hair at the side of my face so that all of my curly locks elegantly fell down my back.

My skin wasn't dark enough to go without a pair of stockings, so I'd picked a black pair, ones so sheer that I'd been worried about snagging them the entire night.

Best thing ever? I was wearing a pair of three-inch stiletto heels *without* worrying about being taller than my date.

Damian still towered a couple of inches above my height, even with me in an outrageous pair of high heels.

No slouching to try to look shorter necessary.

At all.

Somewhere along this UK journey, I'd lost all of my self-consciousness about my body type. Damian had done that for me. I'd learn to embrace myself and my body, because hey, not every person in the world found the same body type attractive.

"You told me," I finally responded. "I think that compliment makes it a baker's dozen now."

He smirked. "Thirteen *is* one of our favorite numbers. And you do look…stunning."

"You look pretty damn handsome yourself, Your Grace," I said impishly.

He looked every inch the debonair billionaire duke he actually was, and more.

Now that we were in *his* territory, his wealth and power were much more in-your-face obvious, but it wasn't the money or his title that really bowled me over sometimes.

It was Damian's aura, the confidence he wore like an invisible cloak, that drew me to him.

Yet, I also knew that some of that was façade, which made him even more fascinating.

There was so much more to Damian Lancaster that most people would never see. He played the part of the billionaire duke so damn well that nobody *looked* for any vulnerability.

Most likely, they didn't dare.

"Are you ready to get out of here and go home?" Damian asked.

Home? Am I ready to go home?

Strangely, I was almost comfortable staying in Damian's gigantic wonder palace of a house in Mayfair.

Probably because we've had sex in nearly every room in the place.

No, that *wasn't* the reason. Not exactly. I was starting to love his home because it was the location where I saw him smile the most, sensed his happiness. We'd laughed a lot during the last several days in that residence, so it felt warm every time we entered, instead of being the ultra-contemporary showplace I'd seen it as in the very beginning.

Sure, it was ostentatious and luxurious. Damian Lancaster was one of the richest guys in the world, so why wouldn't it be? But what made it so inviting was the man who resided there, not the expensive materials that decorated it.

I nodded. "I'm ready."

I tried not to think about how I was going to feel when it came time for me to go back to the United States.

We were going to Surrey tomorrow night for the gala that Bella was hosting, and then what?

The bad press had completely died down.

I supposedly took one of the most eligible bachelors in the world off the market, so people in England were more curious about me than Damian's naked picture.

When I was gone, Damian Lancaster would garner a whole lot of sympathy because a flighty American woman had jilted him. He'd be the victim. I'd be the wicked witch.

Job well done.

Really, my work here was finished.

So why did it seem like it was going to be so damn hard to say goodbye?

But it wasn't like I hadn't known the sad ending to this fairy tale.

Damian held out his hand, and I offered mine immediately, instinctively, because it felt so natural to do it.

The crowd had thinned considerably as we walked through the lobby, but the cries from the other side of the hall were impossible to ignore.

"Your Grace! Wait!" a male voice bellowed as it got closer us. "Your Grace!"

The older man stopped in front of us. Behind him, there was a guy with a large video camera on his shoulder.

"Trenton Brown with *The Sun Times*, Your Grace. I'm a reporter. Would you mind a few questions?" the man asked eagerly.

Until now, we hadn't been approached by reporters. Probably because we'd mostly sought out tourist attractions, and Damian had managed private tours for several of my sightseeing adventures.

Damian sent the man a glare that probably would have had most people backing off. "Since I assume that camera is already rolling, yes, but make it quick. Ms. Ashworth and I are knackered. It's been a long day."

And...it was on. The forward reporter rattled off question after question. Damian answered when it suited him, or when the questions weren't all that personal.

I kept a smile plastered on my face, and my attention on Damian's expression.

Even though he looked more bored than rattled, I knew that he didn't like this type of intrusive publicity. Damian had managed to stay out of the limelight most of his life.

Now, his handsome face was becoming familiar to more than just reporters because he'd been forced to act out this whole charade. Eventually, it might become impossible for him to leave his own home without some kind of security detail.

And he'd hate that.

All of his efforts, and his mother's earlier endeavors to keep her children out of the news, could end up being completely wasted by one single incident that had catapulted Damian into front-page news.

Now, after one scandalous picture, it was like the media had just realized how much people wanted to hear about Damian Lancaster.

Of course, we'd given them a fairy-tale romance to follow.

And Damian had started it with the whole setup orgy thing.

But if I'd ever doubted how much Damian hated being in the public eye, all I had to do was look at his face right now.

He hated it.

"Should we be hearing wedding bells at this point?" the reporter asked craftily. "Will every single woman in London need to cross you off their lists of very eligible bachelors?"

"I doubt very much whether I was ever on those lists," Damian said charmingly. "Now, if you'll excuse us, gentlemen, I'd like to take Ms. Ashworth home. It's getting late."

He didn't wait for those men to accept their dismissal. Damian strode forward with me in tow, and exited the theater.

I stumbled on a large crack in the sidewalk before we could reach the curb. "Ouch! Damn it!"

Damian halted instantly and turned. "Nicole. Are you okay?"

"Fine," I said through gritted teeth. "The damn cement jumped out in front of my big toe."

Not to mention the fact that I'm a major klutz because I never wear a pair of three-inch heels with an open toe!

He didn't acknowledge my joke. Instead, he swept me up into his arms, and carried me to the curb where his limo was waiting. "I'm sorry," he said huskily as he looked down at my face.

I'd wrapped my arms around his neck when he'd picked me up, and I stared back at him, my heart melting. "Don't be sorry. It wasn't your fault. I'm sorry that you're being plagued by reporters now."

He leaned down and kissed me, a sweet embrace that I barely had time to respond to before Damian's driver opened the back door of the vehicle.

My ass hit the soft, creamy leather, and I clambered across the seat so Damian could come in after me.

"Now, let me see that foot," Damian demanded gruffly, as he pulled both of my clumsy feet into his lap.

CHAPTER 29

Nicole

"IT'S THE RIGHT toe, and it's fine," I told Damian, feeling awkward with both of my sandaled feet plopped in the middle of his lap.

He gently removed both of my shoes, and dropped them onto the floorboard. After he surveyed the injury closely through the sheer stocking, he said. "No blood. It looks okay."

"It's good. Really. I just stubbed my toe."

I expected him to give up, and put my feet back on the floorboards.

Instead, he took one foot into his large hands and started to massage it.

After hours of wearing those shoes, my feet were a little sore, and what he was doing to them right now felt like a mini orgasm. "Oh, God. That's nice."

He pushed on a pressure point with his thumb. "Just nice?" he mocked.

It didn't take me long to realize he was teasing me like he had after our first kiss. He obviously wanted to hear that what he was doing was more than just…nice.

"Amazing," I moaned as he picked up the other foot. "Fantastic," I added breathlessly as he massaged my left foot. "Maybe even orgasmic."

It wasn't like I had some kind of foot fetish, but Damian's hands were like magic as he massaged over the cramped muscles of my insole, and forced them to relax.

I stretched out on the long leather seat, and propped my elbows behind me, watching Damian as he soothed away the ache in both of my feet.

"Better?" he asked as he moved to lightly rub my calves.

The feel of those beautiful fingers skimming across the sheer silk of my stockings sent a shiver of longing through my entire body.

He stroked over my knees, and then slowly up my thighs. "I'm more than willing to sooth *any* part of your body that aches, sweetheart," he said in a hoarse, deliciously naughty tone.

I flopped down on the seat, releasing a pent-up breath as my head hit the soft seat cushion. "Damian," I said in a loud whisper.

His fingers stopped their marauding progress as they hit bare skin. "Fuck! How did I not know you were wearing these?"

He'd found the lace edges of my stockings that were held in place by an equally lacy garter belt.

"Because I didn't tell you," I replied in a sultry voice. "I was going to let you discover them later."

"They're sexy as hell," he informed me.

I closed my eyes. God, I adored that barely leashed edginess I could hear in his words. He sounded like he couldn't wait to fuck me, like he'd completely lose it if he didn't. "I wore them for you, Damian. I thought you might like them."

"Mission accomplished if your goal was to make me crazy," he answered tightly. "My cock is hard as a rock."

I opened my mouth to make a smartass comment, and then snapped it closed as his fingers started to explore beneath the scrap of lace.

"Jesus, Nicole. You're so damn wet."

I whimpered as he smoothed a finger over my slick flesh. It didn't take much for Damian to soak a pair of my panties. It had happened as soon as he'd started to massage my foot. "Yes," I hissed in agreement.

"You'll have to be very, very quiet," he advised in a low, wicked tone. "The partition between us and my driver is pretty thin."

I sighed. It wasn't like I could straddle him right now and ride both of us into an amazing orgasm. The seats were enormous, and the windows were tinted, so it would be *physically* possible, but I doubted he was carrying a condom.

I felt the cool air waft over the skin of my upper thighs as he lifted my skirt. "Very pretty," he remarked appreciatively.

The lingerie set *was* really nice. The lace was black, but there were tiny red bows at the top of each stocking, and at the band of the panties. I'd thrown them in my suitcase on a whim. I'd never worn the stuff. Kylie had given them to me as a gag gift for my birthday a couple of years ago, and I'd shoved them into the back of my drawer, assuming they'd never see the light of day again.

I wasn't the kind of woman who wore anything sexy.

Or, at least, I wasn't…until I'd met Damian.

Maybe I'd just never been inspired like I was right now.

His fingers continued to play in my slippery heat, and I let out a squeak as he sought and found my clit. "Feel good, baby?" he asked in an almost polite tone.

"God, yes," I answered tremulously.

He rolled his finger over the sensitive bundle of nerves again, and kept stroking over it lazily until I was ready to shoot off my seat. "Damian," I moaned, my body primed for his.

"You want my cock?" he asked in the same controlled voice.

"Yes, yes, yes," I cried, right before his hand clamped over my mouth.

"Quiet. Remember?" he admonished. His torso stretched out on top of mine.

I nodded and he took his hand from my mouth. "It's hard," I whined quietly.

"Sweetheart, you have no idea how hard it really is right now. I'm going to make you come, but I really don't want to share your pleasure with my driver."

"Tell me you have a condom," I pleaded quietly, my body begging for release.

"I don't," he said. "But it's not necessary right now."

I was panting as I tried to stem my disappointment. I needed Damian fast and hard to satisfy the need he'd stoked inside me.

His whole bossy do-what-I-say prelude had me panting for more.

He was probably enjoying it, but I was a complete mess.

I'm going to make you come.

Ha! He hadn't mentioned that he couldn't do that until we got back to his house.

I started to sit up, but Damian pushed me back down firmly, and then took my right leg and stretched it over the back of the seat until my legs were spread wide open.

He looked at me and put a finger to his mouth in caution right before his head disappeared between my open thighs.

A strangled gasp left my lips as I felt his tongue probing, stroking over the thin lace of my panties.

Holy shit!

I bit down on my bottom lip, trying to hold the mewl of pleasure that sprang to my lips.

Damian teased, his tongue sliding along the edges of my panties, but never making it to the place where I really needed him.

I slapped one hand on the back of the seat, and clawed at the leather as Damian did everything in his power to drive me out of my mind.

"Please," I begged in a soft tone, trying not to be too loud.

Just when I thought I was going to scream in pure frustration, he gripped the crotch of the sexy panties and gave them an enormous tug.

They tore away from my body under the brutal assault, and I heard Damian growl as his mouth covered my pussy.

"Yes, yes, yes, yes, yes," I chanted as he went down on me with very serious intent.

No more playing.

Damian Lancaster was now apparently determined to make me come, or die trying.

I tossed my head from side to side as I panted, waiting for him to bring me the release my body demanded.

It was so damn hard to stay quiet, to stifle the cries that rose to my throat in response to what his wicked mouth and tongue were doing between my legs.

"Oh, my God," I hissed, no longer capable of staying completely silent. "Yes, Damian. Please. Make me come."

I couldn't take any more.

I tamped down a scream of elation as I felt his fingers fill me, working in the same rhythm as that incredible tongue on my clit.

My body began to implode as I felt my climax building.

I didn't care who was listening.

I *had* to scream.

I slapped my own hand over my mouth, and settled for whimpering into my palm as my orgasm hit full-force.

All I could do was lay on the leather seat and tremble in the aftermath. "You ruined me…again," I told him once I'd caught my breath.

He pulled me up as I recovered, and cradled me on his lap.

He nuzzled my ear as he said, "If I keep ruining you, I might just have to marry you, woman."

I knew it was a joke, but my body tensed up a little anyway.

I couldn't find a single witty thing to say to him in return.

Really? Like His Grace would ever marry a nobody American woman like me, shotgun wedding or not?

Maybe I would have laughed at his comment if it hadn't made my heart ache so damn badly.

CHAPTER 30

Nicole

"YOU LOOK ABSOLUTELY beautiful, Nicole," Bella told me as she strode into the sitting room in the east wing of Hollingsworth House.

I did a last mirror check on my appearance. "Because of you," I reminded her.

I'd spoken to Bella this morning, nervous because I wasn't sure I had the appropriate formal wear for her gala.

She'd been insistent that I come to Hollingsworth House right after breakfast.

Who knew that we could search through pictures on the internet, and have a ball gown delivered a few hours later?

"I'll take no credit for how you look tonight, dear. All I did was provide a means to get a dress. The makeup artist and hair stylist were already here for me."

Yes, but...she'd lent me those resources without a qualm. I'd never done such an elaborate makeup job on my own, or a hairstyle with such elegant knots.

Not to mention the beautiful, floor-length red dress Bella had talked me into.

I'd seen the dress as a little fussy when I'd first seen the pictures, but I didn't regret choosing it now. The tight, sheer sleeves that ended at a loop over my thumb had dainty, delicate embroidery that I hadn't noticed in the pictures. Although the bodice hugged my body, the skirt flared at the waist, falling gracefully to the top of my high-heeled shoes.

I felt like a princess. Okay, maybe more like Cinderella when she was cleaned up for the ball. Regardless, I *did* feel beautiful.

There was also the small—or maybe not so small—matter of learning how to waltz. Bella had opened up her ballroom for this event, and she'd employed a small orchestra to play.

Leo had come to my rescue before I'd gone upstairs to start getting ready. He'd shown me the steps, danced with me until I was confident I wouldn't make a fool of myself.

I looked at Bella with gratitude. "You look very elegant yourself, Your Grace," I told her.

She made a face as she replied, "It doesn't matter what I look like. I'm an old woman who already found the love of her life and lost him. I'm perfectly content to sit on the sidelines, my dear, and watch the younger generation mingle."

I snorted. "You'll never be sidelined, Bella, and you know it."

She gave me a small smile. "You may be right. I'm probably a little too ornery for that."

The older woman looked like...a duchess. The ice-blue gown she was wearing complemented her coloring, and the sapphire and diamond jewelry she had around her neck, on her wrist, and adorning her ears were the perfect accessories.

Well, if you could *really* call a fortune in gemstones an "accessory."

I reached out and touched her bracelet gingerly. "These are gorgeous."

"They were a twenty-fifth anniversary gift from Damian's father. I was born in September, so sapphires are my birthstone. They were given to me with so much love that it's been too difficult to wear them until tonight," she said wistfully.

"You loved him very much, didn't you?"

She nodded. "More than I ever could have imagined loving anyone. I've never regretted a single moment of leaving my own country as a young woman, and adopting England as my second home."

"Was it strange?" I asked her. "Coming from Spain to England?"

"It was a whole new world for me, but it wasn't the country—it was the stark difference in social classes that made it so hard to adapt. My family are poor farmers. I wanted better, which was why I was living in the city to get an education. I wanted more, but I certainly didn't aspire to be a duchess, or to suddenly be so rich that I could buy anything I wanted. Most women would give anything for that kind of life, but I was...uncomfortable."

I nodded. "I can see why." Hell, it was disconcerting for me just to be dressed like a princess going to her first ball. I couldn't imagine how Bella had felt trying to make all this her everyday life.

There was a sparkle in her dark eyes as she answered, "I got used to it, but what made it an amazing life was the man I shared it with, and the family we made together. All the money would have meant nothing if I wasn't already happy with the man I'd chosen. Damian's father was worth all the work I had to do to try to fit into his social status."

"But why isn't that class system gone? We're into the twenty-first century. Does it really matter?" I questioned. "Even the royal family is pretty much there for show. It's not like they have any real power in the government."

She wagged a finger at me as she said, "Don't you believe that, missy," she warned. "People can say the society ranking system is dead, but it really isn't. Old money and distinguished titles are still valued, and nouveau riche are looked on as social climbers. It's gotten better over the years, but England is steeped in centuries of tradition, and the English people love their heritage, especially the old money and titles. Nobody has dared to tell them that if they cut themselves, they aren't going to bleed blue."

"Damian isn't like that," I mused. "And neither is Leo." I certainly wasn't about to argue with her. I'd met enough of the elite crowd to know that she was correct.

Bella smiled. "My husband and I didn't want our sons raised that way. We kept them far away from the cameras and ridiculous gossip among the uppers. I can't take credit for who they've become now, though. They chose their own value system as adults, but I can't say that I'm sorry they've basically shunned the snobby, elite crowds. They work, just like their father did, because they realize that they'd be incredibly bored if they didn't. Damian has taken all of his responsibilities a little too much to heart, but I'd rather see him go that direction than to be an unfeeling society twit."

"He works too hard, and takes full responsibility for everyone's welfare," I said with a sigh. "But at least his headaches seem to have stopped, at least for now."

Bella looked at me sharply. "You know about his headaches."

"Of course. How could I not notice? I can see the signs of stress on his face when he gets them, and he gets as white as a sheet. He hasn't had one since the day we were flying across the pond. He's been working from home, so he seems more relaxed, and I've forced him to eat and sleep when I'm around. He'll probably be happy to see me leave." I forced my lips into a smile I didn't quite feel.

"He'd be far better off if you stayed," Bella said adamantly. "But I don't suppose he's gotten around to talking to you about that yet."

"I can't stay, Bella," I said wistfully. "I'm American. My entire life is back in California. My business is there, too. Besides, Damian hasn't asked me to stay longer. All we need to do now is sign our contract for Lancaster International and I'm done."

"Oh, he will ask," Bella said in a sly tone. "I've never seen Damian as crazy about a woman as he is about you. He's not the kind of man who seeks out relationships, Nicole. He swore he'd never marry, but I knew he'd change his tune when he found the right woman. I knew when my eldest son fell, he was going to fall hard, and I was right. He's like his father that way. There was only one woman for my husband, and that woman was me. Like his father, Damian will chase you to the ends of the earth if he has to until you agree to marry him. Mind you, that kind of love is pretty intense, but it's also exhilarating. You'll never accept anything less after a man has loved you that way."

Unfortunately, I was well aware of the euphoria that came with loving Damian Lancaster. I knew what it felt like to have all that intense male attention focused directly on me.

"I'm in love with him, Bella," I confessed before I could think better of doing it. I didn't have a mother anymore, and she was the closest thing I had to a parent figure. "But Damian has never claimed to want anything permanent. He's never said that he loves me. All of this was a game we played to fix his reputation, and a brief interlude of sightseeing. Let's get real. He's a billionaire duke. His life is here in England."

Bella shot me a dubious look. "Strange how all of that can be worked out if the feelings are there," she said in a gentle tone. "Don't give up on him, Nicole. He might be a little slow to say the words, but Damian is crazy about you. He's just so tied up in knots about the way that he feels that his head isn't on straight. He'll ask you to stay. The question is: do you care enough to do it? If you don't say yes, I fear he'll end up moving to America to camp out on your doorstep."

I let go of a startled laugh. "I doubt that very much, Bella. Damian belongs here."

"Maybe you should consider whether or not you could eventually call England your home then," Bella instructed. "Understand, sometimes those private jets come in handy if you want to spend some time in the States with your family."

I shook my head slowly. "I don't really have any family there anymore. My mom died over a year ago. She was pretty much all I had. I have some great friends there, though."

"They're just a plane ride away, and it doesn't hurt to have the Lancaster fortune at your disposal." Bella held up a hand as I started to protest that I didn't want Damian's money. "I already know you're not after his money, Nicole. All I'm saying is that it's a nice perk that comes with loving a billionaire, and the Duke of Hollingsworth."

Since I was certain Damian and I were never going to be married, I placated her by murmuring, "I'm sure it is."

"Well, here I've been prattling on and on when I actually came here to give you this."

I noticed, for the first time, the box she was holding as she offered it to me with an explanation.

"Damian called me. He's tied up with something work-related, so he wasn't sure he'd get here before the gala to give this to you."

The rectangular wooden box was heavier than I expected when I went to take it from her. "What is it?" I asked curiously.

She nodded at the gift. "You'll see. Open it."

I fumbled with the old-fashioned catch on the box before it finally unlatched, and I was able to lift the lid. My hands began to shake as I saw exactly what was hidden inside. "Oh, my God. These are beautiful."

I had no doubt the necklace, bracelet, and matching earrings were also worth an outrageous amount of money.

They had to be vintage, but the sparkling diamonds were timeless. The necklace was made up of a large string of diamond-studded dainty flowers that were shaped like daisies. The bracelet and earrings matched the necklace in design. Together, the set was extremely flashy, all of the diamonds sparkling in a nest of red velvet.

"Damian wanted you to have them," his mother said with a touch of smug I-told-you-so vibes in her tone. "They belonged to my husband's mother, Damian's grandmother."

"Then they really are priceless. I can't take these," I said, my voice more than slightly panicked.

"Nonsense," Bella said as she took the box, set it on a small table, and took out the necklace to fasten it around my neck. "They're perfect with this dress, and every female at the party will be sporting their own collection of jewelry. Don't you like them?"

"O-of course I-I like them. But they look like something from the Crown Jewels. I can't wear them. I'll be terrified all night that I'll lose something. Don't they belong to you?"

"They did," she acknowledged. "They were given to me when I was younger, and I gave them to Damian. The design is way too young for me. I stopped wearing them years ago. My son is lucky I held on to them for him. He's never had any desire to gift them to a woman until you came along."

I stood still, unable to move as she fastened the bracelet around my wrist, and then handed me the earrings to don myself.

She waved for me to put them on, and I had to turn toward the mirror again to put the posts into my ears. They were heavy, but not unbearably so, and when I turned back to Bella, she beamed approvingly at me.

"Gorgeous!" she exclaimed happily. "They do look lovely with that dress. You sparkle now, dear."

Bella was right. I'd caught a glance of myself in the mirror. But... "Bella, I can't do this. I can't wear these. I'm not one of those women who can flash jewels like they're nothing but a status symbol, and without thinking about the fact that what I'm wearing in jewelry could probably purchase a nice house in Newport Beach."

She snorted. "Not even close. I have a dear friend who has a vacation home there, and that set of jewelry wouldn't do much more than make a down payment. Don't think about the cost, Nicole. The Lancaster fortune is vast. For my son, the cost is a pittance. Think about the sentiment. Damian wants you to have them."

I fidgeted nervously. "I know he was being considerate and sweet. But we don't have that kind of relationship. He's not supposed to give me lavish gifts. I don't want him to do that."

I was so torn. The last thing I wanted to do was hurt Damian by not wearing something he'd given me. On the other hand, it was just too much.

Bella took my shoulders and turned me toward the mirror. "Look at yourself, Nicole. The set suits you perfectly. Isn't it better for the jewelry to be worn and appreciated than to sit in a box, collecting dust?"

Well, when she put it that way, yes.

I put a careful finger on the glittering diamonds around my neck. "I'm still terrified."

"Feel the fear and then learn to ignore it," Bella advised. "That's what I did. Take Damian's gift in the spirit that he gave it to you."

I let out a long sigh. "I'll wear them, but I'll talk to Damian about keeping them after this gala is over."

He was getting his grandmother's jewelry back, but I didn't want to drag Bella into the argument.

Bella shrugged. "Then my job is done. You look ravishing. My son can take it from here. He can be very persuasive."

I caught her eyes in the mirror. "Bossy, you mean?"

She winked. "Sometimes, the Lancaster male tendency to be a little bit domineering isn't all bad."

My heart tripped as I thought about the way that Damian had taken complete control of my body the night before, after the theater.

I certainly didn't mind surrendering to him in bed when he was in the mood to be bossy.

But is that really what Bella had meant?

As I looked at the gleam in her dark eyes, I was pretty sure *that* was exactly what she'd been getting at, but she just hadn't said it outright.

"Are we all ready to get this party started?" Leo boomed as he strode through the open door. He offered one arm to his mother, and the other to me.

"Ready as I'll ever be," I mumbled as I took his arm.

"Watch out for the women who look like helpless kittens," Leo said, bending his head toward me. "They actually do have claws."

"Meow," I answered with a little purr, letting him know I had a very sharp set of teeth, too.

"That's my girl," he said with a grin.

CHAPTER 31

Damian

"COME DANCE WITH me, gorgeous," I demanded as I laid my hands gently on Nicole's shoulders.

Maybe I had been a little late because I'd run into traffic on my way to Surrey from London, but I was here to claim my woman now.

When I'd entered the residence moments ago, I'd made a beeline for the ballroom, only to find a major crush of people filling the large room almost to capacity.

Nicole's back was to me, and there was an abundance of pretty blonde women present, but I'd identified *her* immediately. I'd know my woman in a crowd at any time, under any circumstances. It seemed that I just gravitated toward her naturally.

Maybe it was her height that ultimately gave her away, but I hadn't been paying much attention to that. It was the more subtle nuances that seemed to beckon me.

The way her shoulders shifted a little as she used her hands to talk.

The tilt of her head when she was listening.

The fact that she always stood still with one heel perched slightly off the floor.

The graceful arch of her neck and back.

I couldn't miss the fact that the young Baron Whitewood looked completely enthralled with Nicole, and perhaps needed some help getting his tongue back into his mouth.

The two men flanking him looked equally enamored.

So I'd pushed through the crowd to stake my claim.

Those three bastards could just look elsewhere.

Nicole Ashworth was already mine.

I had to literally catch my breath as she turned, smiling broadly as she saw me. "Damian. I was getting worried," she said, sounding as breathless as I was right now.

"I'm sorry," I said with real remorse. "I got tied up in traffic."

"You're here now," she said softly. "I'm just glad you're okay." She threaded her arm through mine.

"Gentlemen, please excuse us while I have a dance with Nicole." Honestly, I didn't give a damn if I got their approval or not; I was hauling her away from all three of them.

Baron Whitewood slapped a hand to his chest dramatically. "I'm not sure I can endure the disappointment of losing the company of such a spectacular woman. Bring her back to us when your dance is over, Damian."

Yeah, over my dead body will you ever get within shouting distance of Nicole again, Baron.

I was a man, and it was perfectly evident that he'd been trying to charm Nicole out of her knickers. *Bastard.*

"It was very nice to meet all of you," Nicole said to them with a gracious smile.

"Not that nice," I growled into her ear as I escorted her to the dance floor.

The only damn thing I was grateful about at the moment was that Mum had left her with three people who would never mention Dylan's name.

Other than that, I saw no redeeming qualities in any of them, and I sure as fuck hadn't liked the way they'd been looking at Nicole.

Her brows drew together as she looked at me. "They were all very pleasant. I think I prefer the company of the gentlemen here to the ladies. The women aren't blatantly rude, but some of them are very snide. They want to know who my people"—she made an air quote with her free hand—"are, and where they come from. They sounded like nineteenth-century throwbacks of some kind."

I grinned at her assessment as I wrapped an arm around her waist. "They are," I agreed readily. "Not all of them, but a few are wrapped up in a small world that revolves around their own status, and they love putting people they don't consider their equals down to elevate themselves. It's all rather twisted."

I'd grown up in this world, but that didn't mean I liked it.

"Does your mother really have to invite those people?" Nicole asked as she took my hand, and I led her into a waltz.

I was surprised by how well she followed my lead.

"Technically, no, she doesn't. Believe me, she already cut a large list of the cats off the guest list. But a few are daughters and sons of some of her own friends, so she doesn't really want to offend the older generation she actually likes."

Nicole nodded slightly. "I could see why that would be a problem, and those women don't matter. I think a few of them might be jealous because they think I stole a very eligible bachelor from their grasps."

"I wasn't interested in a single one of them," I denied.

"Maybe not, but they might have been hopeful. You are the most handsome man at this gala," she answered earnestly.

"That man would be Leo," I corrected her, but my damn heart was still singing some happy little tune because she *thought* it was me.

She stumbled a little. "Oops. Sorry." She got back into step easily. "Leo just taught me how to waltz earlier today, so I mess up sometimes. And just for the record, I don't think your brother is the most attractive guy here. Maybe he was *before* you got here. But, now…nope. Sorry. Not even a close competition."

Jesus! She was learning exactly how to render me mute before I even had the chance to get jealous. "I hope Leo was a gentleman," I muttered.

"He was," she answered merrily. "He was even polite every time I stomped on his foot. I'm actually surprised he can still walk."

"I can't even begin to describe how beautiful you look tonight," I told her honestly.

I wished I could find the words to tell her that she outshone every woman present, that she was like a bright light that I couldn't help but chase.

I had no idea what kind of spell I was under with Nicole, but I'd stopped giving a damn about finding the answer to that question.

She made me feel like I was completely alive after spending most of my adult life in a bubble, trying to live up to the role I had as the eldest adult Lancaster male.

I couldn't go back to the man I was before; I didn't want to go back.

I just wanted…*her.*

"We have to talk after the gala," I told her solemnly, feeling guilty as hell because I *wasn't* entirely the man she thought I was. I couldn't lie to her anymore, or evade the truth. I couldn't keep her by my side when she didn't know about Dylan. I'd gotten damn lucky that nobody had slipped up, or mentioned his name yet, but it was bound to happen at some point, and I wanted the truth to come from me.

Dylan was a huge part of my life that I'd managed to keep hidden until now, and honestly, I wasn't even afraid of telling her anymore. I just wanted Nicole to know me. All of me.

Her face softened. "Is everything okay?"

I swallowed the huge lump in my throat, the one that was threatening to choke me to death. "Yeah. I just need to tell you something that I should have told you about a long time ago."

I'd made my choice.

And I hated myself because it had taken me so long to do it.

If it was going to come down to protecting Dylan or this woman who I loved more than anyone else in the world, Nicole was going to win, hands down.

My twin was making his own problems at this point. I'd help him with whatever he needed in the future, and I'd support him when and if he decided he wanted his life back. But I wasn't willing to risk my relationship with Nicole by taking the rap for any of the idiotic things he did in the future.

"That sounds a little ominous," Nicole observed.

The waltz ended, and I took her hand to lead her off the dance floor. "It's not," I assured her. "There's actually a lot of things we need to discuss. Like you deciding that you want to stay here in England with me instead of going back to the States."

Fuck! Now why in the hell had I brought that up right now?

I found a quiet corner and pulled her into it. I needed to explain, and I didn't want to scare the shit out of her. I took her hand. "I want you to stay, Nicole. We can sign the agreement with Lancaster, and you could work on developing more business here in the UK." I didn't say it out loud because I already knew she'd protest, but let's face it, there was no end to the business I could send her way. I had a hell of a lot of connections both in the UK and Europe.

Her eyes went wide as she leaned her back against the wall. "You actually want me to stay?"

I nodded. "I do."

"But my whole life is back in the United States. I know you aren't asking me to stay forever, but I can't be away from ACM for much longer."

Oh, hell yes, I *was* asking her to stay forever. That was exactly what I wanted, but I wasn't quite sure I should blurt that out right now. She already looked confused as hell. Did I really want to give her a chance to turn forever down flat? "Then stay another month or two," I suggested. "I don't want you to go right now."

Or ever! Definitely not ever.

I continued, "Kylie is doing a great job operating your domestic business. Stay and work on expanding here."

I'd settle for temporary if it would eventually get me to forever. I needed more time, and a clean slate to work with after I told her about Dylan.

If she could get over the fact that I hadn't told her the entire truth about the orgy and naked picture, I'd do everything in my power to make damn sure she fell in love with me.

My gut ached as I watched the expression on her face. There was a lot of uncertainty in those beautiful blue eyes, and I wasn't sure what to make of it.

"I don't think I can actually open an office in London. It's too expensive."

I had a plethora of commercial property in the city I'd gladly hand over, but I answered carefully, "You can figure that out later. You can do a temporary office upstairs at the house, and stay with me."

Her eyes grew wide. "You want me to actually stay at your gigantic palace? Convert one of your upstairs bedrooms into an office?"

"Of course. I just said I wanted you to stay."

I didn't give a damn what she did to my house. She could blow up the whole damn thing as long as she left us a room with a bed.

"Damian…I-I don't—"

I put a finger to her mouth to keep her from answering. "Don't answer right now. Think about it, Nicole. We'll talk after this ridiculous gala is over."

In the meantime, I needed to find a way to stop her from saying *no* like she nearly did just a second ago.

She nodded slowly. "Okay. I'll think about it. Right now, I really need to pee."

I glanced toward the powder room my mother had set up for the guests. "There's a line for the loo down here. Do you want me to take you upstairs?"

She smiled. "I know where it is. I think you should find your mother and let her know you're here."

"I should," I agreed. "I'll see you back down here in a few minutes."

"Damian?"

My head came up sharply, and my eyes locked with hers.

She continued, "I don't want you to think that I don't want to stay…" She paused. "Never mind. We'll discuss it later."

I wanted to call her beautiful ass back as I watched her depart from the ballroom. Her unfinished comment made me edgy, concerned that her words might have been a prelude to a really large *no* decision.

I shook my head as I looked around for my mum.

Letting Nicole say no to staying here wasn't an option.

Well, unless she had no objection to me going back to the US with her.

The whole geography thing didn't really matter as long as Nicole ended up somewhere with…*me.*

CHAPTER 32

Nicole

AFTER I USED the bathroom in the east wing, I rifled through the fridge in the sitting room and found myself a cold bottle of water.

I was a little sweaty, so I'd taken the time to cool off and fix my makeup.

Honestly, I'd just needed a few moments outside the crowd to digest everything Damian had said to me.

He wants me to stay. He doesn't want me to go. And what in the hell did he need to tell me that he hasn't already said?

I took a few gulps of the water, and a couple of deep breaths.

My heart had been doing a happy dance when Damian had asked me to stick around, but my head was telling me I needed to hightail it back to California before Damian Lancaster had a chance to break my heart.

"Who am I kidding?" I said aloud to the empty room. "It's *already* going to break my heart to leave him."

And it certainly wasn't going to get any easier if I stayed for a month or two longer, because I'd *know* the end was coming. I'd probably be doing a countdown to my broken heart every single day.

What am I expecting? A declaration of his undying love and a confession that he can't live without me?

I let out a long sigh, hating myself for allowing Damian to get close enough to break my heart.

I should have known that I wasn't the kind of woman who could do a wild fling. Not with somebody like him, anyway.

Bottom line: I loved Damian so much that it was going to shatter my heart into thousands of little pieces to say goodbye to him, whether that happened tomorrow, or in a month or two.

I downed the rest of the water and dropped the bottle into the trash, wondering if Damian wanted me to stay out of a misguided sense of gratitude.

Does he just want to help my company expand because I'd helped him out of a tight spot?

That was possible, although I had to admit that I didn't think that was the entire reason for his offer to hang around.

There was some mind-blowing passion and sex involved in our relationship, and I had no doubt that Damian cared for me.

Unfortunately, that just wasn't enough.

I needed to get back downstairs. Nothing was going to be resolved before Damian and I had a chance to discuss it later.

I was heading toward the door when I heard a muffled noise coming from the master suite Damian had used when he'd stayed here.

It had almost sounded like...a feminine laugh.

I shook my head, and was determined to ignore it when I heard a deep, male voice, too.

What the hell?

I stepped nearer to the closed door, wondering if the old estate had a resident ghost or two, and I listened.

There was a giggle.

And then a moan.

Followed by that deep voice.

I couldn't make out words, just muffled sounds.

I should go. It's none of my business if somebody found their way upstairs, right?

The problem was that nobody should be *up here*. The stairs were blocked off, and only the family was allowed upstairs.

Well, and me. I was allowed past the chain, but only because Barnaby knew me, and I'd already been a guest here.

I slid a little closer, close enough to put my foot on the bottom of the door and apply a little bit of pressure to it.

I had to know if someone had snuck up here to steal something. There were priceless furnishings everywhere.

If I could do something to protect Bella's home, I would.

The door wasn't completely latched, so it opened a crack.

In for a penny, in for a pound.

I grasped the doorknob and pushed the door open wide, ready to run if I saw anything I couldn't handle.

There was only a male and a female in the room, and the two of them didn't appear to be stealing anything.

If they were, they were doing it half naked on the bed.

The pretty brunette female was half out of her pink ballgown, while the male was bare from the waist up. His lower body was covered by a sheet, so I didn't know if he was completely nude.

And I really didn't *want* to know.

I'd obviously interrupted something very intimate, and my cheeks flushed as I grabbed for the doorknob to close the door again.

I could tell Damian, and let him decide if he wanted to investigate.

I was way too mortified about interrupting a private moment to deal with *this* situation.

The door creaked as I started to close it, and I cringed when the guy on the bed suddenly swung around to face me.

Busted!

"Well, hello, beautiful. Please come in. Three is never too many in my bed," he said in a welcoming tone.

Oh, dear God!

I put my embarrassment aside long enough to realize that I knew that face.

I knew that gorgeous body.

There was no mistaking those distinctive, peridot-green eyes.

And I *definitely* recognized that deep voice with a British accent, even though the tone was somewhat different.

"Damian?" I'm not sure why I asked, because I already knew exactly who was lying in that bed with a hand up the skirt of the woman's pink dress.

My entire world upended, and then started to spin.

"Why?" I cried out like a wounded animal, keening the single word as tears flooded my eyes.

Damian stared back at me with an empty-eyed gaze I'd never seen before.

No embarrassment.

No remorse.

No affection.

There was absolutely *no emotion* radiating from those beautiful eyes at the moment, and it completely crushed me.

Deciding that I didn't really need to know *why*, I fled.

I slammed the door closed, went and retrieved my purse and clothes off the couch, and then sprinted out of the east wing, visions of Damian's smug, detached expression still haunting my brain.

"No! Wait a minute!"

I heard Damian's call from the bedroom as I made my escape. I ignored it. Did he *really* think he was going to talk me into a threesome?

Bastard!

"It's not like he ever promised me exclusivity or anything," I whispered harshly as I rushed down the hall and toward the stairs. "He never promised me anything. Nothing."

My brain was trying to convince my heart not to break. Unfortunately, it wasn't working.

My vision was blurred from the tears coursing down my face, and I decided to try harder.

It was my problem, not his. He was free to fuck any woman he wanted. There was no commitment between the two of us. There never had been. I'd always known it was a fling, right?

Maybe so, but…I just didn't see him as the type of guy to do that in his mother's house, or during one of her events.

Or while another woman he was currently fucking was in the same damn place!

He'd looked just like he had in that damn orgy picture, his eyes wild with what I could assume was lust.

"My mother used to say that a leopard never changes its spots. I guess she was right." I panted as I ran down the stairs.

What in the hell is wrong with me? Had I really bought that story about the whole orgy thing being a setup?

Yes. Yes, I had, and I wasn't a stupid woman. I'd believed Damian Lancaster because I'd *wanted* to believe him, not because it really made sense.

Dammit! I cursed when I couldn't get the chain undone at the bottom of the stairs. So I simply ducked under the barrier, and raced through the crowd to get out the door.

All I wanted was escape.

From this house.

From the memories of Damian and me together.

From every snobby rich person present who would never understand the kind of pain I was suffering right now.

"Nicole. Wait! Where are you going?"

For an instant, I thought it was Damian calling my name, but it was Leo, and he caught up to me the moment I got outside.

"Nicole!" He grabbed me by the shoulders to stop me. "What in the hell is wrong? You were running like the house was on fire."

I could hardly lie to him. I was probably a mess. My tears were falling hard and fast, so I knew my makeup was beyond repair, and probably smeared everywhere.

"I have to get to Heathrow, Leo. Something happened. It's an emergency. I'll explain later. Can you help me?" My voice sounded pathetic, even to my own ears.

My only thought was to put as much distance between myself and Damian Lancaster as possible right now. I had my passport and ID in my purse, and the clothes I'd worn to Bella's home this morning.

Damian could send me the rest of my things. It was the least he could do. I never wanted to step inside his ridiculous castle again.

Leo nodded solemnly. "Of course. I'm sorry, Nicole, whatever it is that happened. You look terrible. Do you want me to find Damian? He'd want to be here with you."

I shook my head vigorously. "No! He already knows. I just need to get to the airport."

Leo motioned to Damian's driver, and the Phantom moved forward.

"Isn't Damian going with you?" Leo asked as I rushed to the limo.

"Not this time," I babbled. "He has work, and this is...personal for me."

Well, that wasn't *exactly* a lie, but my explanation was probably about as clear as mud.

Luckily, Leo didn't question me further. "Take care of yourself, Nicole. Damian can tell me the rest."

I threw myself into his arms because I couldn't let myself leave without saying goodbye to Leo. He'd been good to me, and I'd started to become silly enough to consider him the brother I'd never had. I'd call Bella later and thank her for everything she'd done for me. I wasn't strong enough to talk to her right now without throwing myself in her maternal arms and sobbing like a five-year-old child.

"Oh, wait!" I said to Leo when I pulled myself away from him.

I pulled my earrings off, then the bracelet, and finally the necklace. "Please give these back to Damian. They were just a loan for tonight." I pressed the diamonds into his hand before I jumped into the back seat of the Phantom.

"Be safe, Nicole," Leo called out, and then he closed the car door.

"Where to, Ms. Ashworth?" the driver asked politely.

"Heathrow Airport please," I said loudly as I started to search my purse for my phone.

I had no idea how I was going to get out of England tonight, but I'd search for flights and standby possibilities on my way to London.

Tears blurred my vision, and I quickly reached for the button to close the partition between me and the driver as we got in motion.

And then, finally, I let go of the sobs that had been screaming for release since the moment I'd found the man I loved in bed with another woman.

Maybe I didn't have the right to be brokenhearted since Damian had never promised me anything more than what we'd had.

But I was.

I was devastated, and I sobbed halfway to London, whether I had the right to my pain or not.

CHAPTER 33

Damian

"I'D LIKE TO go find Nicole." Mum had tried to drag me to *another* group of people I hadn't seen for years, but I didn't follow her this time.

Nicole had probably arrived back downstairs a long time ago, and I was tired of greeting people without her.

I was relieved when I saw Leo coming toward us. Maybe he could take over for me while I went in search of Nicole.

"I've been looking for you," Leo told me. "I wanted to see if everything was all right with Nicole. I hate to say it, but she didn't look good when she left."

"Left?" I questioned. "Where in the hell did she go?"

Leo shot me a confused gaze. "I thought *you* knew. She said you did. She took off for Heathrow almost an hour ago. I put her in the Phantom myself. She was crying, Damian, and she looked pretty frantic. She said she had an emergency. Something bad happened, but she said that you already knew about it. For some reason, she took off the jewelry she was wearing and asked me to give it to you. I had Barnaby lock it up."

Fuck! "I don't know a damn thing. She went upstairs to use the loo, and I haven't seen her since she came back downstairs. I assumed she was mingling until we caught up with each other. Why in the fuck was she crying?"

Every single one of my senses was starting to alarm as I strode toward the stairs, went under the chain, and took the steps two at a time.

I told myself not to panic as I entered the east wing, but my voice of reason wasn't responding.

"Maybe she left a note then," Leo said reasonably as he and Mum followed behind me. "Do you think she found out about Dylan?"

"Fuck! I hope not!"

"I doubt it," Bella commented. "She'd be upset, but not that upset."

The three of us made short work of searching the sitting room and the master suite she'd used when she'd been staying here in Hollingsworth House.

There was no sign of her anywhere.

Mum didn't try to hide her concern. "She took her purse and the clothes she was wearing this morning."

"Fuck!" I raked a frustrated hand through my hair. "Why in the bloody hell did she leave without saying anything? That's not like her. She's not the flighty or dramatic type, and she wouldn't go without saying something."

"Maybe she had a family emergency, Damian," Leo suggested.

I shook my head. "She's an only child, and her parents are gone. She doesn't have any close family anymore. Friends, yes. But not family."

"She said it was personal," Leo said thoughtfully. "So maybe something happened with one of her friends."

"That doesn't make sense," I said in a raspy voice. "She would have talked to me first. No one can get her to America faster than I can in a private jet."

"She wouldn't tell you if she thought you were a total wanker," a deep voice said from behind us.

I whirled around, and saw Dylan leaning nonchalantly against the doorjamb of the second master suite in the east wing. The room I'd used when I'd stayed here with Nicole.

"What in the fuck are you doing here?" I growled as I strode up to Dylan. "I thought you were in California."

"Such a warm welcome from my twin brother," Dylan said dryly. "It's good to see you, too, Damian."

"Now probably isn't the time to fuck with him, Dylan," Leo warned. "We're looking for some sign of Nicole. Have you seen her?"

"Tall, beautiful blonde in a red dress, wearing Gran's jewelry?" Dylan questioned.

"Yes," I ground out. I needed to be civil with Dylan until he told me everything he knew.

He continued. "She barged into a…brief liaison I was having with an old girlfriend. I invited Nicole to join us, but I'm guessing she isn't the type to play." Dylan's nonchalant tone was more than I could take.

I snapped, and fisted the T-shirt he was wearing. "She thought you were *me*, didn't she? Nicole thought I was shagging another woman when she was right here in this house."

The fact that Nicole had actually believed my twin was me was almost inconceivable, but what else was she supposed to think? She didn't even have an inkling that I had an identical twin.

Dylan raised his brows. "Technically, we weren't shagging. Just a little foreplay." He hesitated before he added, "Apparently, this woman means something to you."

"Yes, she means something to me, you bastard," I snarled. "I fucking love her, and just the thought of her fleeing this house in tears, upset and alone, makes me completely insane."

Dylan grabbed my hands, and I let him go because I wanted to do it. Maybe I *did* want to kill him, but I was more interested in getting to Nicole. I could deal with him later.

"She thought I was you," Dylan confessed. "She said your name when she saw me. It was like she had no idea that you had an identical twin."

"She doesn't," I rasped. "She has no idea. If I'd just fucking told her, she wouldn't have run off that way. She would have known that it wasn't me. But I didn't tell her because of the goddamn promise I made to you."

I had absolutely no doubt in my mind that if Nicole had known I had a twin, she would have instantly recognized the fact that it wasn't *me* in that bed.

I hated myself for never telling her, for allowing her to think for one single bloody second that I'd be fucking another woman when all I'd ever wanted was her.

"Dylan, I want you to leave," my mum said sternly. "Get your things, and get out of here before Damian tears you apart while we all cheer him on for doing it."

Dylan scowled. "You invited me here."

Mum shot him a disgusted look. "Not so you could cavort around with women. Or ruin the best thing that has ever happened to your brother."

"You invited him here?" I glared at my mum.

"Yes, but he arrived earlier than I expected. I was hoping he was ready to come home. Obviously, he's not. I'm sorry, Damian. I asked Dylan to stay out of sight."

"I did," Dylan snapped. "She walked into a private room."

I ignored Dylan, and looked from my mum to Leo. "I have to find Nicole. She could be getting close to Heathrow by now. I'm not letting her leave England until she knows the whole truth, and exactly how I feel about her. Once she knows, she can make her own *informed* choice about whether she wants my sorry ass or not."

"Let me call her," Bella offered.

"I'm going to try to get in touch with her on the way to the airport," I barked back at her as I headed toward the door.

"I'll try to find out if she's there, and if she has a flight out tonight," Leo called after me. "You'll have to drive. I sent Nicole in the Phantom."

I dug into my pocket for my mobile as I made my way downstairs.

I cursed and shoved my phone back in my pocket when she didn't pick up.

Of course it went to voicemail. I was probably the last person she wanted to talk to right now.

She hated me, and worse yet, she was under the impression that I'd betrayed her by grabbing the first available woman at this gala, and taking her to bed.

Nicole should know better, but could I really blame her?

This was my fault because I'd had my head up my ass when it came to my twin brother.

I reached for my keys as I exited Hollingsworth House, grateful that I'd driven myself here in my Ferrari.

I was going to need a fast Italian sports car to get my ass to Heathrow if I was going to catch the woman I loved before she ran away back to America with my goddamn heart.

"Damian!" I heard Dylan yell my name, but I didn't stop.

He caught up with me just as I got to my car.

"I'm sorry," he said, panting from the effort he'd made to chase me.

"Not good enough." *Jesus Christ!* Did Dylan really think I wanted to talk to him right now? "You hurt the woman I love, and if you ever do it again, twin or not, I'll lay your sorry ass up in the hospital. And just for the record, I've kept my promise, but two years of doing it is more than enough."

"You really *do* love her," Dylan said, sounding astonished.

I turned to face him. "More than anyone else in this world, and that includes *you*, brother. I'm done covering for you. I'm done giving a damn whether you decide to join our family again. You crossed the line with me tonight, Dylan, so don't expect me to ever welcome you back with open arms unless you stop being a prick and start being a brother to me again. Even then, I may not forgive you if I lose Nicole. I won't give a damn about anything."

Every word I said to Dylan was true. I'd loved the man he used to be, but I despised what he'd become, and if Nicole *did* decide to forgive me, I'd never put this wanker's needs before hers. *Ever.*

"What can I do to help?" Dylan asked sullenly.

"Stay the fuck out of my way." I didn't give two shits about Dylan's problems right now.

I pushed by him, got into my car, and never looked back to see the dismal look on Dylan's face as I focused all of my attention on getting to Heathrow before Nicole could board a plane that would fly her right out of my life forever.

CHAPTER 34

Nicole

I'D FOUND A seat in economy for a Transatlantic Airlines flight that was leaving early the next morning.

And bonus! I was booked in an aisle seat, so I wouldn't have to crawl over my fellow passengers every time I needed to pee.

I tried to make myself comfortable in the chair I'd found not far from my departure gate. There weren't any flights scheduled out of this particular gate right now, so it was quiet, and devoid of other travelers.

The perfect place to spend the night wallowing in self-pity and misery.

I'd spent over an hour talking to Kylie on the phone after I'd booked my flight. I was pretty much cried out, and all that was left was my desolation and my desire to get back to California so I could step back into a normal life again.

However, I knew nothing would ever be quite the same for me again.

Damian Lancaster had changed the way I saw myself so profoundly that I knew I'd probably never look at myself in a mirror the same way again.

Okay, maybe *that* was a good thing, so after I put my heart back together again, maybe I could find one positive in my fling with Damian Lancaster.

I took a gulp of the enormous coffee I'd purchased. There was no sleeping for me tonight. Unfortunately, I was going to have way too much time to think since I didn't have my laptop or anything else to occupy my brain.

Maybe I could find something to do on my phone, but it was currently next to me, charging.

As I glanced at the table where my phone rested, a discarded newspaper caught my eye. I picked it up, hoping the royals had created some kind of scandal to distract me.

My breath hitched as I stared at the front page of today's paper, and saw the headline.

IS IT LOVE AT HER MAJESTY'S THEATRE?

I ignored the cheesy headline. I didn't really care about the article, either, but my eyes were instantly drawn to the two side-by-side pictures of me and Damian.

A photographer had caught the moment when Damian had picked me up after I'd stubbed my toe. The first image was almost mesmerizing. With a snap of a shutter, someone had captured the concern in Damian's eyes as he'd looked down at me with an expression so full of affection and warmth that it made my heart race.

The second one froze Damian and me while we were in motion, sharing that brief but incredibly tender kiss before he'd placed me in the back of the limo.

The tear ducts that I'd thought were completely empty suddenly pushed a bucket of moisture into my eyes, and my vision clouded.

I'm not imagining things. He really does look at me the way I remembered. I don't understand how he could care about me, and still act the way that he had in the east wing.

Two huge droplets led the march down my cheeks, and the rest followed like another dam had broken.

I slapped the paper back onto the table, making sure the images were facedown.

It doesn't matter how he looks at me when he's fucking any woman he can find after that.

I was angry at myself, and I was brutal when I swiped all the tears from my face like I was trying to scrub away every memory I had of Damian.

Trying desperately to put him out of my mind, I watched people rush down the throughway from my seat outside of the crowds.

I found it interesting that people in airports always seemed to be in such a big hurry, trying to get to where they were going in as little time as possible, only to arrive at security or at their gate and…just wait.

I closed my eyes and tried to wipe *everything* out of my mind. I breathed in slowly, and then out.

Although I'd never been able to meditate like Kylie could, I was willing to try almost anything at the moment to erase the image of Damian naked and in bed with another woman completely out of my head.

I couldn't believe he'd actually had the gall to call me *beautiful* while he had his hand under the skirt of some stunning brunette!

Had I been starting to forget that he had his picture taken with an entire bevy of gorgeous nude women at an orgy?

How did I ever allow myself to forget that, or let myself believe the excuse that it was all a setup?

Why? Why? Why?

It was the answer I'd wanted *immediately* after seeing Damian half naked, seducing a female who wasn't…me.

I guess I *still* wanted that answer.

I mean, seriously, the man *had* to be some kind of nymphomaniac or sex addict. Damian and I had barely let a couple of hours go by without having some kind of sexual encounter. To be honest, we'd been fucking like bunnies the entire week because we couldn't seem to get enough of each other's bodies.

"Dammit!" I said out loud. This whole meditation thing didn't seem to be working. At all!

"I hate to intrude on whatever it is that you're doing," a smooth baritone said from the chair next to me. "But I really do need to talk to you, love."

My eyes popped open. I turned my head and groaned. Not that I didn't *know* exactly whose voice I'd just heard, but the verification was painful.

"Well, I don't want to talk to you." I hated the fact that I sounded like a spiteful child. "I have a flight to catch. I'd appreciate it if you'd just…go away."

Damian was still dressed in his tuxedo, just like I was still wearing my formal gown. I planned on changing into the jeans and top I'd worn to Bella's this morning before I boarded my flight.

"I can't let you go until you hear everything, Nicole, and then I'll let you make your own decision. I won't promise that I won't try to change your mind if it isn't the resolution I want, but if you really want to board that flight, I'll let you."

"You'll *let* me? Excuse me if I was under the impression that England was still a free country." My voice was oozing sarcasm, but anger was the only thing that was going to stop me from breaking down in tears, so I'd use that outrage.

He shrugged. "I do own the airline you're flying, so I could very easily keep you from boarding that flight."

Had he really just said that? Had he actually threatened me to get me to listen to him? Bastard!

I glared at him. "Oh, my God. You're such a…wanker."

His lips turned up in a sad smile. "Well done, beautiful."

Ugh! "Don't ever call me *that* again. Not after you used that ridiculous pet name to invite me into a threesome."

"Did I?" His expression looked troubled.

"Yes!" I snapped. "You've forgotten already?"

He shook his head. "Then I'll never use it again, love. I promise."

I let out an exasperated breath, not sure if the current pet name was better than the old one. He didn't *love me,* so it was as artificial as his apparent concern. "I'll give you five minutes, but only because I want to get on that plane, and then I'm done. If having your say will make you leave, then by all means, go on. But I'll probably go find security when your five minutes are up."

"And do what, gorgeous? I'm the owner of one of this airport's busiest airlines."

There was nothing I wanted more than to slap that smug look off his face right now. He was damn lucky that I didn't have enough serious anger issues to make me resort to physical violence, but that didn't mean I wasn't tempted.

The thing that really pissed me off was that…he was right. It *would* be my word against the word of the CEO and owner of Transatlantic Airlines. Security was more likely to boot *me* out of Heathrow than *Damian.*

And God, just the fact that he carried *that much* weight and power had steam coming out of my ears.

"That doesn't make it okay for you to harass me." My tone held more fury and bitterness than I'd heard come out of my mouth in my entire life.

Dammit!

"I didn't say it did," he acknowledged.

I crossed my arms over my chest. "The clock is running. Four minutes."

"Don't rush me. I want to say this right. I have a feeling I'm only going to get one chance," Damian said in a husky, unusually hesitant tone. "I feel like my entire life depends on whether or not you believe me right now, Nicole."

"Why don't you just try being honest?" I suggested wryly. There was something about his desperate expression that *almost* got to me, but I tamped that shit down in a hurry.

"Honesty it is then," he said grimly. "I should have been *completely* honest with you from the moment we met. I don't know much about that encounter in the east wing because the man you saw in that bed wasn't me, Nicole. It was my identical twin brother, Dylan."

As I tried to let his ludicrous explanation sink in, Damian reached for his wallet, took a few things out, and handed them to me. "These are a few photos that Barnaby took at Mum's birthday party three years ago. I have more, but not with me. I'll provide anything you want as proof. Our birth certificates, more pictures, even family videos of the two of us together."

My hands began to shake as I looked at the small photos. As incredulous as his scenario seemed, I *was* looking at pictures of Bella, Damian, Leo, and the guy who must be Dylan right *next* to Damian.

Damian wore his hair cropped a little shorter than Dylan, but otherwise the two of them were like mirror images of each other.

"This can't be possible," I whispered as I traced the outline of Damian in the picture.

"You know which one is me?" he asked curiously.

"Yes, now that I know that someone exists who looks just like you." I pointed at Damian in the photo.

I couldn't put a finger on *why* I knew, but I was pretty sure it was the eyes that gave Damian away. He looked so serious next to his twin, who had a different, devil-may-care expression on his face.

Damian was smiling in the picture, but his eyes were thoughtful, like he had the responsibility of solving every world problem in existence.

Dylan looked just the opposite, like he didn't have a single worry in the entire universe.

"My mother and Leo are the only ones who can usually tell us apart." Damian pried the photos out of my hands and put them away. "I'm older than Dylan by a matter of minutes. We've always been very different, but he was my best mate, anyway. Until about two years ago. Something happened to Dylan. He lost someone he loved. My brother suddenly dropped out of his life, became reckless and started doing some crazy things that he would have never even contemplated doing before. He's out of his mind on alcohol the majority of the time. In the beginning, I gave him space, let him act out without suffering the consequences. He wanted me to help him disappear completely from the public eye, and I did everything I could to make that happen."

My mind was reeling, trying to take in everything Damian was telling me.

Why would he lie about something like this? But I knew Damian *wasn't* lying this time. All of the information was too easily verified *not* to be the truth.

And yet, my brain was having a difficult time accepting it.

"So are you trying to say that the orgy picture was Dylan and not you?" I scrutinized his expression, trying to read his eyes.

He nodded. "Yes. I gave Dylan my promise that I'd keep him out of the public eye. I thought he might be getting better when I saw him at our residence in Beverly Hills, so I didn't want to out him. This Dylan isn't the brother I knew, Nicole. Dylan used to be a man I respected; a man worthy of everyone's trust. I wanted my twin brother back, the man he was *before* he went off the deep end."

I lifted a brow. "So you took the blame, and didn't feel like you could trust me with the truth?"

"Yes… No… Fuck! I don't know what I was thinking, Nicole. You and I barely knew each other. And I'd given Dylan my word that I'd do everything possible to make him disappear while he was trying to get his head on straight."

I kind of got what he was saying. Damian had no reason to trust me back then. One slip to the media, and reporters would have been all over Dylan like rabid hounds.

"Why didn't you tell me once we got here? Or after we'd already performed every possible sex act together?" I asked, unable to keep the hurt out of my voice.

I knew Damian, and I understood why he'd never wanted to break his promise. For a guy like him, his word was even more serious than a written contract, especially when he gave it to someone he obviously loved.

"I think my motivations were entirely selfish by that time," Damian said morosely. "I was afraid you'd walk away. No matter how many excuses I came up with, that's the truth."

The icy wall I'd erected around my heart over the last few hours cracked just a little. I knew Damian had to be telling me the truth about Dylan. It was really the *only thing* that made sense, even if the story did sound completely crazy.

I'd been confused when I'd seen Dylan in bed with that woman because I'd thought I *knew* the real Damian. Him hopping into bed with another female during his mother's gala had been so contrary to the man I'd come to know and love. If I hadn't seen it for myself, I never would have believed it.

None of the bad stuff is Damian's doing. Well, except the lying. That's pretty bad.

I felt like the last piece of the Lancaster puzzle was falling into place. Everything that hadn't seemed like Damian *hadn't* really been Damian. It had been a man who wasn't *Damian* at all.

I took a deep breath and let it out before I asked, "Why have I never seen any sign that you have a twin? Nothing. I did a deep dive on the internet for the last few years, and there's no mention of him at all."

"I paid a pretty savvy company a ton of money to make Dylan disappear from the internet two years ago." Every word coming from Damian's voice was pulsating with regret. "I knew bringing you here was a risk, but I tried to make damn sure that you didn't talk to anybody who would mention Dylan's name at those charity events we attended. I told you at the gala that we needed to talk after it was over. I've known for a while now that I couldn't take the risk of you finding out the truth from anybody but me."

I sat there silent for a moment, trying to take in just how much work it must have taken to pull off this entire ruse. "So the PR agent actually got played," I said in a husky whisper.

"Not intentionally," Damian rushed to assure me. "All this started long before you, Nicole. I made my brother a promise when he was at the weakest point of his life, and I meant to keep it. I've been putting out fires for Dylan for the last two years by either squashing any press information or letting people think it was me and not Dylan who pulled some asinine stunts. If I took the blame, those small articles were eventually deleted. But I knew I couldn't resolve the naked orgy thing that easily. It was front-page news way too fast, and big social media news by the end of the day."

Jesus! It was going to take me a long time to work all of this out in my head.

"I believe you," I said on a sigh. "Honestly, as unbelievable as it sounds, it's the only thing that really makes any sense. I just wish you would have trusted me enough to tell me the truth once we got here to England. I take it that Bella and Leo were in on the deception, too?"

He shifted in his seat uncomfortably. "Yes. I'm sorry. Everyone at Hollingsworth House knew not to mention Dylan's name, too, but they didn't know why. Please don't blame either one of them. Mum adores you, and so does Leo. In their defense, they both hated the fact that you were in the dark about Dylan."

"In the end, they're *your* family, Damian. If nothing else, I've definitely discovered that the Lancaster family is loyal to their own blood." Damian was the perfect example of that. He'd supported Dylan at the cost of his own reputation, and I knew how annoying it was for him to be in the public eye, even for *good* PR. "Why is it that nobody suspected Dylan?"

Damian shrugged his shoulders. "I think everyone assumed he was keeping a really low profile to mourn his loss, and get through it. It was probably a lot easier to believe it was me."

"Even though you've never done anything like that before?"

"Truthfully, neither has Dylan. At least, he hasn't as far as the general public knew. I owe you for everything you've done, Nicole. I'd much rather be a smitten billionaire duke than a man-whore."

I locked eyes with him, and even though he was smiling ruefully over his joke, I could see the inherent hurt in those expressive green eyes. "Dylan's hurt you. A lot."

He nodded, not even trying to hide the truth. "He has, but he crossed the line this time. He hurt *you*, and that's totally unacceptable to me. I'm done covering for him, and trying to protect him. It's been two years. I've given him his space and time to work everything out. He's on his own if he wants to keep acting like a wanker. I have to learn to accept that I've done all I can. The ball is in his court now."

There was an uncomfortable silence for a few seconds before I broke it. "Thank you for coming here to explain everything. It doesn't fix what happened, but it helps me understand it better. I'm glad that I wasn't exactly sleeping with the devil."

Damian stood. "Don't leave like this, Nicole. Not now. And for God's sake, not in the *economy section* of my airline. The seats definitely weren't made for tall people like us. Come home with me. *I'll* fly you back across the pond myself if that's what you really want, but you look exhausted right now. Let's sleep on this. Let me show you all of the pictures and videos I have of my family, and give you a chance to meet with Mum and Leo. My little brother is insisting now that he won't leave until he gets to talk to you, and make sure you're okay."

As I looked up at Damian's tormented expression, I was tempted to accept. I felt physically and emotionally spent, and I wasn't sure I'd gotten all the information I wanted to get complete closure.

Maybe I'd never quite get over Damian, but I needed to try. If I didn't, I'd be completely scarred for life.

I wavered. Maybe I should go with him. I did leave everything at his place, even my laptop.

"Come. With. Me." His voice was little more than a growl as he held out his hand. "Please."

It was that damn "please" word that really tempted me to take Damian's hand. He was a man who probably never had to ask for anything, but he had. For…me.

I let him pull me to my feet. "I'm not sleeping with you, Damian. Our fling is officially over."

He grinned, and my heart rolled over inside my chest. "You *are* technically occupying the second suite at my house. But I must warn you that the shower isn't nearly as good as mine."

I rolled my eyes. "I need you to promise that you won't try to charm me out of my panties."

"Full disclosure in the interest of keeping everything honest with you from this day forward; I won't push terribly hard, but don't expect me not to try to change your mind."

I gathered up my phone and charging cord. I'd picked up the bag containing my clothes from earlier in the day and then…I panicked.

I can't do this! I can't do this! No matter how much I needed more closure, I couldn't spend another moment alone with Damian.

Being with him for even *one more day* would probably completely destroy me.

I loved him too damn much, and my heart was too fragile right now.

"I'm sorry." My voice sounded raw, and the dam that held back my tears of pain opened wide again. "I can't do this. I can't go with you. I'm already broken."

"*Jesus Christ!* Don't cry, Nicole." Damian's tone was tender and rough. "Just come home with me. I'll make all of this right. You're not broken, love."

"I am." My words came out in a strangled sob. "I can't go with you. I need to be on that flight early in the morning."

Damian scrubbed a hand through his hair in apparent frustration. "I can't fucking let you go. Not like this, and probably not ever. I know I said I would, but I was lying. Not to you—to myself."

"Y-you have no choice but to let me get on that plane." I couldn't give in to him.

His eyes were wild when he answered. "You think you're broken? Then bloody hell, I'll fix you. I'll put every single gorgeous piece of you back together again, Nicole. I promise."

My chest was so tight I could hardly breathe. Damian Lancaster had just made *me* a vow, but no matter how hard he tried to keep it, I knew I needed way more than he could possibly give me.

Before I could open my mouth to say another word, Damian cursed, "Fuck! What in the hell am I doing?" I watched him as his expression went from dogged determination to complete desolation and despair before he continued in a resolute tone. "I came here to plead for forgiveness, Nicole. Instead, I'm trying to bully you into submission. Coming with me has to be your choice, not mine. It wouldn't feel right anyway, not unless you really want to be with me. I give you my word I won't interfere, at all. You know the truth now. The ball is completely in your court, love. I'll do whatever you need from me. You can leave on that flight in the morning, come with me for the night, or however long you can stand to be around me, and I'll make sure you get home safe in my jet whenever you want to go." He stood. "Just don't expect me to go too far until you're safely on that plane this morning, and please know I'm willing to take whatever you give me. On your terms this time."

Without another word, Damian Lancaster turned, strode into the crowd and disappeared.

But he hadn't departed before I'd gotten one final look at his face. He'd looked completely ravaged, wrecked, and defeated.

I picked my jaw up off the floor, and closed my mouth.

What in the hell had just happened?

Had Damian really just left after making himself as vulnerable as a person could be?

He'd made it clear exactly *what* he wanted, yet he'd walked away from me without a single one of those things.

So I could decide what was right for me.

For a man as strong-willed as Damian, I knew just how hard it was to give up his power to someone else.

But he had.

For me.

My ass stayed planted in my chair for nearly an hour, my mind trying to absorb Dylan's existence, and more importantly, the hell he'd put Damian through.

In the end, I couldn't put all that much blame on Damian. He'd been caught between his loyalty to a brother he obviously loved deeply, and me. And he *had* planned on telling me, even though he'd still be taking a risk.

I swiped away the tears that had intermittently poured down my face during my emotional turmoil for the last sixty minutes.

Suddenly, I realized that I couldn't just catch that flight in the morning, and forget the last few weeks had never happened. I couldn't leave Damian feeling like he did right now. Yeah, I realized that he couldn't give me everything, but *dammit!* The man had been willing to trust me; it just hadn't happened as early as I would have liked.

My heart was still aching from his expression when he'd turned and walked away, and it was obvious that he'd meant exactly what he'd said.

He *wasn't* coming back.

He *wasn't* going to interfere if I needed to escape.

"Shit!" I mumbled anxiously as I gathered my stuff. "I have to talk to him. I can't leave this way."

No matter how many differences there were between us, I *wanted* to give Damian his power back, because I didn't need it. I was strong enough on my own. He'd taught me that, so I wasn't about to leave him vulnerable and defenseless.

I couldn't.

I sprinted back into the throughway, looking at every single face as I made my way toward the exit.

I finally stopped, panting from exertion, as I saw who I was looking for sitting at the very last gate before security and the exit.

Damian's head was down, his elbows on his legs, his broad shoulders slumped.

Pain ripped through my entire body as I watched him, hating the fact that he was hurting as much as I was, even if it wasn't for the same reasons.

I strode to where he was sitting, touched his shoulder, and held out my hand. "I could really use a comfortable bed right now. I'm exhausted. I'm not even going to try to pretend that I'm over all of this, but we'll talk when we're both rested, and then I'll go."

The moment his head jerked up, I knew I'd *never* forget his expression as relief flooded his features, removing the anguish that had been there seconds ago.

He was on his feet so fast his body was almost a blur, and he snatched the hand I was offering. "You won't regret this, Nicole."

I swallowed hard as the two of us walked toward the exit. "You broke my heart, Damian."

"Then I'll bloody well fix that, too," he grumbled.

And just like that...Damian Lancaster took his power back, like he'd never given it to me in the first place.

My lips kicked up into a small smile of satisfaction.

I'd fallen in love with this bossy, powerful, kindhearted, honorable man, and no matter how much it hurt, I'd much rather leave him this way.

CHAPTER 35

Nicole

BY NOON THE following day, I felt like I hadn't left a single stone unturned.

I'd spoken to Bella and Leo at length, and saw all of the pictures Damian had hidden away. I was now completely convinced that Dylan was his identical twin, no matter how crazy it all seemed.

I sighed, glad that I was feeling more like myself today. Except for a few slightly uncomfortable interactions when he'd brought me the evidence of Dylan's existence, Damian and I had hardly spoken yet.

We hadn't said much on the ride home from the airport, and I'd fallen into bed as soon as we'd reached Damian's house, so mentally and physically exhausted that I hadn't been ready to talk.

The subject of my thoughts came walking into the living room seconds later. "I made you some breakfast. You didn't eat anything this morning."

I smiled at him warily. "I've been busy. What's for breakfast? You do realize it's almost noon."

He handed me one of the plates. "Pancakes. It's the only thing I really know how to cook. Every Sunday was family day in the Lancaster home. When we were kids, me, Dylan, and Leo used to spend the morning with our parents in the kitchen, making as many pancakes as we could eat."

I looked at the plate as Damian took a seat next to me on the couch and began to devour his own food.

"They don't look like pancakes," I observed.

"Our pancakes look more like crepes," he explained between bites. "They're unleavened and thin, and we top them with anything and everything. I went with maple syrup for yours to make you feel more at home."

I picked up my fork, trying not to smile. He'd *definitely* gone with maple syrup, and he hadn't been stingy about it. The English version of American pancakes on my plate were literally drowning in syrup.

I took a big bite. "Oh, my God. These are fantastic." They *tasted* more like crepes than pancakes, too, but I happened to love crepes, even if they did go straight to my ass after eating them.

He nodded. "Eat. Unless I missed it, you haven't consumed much since yesterday morning."

I was ravenously hungry, and I made short work of the pancakes.

Once I was done, I got to my feet to go rinse my plate and put it in the dishwasher. Damian was right behind me, so I did the same with his, too.

I couldn't say he'd totally regained his previous demeanor. He still seemed repentant over everything that happened, but a whole lot less shattered than he'd been the night before.

I turned around when I was finished, and looked at Damian. "I'm ready to go home now. I think I have all the answers I need. I'm going to try to get a flight out tonight or early tomorrow morning."

I'd gotten all my answers, and Damian seemed more like himself, but being around him was killing me.

That's why I *had* to go as soon as possible.

"I know I need to apologize again for everything that happened." Damian's voice was low and rueful. "Last night included. I didn't even think about the fact that I was overpowering you, or that my actions might make you feel like less of a person until I pulled my head out of my ass. I had no business trying to *make* you stay, in any way. I'm sorry, Nicole. I wanted to help you, not hurt you. You looked so damn exhausted and disheartened that I temporarily lost it."

And just like that, my heart melted. I actually believed that he *hadn't* thought about the fact that he was taking advantage because he'd never been anything *other* than Damian Lancaster. The man was a fixer of problems, so his intentions were probably in the right place, even though his execution had sucked during the first part of last night's discussion. "Apology accepted. Just try to remember that not every single person in the world has the same privileges you do."

"Say you don't hate me for doing it." His words were actually a request and not a demand.

For the first time, I actually saw true fear in Damian's eyes, and I realized I actually wielded my own power over him. For some reason, he didn't want to lose my respect, and that made him vulnerable, but I wasn't about to take advantage of that susceptibility.

I shook my head. "No. I was just angry at the time."

"And do you plan on forgiving me for being a lying wanker?" His voice was a little lighter, like he was relieved I didn't hate him.

I understood his motivation, and his desire to take care of his twin brother. It was just what Damian *always did*. The man was a caretaker, and I couldn't really find fault in a characteristic that had been part of the reason I'd fallen in love with him in the first place.

"I really need to know if you're ever going to be able to forgive me, Nicole," he said, more impatiently this time.

"I think I already have." My voice was sad and wistful. "It hurts that you felt like you *had* to lie to me, and that you roped your mother and Leo into those lies, too. But I can hardly fault you for trying so hard to protect a twin brother you love."

Damian prowled closer until he was right in front of me. "I told you that it wasn't about *that* once we got here to England, Nicole. Were you hearing me last night? My motivations changed. At some point, it wasn't about Dylan anymore. It was about us. I was afraid you'd walk away. I wanted more time."

I nodded. "I'm having a really difficult time buying that you kept up that whole ruse just to be with me. I know it was mostly all about Dylan, and I'm okay with that."

His expression was intense as he slapped a hand down on each side of my body, trapping me against the counter and his muscular form. "Bloody hell! *I'm* not okay with it, Nicole. Not at all. I'm not okay with *any of this*. Soon after we got here to England, it was *all* about me. *My* desire to be with you. *My* need to make you mine. There were times that I was losing my fucking mind because of the way I feel about you, and you're okay with thinking this was all about my twin brother?"

I tilted my head and got lost in Damian's wild eyes. He looked like a feral animal in pain, and I had to stifle the urge to soothe him.

He kept going like a floodgate had opened, and he couldn't stop the words from flowing out of his mouth. "You want to leave? You're calmly telling me you're ready to walk away from me, from us, from this crazy attraction that's unlike anything I've ever felt in my entire life? Well, it's not happening. How many ways can I tell you that I love you, Nicole? That if you leave, you'll be taking my heart with you, and I probably won't survive it? I'm not good with words, and fuck knows I'm not used to expressing myself, but I'm willing to find every way possible to make you believe that I love you. I need you, and there's no way in hell that I'll ever be happy if you aren't with me. Just give me…some time. I'll figure out a way to make you believe all of it. Every. Single. Word."

Damian's chest was heaving by the time he was finished. His eyes had turned a stormy green, and my heart tripped as I said breathlessly, "You've never once said that you *loved me*. Yeah, we've always had this intense sexual thing going on—"

"It's not just sexual. Not for me," Damian growled. "Granted, there isn't a single day that I don't very much want to fuck you until neither one of us can move anymore, but it goes way beyond that. The second you walk into a room, and I see you, I feel like the whole damn world looks different for me. Brighter. Happier. Like I've finally found someone who sees the real me, and not Damian Lancaster, billionaire duke. And you actually seem to like the man you see. Could I have been so wrong about us, Nicole?"

Tears started to clog my throat, and I couldn't contain the endless stream of them pouring completely unchecked down my face.

Damian Lancaster loved me, and my world was never going to be the same because of it.

I hated the way he was hurting right now, but he'd put his whole heart out there, completely vulnerable and raw, to try to explain how much he loved me.

He'd actually laid his heart at my feet twice in less than twenty-four hours, but I'd been too damn guarded to see it.

I shook my head. "You weren't wrong, Damian. I think I fell head over heels in love with you the moment I tumbled into your lap on that plane. I think it was *that damn kiss*. I've just been so afraid because I felt too much—"

"You can never care about me too much, Nicole," he interrupted. "Never. I'm *always* going to want more. I'm obnoxiously greedy when it comes to you."

I started to sob all of my relief into the button-down shirt he was wearing, and Damian simply wrapped his arms around me and let me get it out. "*Christ!* I hope this is a happy cry," he muttered against my hair. "Fuck! Never mind. I think *any time* you shed a tear, it's going to kill me, happy or not, but I can live with that. Just marry me, Nicole, and put me out of my misery. I'll make sure you *never* feel broken again."

I sobbed harder.

He stroked my back. "Wrong time to ask you to marry me?" he asked in a concerned voice. "We can work it out somehow, love. I'll live in the States with you if you don't want to stay here. Or we can divide our time to be in both countries for part of the year. We'll figure it all out. Just please fucking say *yes*."

He sounded so damn nervous that I was going to turn him down that I pulled back and started swiping the river of tears off my face. "Yes. Of course I'll marry you, Damian. Now that I know you love me, nothing can drag me away." I put my arms around his neck.

Relief flooded his expression. "Not quite sure how you missed it. I thought it was perfectly obvious."

I tilted my head to look at him. Maybe, if I took all of the clues together, I would have concluded that he could *possibly* be in love with me. I guess it was just too farfetched to imagine that someone like Damian Lancaster could ever be madly in love with me. "You're Damian Lancaster, billionaire Duke of Hollingsworth. And I'm just your average middle-class American female. We come from two completely different worlds, Damian. Honestly, under normal circumstances, our two worlds never even would have collided."

He grinned as he tucked a stray lock of hair behind my ear. "*Technically*, our worlds *didn't* actually collide. Your gorgeous, curvy ass collided with my painfully hard cock, and I knew I'd never be the same."

I giggled. I actually *giggled*. Again. But I didn't give a damn. I'd probably always feel giddy when Damian was around. Knowing that he loved me, and desperately wanted to marry me, was pretty damn heady and intoxicating.

I started to unbutton his shirt. "Is that so? And what exactly did you want from me on that plane ride, Your Grace?"

"You know exactly what I needed, woman," he said hoarsely.

I reached for the zipper on his jeans. "I'm not sure that I do know," I teased. "Maybe you should show me."

Elation flooded my soul, and my body wanted in on the action. I needed to be close to this man, as close as I could possibly get.

I didn't want to think about the fact that I'd nearly lost him just because this particular ending had seemed like a fairy tale that could never really happen.

It had been ridiculous thinking, really, because all of the trappings that I'd thought made Damian an impossible match were just…things. Circumstances. His title. His social status. His enormous wealth. I hadn't fallen in love with those. Damian was just a man. Okay, he *was* an *exceptionally hot* guy with a panty-dropping sexy British accent, but I'd fallen in love with *the man*, not his wealth and power.

I never got past taking off my jeans and panties, and Damian didn't get beyond freeing his cock.

He kissed me with a fiery passion that left us both panting when it was over.

"Fuck me, Damian," I murmured against the hot skin at his neck. "I need you."

After he rushed to fish a condom out of his pocket and roll it on, he grabbed my ass and easily put me onto the counter. "Never let it be said that I won't give you *everything* you need, gorgeous."

I moaned as he buried himself to his balls inside me. "God, yes."

"Jesus, Nicole! You're so fucking wet. You feel so damn good that I could happily die right here, right now," he said with a groan.

I was gasping for air as my inner muscles adjusted to accept Damian's large, deliciously hard cock. "You're not dying right now," I insisted. "Fuck me, Damian. Love me. I need you."

He started to move, and the two of us got completely lost in each other. Damian fucked me like a madman: hard, fast, and with a frenzied urgency that matched my own.

Damian loves me. He really loves me.

My heart was soaring, and I was clawing at his shirt by the time my climax hit me. "Damian!" I screamed, the sound echoing through the entire house. "I love you."

Telling him how I felt *out loud* gave me as much mind-altering release as my climax.

"I love you, too, baby." Damian's voice was raspy and guttural. "Don't ever forget that."

I tightened my legs around his waist, wanting to savor the moment. Damian's big body shuddered as he found his own release. His forehead dropped to my shoulder, and I savored every second of that post-orgasmic bliss.

For a few moments, the only sounds in the kitchen were our ragged breaths as we struggled to recover.

I had no idea what I'd done in my life to deserve a man who loved me like Damian, but I'd spend every day for the rest of my life being grateful for the kind of happiness he gave me.

"Don't make me wait long to be able to call you my wife, Nicole." Damian's voice was rough and insistent as he lifted his head from my shoulder. "I'd like to get my sanity back as soon as possible. Fuck! Scratch that. You're always going to make me crazy, but I'd rather lose my mind married to you, if you don't mind."

"I don't have a single reservation," I assured him with a beatific smile on my face. "We can make it official whenever you want."

Damian wanted to claim me somehow, and I was just as restless for him to be mine.

He toyed with my hair absently. "Let's do it here. We'll fly Kylie and Macy here for the wedding, if you're okay with that. I think I can pull everything together in a month or two with Mum's help."

"That's fast." Not that I really minded.

He sent me a wicked smile. "I want to get it done before you change your mind about taking me on for the rest of your life."

I rolled my eyes. "It's going to be a monumental task, but I think I can handle it, handsome."

Like it wasn't every woman's dream to marry a man like Damian?

"Handle *me*, you mean?" he teased. "I think you've become very adept at doing that."

"I love you," I told him as I stroked a palm over his strong jawline. "I don't need to handle you. I love you just the way you are, Your Grace."

"I feel the same way, love. So marry me as soon as we can get the wedding set up? My jets and my airline will be at your disposal to bring anyone you want from the States to us. We can go pick out rings later today." He caught an errant tear from my face and wiped it away.

"The rings can wait," I informed him as I nipped at his ear. "Right now, I just want you. Take me to bed, Damian."

"Scandalous!" he murmured in a sexy, highly aroused tone as he buried his face in my neck and picked my ass up off the counter. "It's barely afternoon, woman."

"I'd like you to fuck me until it's dark, feed me, and then take me back to bed again. Do you have a problem with that plan, Your Grace?" I asked playfully.

"None at all, Your-Grace-in-waiting," he shot back as he carried me toward his room.

What?

Wait!

Shit!

"Do I *really* have to become a duchess if I marry you?" I asked him, my voice panicked. "I'd rather leave all that stuff to your mother."

Damian tossed me onto the bed with an uproarious, booming laugh. "You have to be the only female I've ever met who *doesn't* want to be a duchess."

He got busy taking off the rest of my clothes, and then he shrugged out of his open shirt. He kept going until he was gloriously nude, and then joined me on the bed.

"I'm American. I don't give a damn about a title. I don't. I *really* don't. Seriously. I'm not kidding, Damian." My protests got weaker as his hot, bare skin slid sensually against mine.

His lips and tongue caressed the side of my neck, and suddenly, every negative, nervous thought fled my brain. "Oh, Damian," I whispered, my heart overflowing with love and tenderness for this incredible man I loved.

"I love you, Nicole," he said huskily.

I sighed. Maybe being a duchess wasn't such a big deal after all.

CHAPTER 36

Kylie

"WHO IN THE fuck are you, and why are you here? Never mind. Just go away and stop pounding on my door."

I lowered the fist I'd been using to bang on the door now that Dylan Lancaster had finally opened the door of this outrageous home.

I'd rung the doorbell for two minutes straight, and then resorted to hammering on the door for several more minutes before Dylan had finally popped his head out.

I wasn't about to...go away.

Not in the near future, anyway.

I plowed past him and into the foyer of the Beverly Hills mansion, a rolling suitcase in tow, and my miniature beagle, Jake, cuddled against my body.

I took a deep breath as I turned to face him. "I don't really have to ask if you're Dylan Lancaster. You do look a lot like Damian. Although I do have to say that your brother looks a lot...healthier."

I stared at Dylan, assessing his bloodshot eyes, unkept attire, and his general malaise.

His eyes were the same color as Damian's, but Dylan's didn't seem to have a single spark of life in those pretty irises. What a shame, because I'd always thought Damian's eyes were one of his best features.

Dylan slammed the door. "I'll ask you again. Who in the fuck are you? And what do you mean that Damian looks...healthier?"

I smirked because I knew I'd hit a nerve. Obviously, Dylan didn't like being compared to his elder twin.

Jake squirmed in my arms, so I put the miniature beagle down on the floor. He was well potty trained, and he wasn't a chewer. "I mean that you look like the anti-twin. Your eyes are bloodshot, you're way too skinny, probably because you prefer to drink your meals instead of eating them, and your general sense of style with your clothing is horrible. Not to mention the fact that you need a haircut, and possibly a shower because I can smell you from way over here."

Okay, I really *couldn't* smell him, but I'd much rather nip the cleanliness thing in the bud. There was absolutely nothing worse than a guy who reeked, and I was going to have to be around Dylan every single day.

"I do not stink. I shower every single day." His answer was haughty, and he sounded somewhat offended.

Since I wasn't about to get close enough to him to sniff for myself, I ignored his comment. "Don't you have caretakers here?"

I could have sworn that Nicole had mentioned a couple who lived here, and managed the estate.

Dylan glowered at me. "They're on vacation somewhere in the Caribbean. I didn't expect to be back here so soon. Now tell me who you are and what you want, or I'll throw your ass out of here."

"Oh, yes. I forgot. You *were* staying at Hollingsworth House until your mother decided that it wasn't appropriate behavior for you to fuck a female under her roof while she was throwing her gala. Not to mention the fact that you broke Nicole's heart. Is that why you ran back here like a coward instead of telling Nic that you were sorry?" I plastered an innocent look on my face while I waited for his answer.

Bastard!

He had no idea how much I wanted to put my knee in his balls for making my best friend cry.

"I was in a private bedroom, for fuck's sake. It wasn't like I knew she was going to come and watch," he said testily.

I folded my arms over my chest. "But you apparently had no problem if she wanted to join you and your girl-toy."

Dylan glared at me. "She wasn't a girl. The *woman* was thirty years old, and as for Nicole, I thought the more the merrier. How was I supposed to know that my brother was madly in love with her? Damian has never fallen in love with any of the women he's shagged."

Don't do it, Kylie. Don't punch the bastard in the face so hard that he can't talk anymore.

I was usually more patient, but Nicole was my best friend, so it fried my ass to hear Dylan referring to her like she was just another fuck for Damian.

Since it wouldn't exactly start us out on a good footing if I punched Dylan, I resorted to insults. "Seriously? I doubt you could handle one woman in the shape you're in, much less two. And by the way, Nicole *is* my best friend, so if you say anything bad about her, I'll put my knee in your balls until you sing soprano. Do we understand each other?"

Dylan's expression turned dark. "The shape I'm in? What in the hell does that mean? I'm thirty-three years old. I'm perfectly capable of handling any number of women in one night."

I snorted. "I noticed you didn't say you could actually *satisfy* them. You probably are capable of *pawing* them, but not much more than that."

The visual for that whole scenario wasn't exactly pleasant, so I made a face and shut down the image of Dylan petting a harem of women.

He let out a low, throaty sound as he moved toward me. "You know nothing about me. I don't really think I even care anymore who you are. I just want you to leave. I don't even know why I'm having this unpleasant conversation with you. I don't give a damn what you think. Go. And take that miserable excuse for a hound with you."

I tilted my chin up as he got close enough to grab me. "I'm not going anywhere."

Dylan started to crowd me, so I stepped back, even though I didn't really *want* to back down.

Really, he wasn't *terribly* skinny, and he *was* extremely tall. I was five foot seven, over the average height for a female, but Dylan towered over me. I didn't like his menacing expression, either.

With my back against the wall, I put my palm out to keep him from moving any closer. "Back off."

Dylan smirked as he took another step closer. "Could it be that you're only brave from a distance, Red?"

God, I hated it when people made fun of my hair. "Fuck off, Lancaster."

"Is that an invitation?" His voice became low and seductive.

I wouldn't say I was afraid of Dylan Lancaster, but I was more uneasy with this new, provocative Dylan than I had been with the asshole.

He's trying to throw me off-balance. The bastard is trying to make me nervous.

I met his gaze and refused to look away, even when he placed his palms against the wall, trapping me between his arms.

"It's not even close to an invitation," I scoffed. "I wouldn't screw you if you were the last man on earth, and my hormones were running rampant."

I'd be damned if I'd back down from someone like Dylan Lancaster. He was a man-whore, a spoiled rotten billionaire who treated women like their only purpose was sex, and to plump his already over-inflated ego.

"Is that right, Red?" His deep baritone was captivating now.

I took a breath and released it slowly, determined not to give an inch. Unfortunately, I realized that Dylan had been right. He definitely didn't *stink.* His scent was musky, masculine, and he exuded something that reminded me of sex, sin, and hot, sweaty nights of carnal pleasure.

Shit!

"Get off me, Lancaster," I insisted, never allowing my gaze to waver.

"I'm not on you yet, Red," he answered huskily.

I was wrong about his eyes!

I froze as I noticed that his irises were darker, and filled with something that looked like…sheer, unadulterated lust.

Holy shit!

"Last chance. Back the fuck off." I hated the fact that my voice sounded slightly panicked.

I was honest enough with myself to admit that it wasn't fear that was making me edgy.

It was Dylan's eyes, his sexy British accent, and the way that he was looking at me right now.

I could handle the asshole.

I wasn't so sure about the sexy Brit persona.

I took another deep breath, and then bit back a groan as I was overwhelmed by Dylan's I-want-to-fuck-you-int o-multiple-orgasms scent.

He lowered his head until I could feel the warmth of his breath on my lips. Those puffs of air smelled minty and fresh, making me want to grab him by the hair and yank his head down until I could taste that hint of peppermint on my tongue.

"What are you going to do if I kiss you, Red?"

"Don't do it," I warned him.

No matter how much my body was clamoring for Dylan's touch, I wasn't about to let this asshole manhandle me like he'd done with countless women before me. Dylan Lancaster was playing with me. I was simply his...entertainment.

He grinned, and the action lit up his entire face. "Now that sounds like a challenge," he said.

I pushed against his chest. "It's not," I snapped.

My entire body tightened as his mouth landed on mine, and his lips coaxed me to respond.

For a moment, I couldn't fight the attraction, and I opened, allowing Dylan's lazy but thorough exploration.

My arms snaked around his neck, and I answered every blatant caress of his tongue.

He teased.

He tempted.

He tantalized.

And oh, my God, the man could provoke a reaction from an inanimate object with a kiss as sinful as his.

Kylie! What the fuck are you doing? He's a male slut, and you know it!

I squeaked as I tried to move away from temptation by turning my head, and breaking lip contact. "Let go of me."

Dylan's body stayed exactly where it was, and he tried to connect our mouths again.

If he doesn't move, I'm screwed. I'd let myself get sucked right back under his spell again.

So I did what I'd already thought about doing earlier.

My knee came up in a quick motion of desperation, and connected directly with my target.

"*Fuck*!" Dylan let out a groan as he let me go. "Bloody hell! Why did you do that?"

I scrambled away from the wall, and moved until there was nothing behind me but air. I watched Dylan as he clung to his family jewels, and sucked air in and out of his lungs like it was the most difficult task he'd ever done.

"I told you to let go." Honestly, I did feel a little bit guilty. I had led him on. A little. Not on purpose, but my hormones had gone from zero to overdrive in less than a second when he'd kissed me.

It had taken my brain a little longer to catch up.

"You wanted that as much as I did," Dylan accused.

"You caught me off guard," I argued. "And then I remembered that you were a man-whore, and I *definitely* didn't want it. I didn't knee you *that* hard. It could have been worse. You're still a baritone."

Dylan's breathing evened out, but his hand was still protectively holding his junk. "I don't give a fuck who you are—leave this house. Now."

I shook my head. "Not happening, big guy. We never really got around to introductions, but I'm Kylie Hart. My best friend is going to be marrying your brother in approximately six weeks. I'm here to make sure nothing goes wrong, and there's no more negative press, here or in the UK, before that happens. Damian and Nicole deserve this time stress-free to plan their wedding, and spend some quality time together without having to put out fires that *you* create."

"I'm not planning on raining on their parade," Dylan grumbled.

I beamed at him. "Good. Then we'll get along fine."

Dylan grimaced as he stroked his crotch like he was trying to decide whether or not I broke something vital before he said, "I don't need a goddamn companion."

"Oh, I'm not planning on being your companion, Dylan." I reached down to scoop up Jake. "In six weeks' time, you're going to clean up your act, and then you'll fly back to London for the wedding. After that, I don't give a damn what you do because Damian and Nic will be on their honeymoon."

"I'm not going to the wedding."

Oh yes, you are.

I curled my fingers around the handle of my suitcase. "I assume the bedrooms are upstairs?"

"You're not going upstairs," he growled. "Leave."

"This isn't your house, so technically, you're a squatter," I informed him. "This place belongs to Damian because you signed everything over to him. And I highly doubt he's going to kick *me* out. Believe it or not, he likes me."

He raised a brow. "I highly doubt that. You're a thoroughly unlikable female."

I laughed. "I'd be completely likable if you weren't such an asshole."

I could see the muscle in Dylan's jaw twitch, and I knew he was losing his patience, if he ever had any to begin with, so I said, "I'll just show myself upstairs."

"If you think you can tolerate six weeks with me, you're delusional," he said.

There was something in his voice that stopped me from tossing back a smartass reply.

Something desperate.

Something vulnerable.

Something…tormented.

I hated the fact that I couldn't completely harden my heart when it came to Dylan Lancaster. I didn't exactly like him, but he *had* suffered significant loss.

I headed for the stairs with my suitcase in tow. "We can do this easy and friendly, or you can make it hard. Your choice."

"What are you, my mum?" he taunted.

"No, I'm your new babysitter for the next six weeks." I kept heading for the stairs without looking back at him.

"You'll be gone in twenty-four hours!" he called after my retreating figure.

My heart ached because I could hear a little bit of fear in his tone, like everyone before me had abandoned him, so he just expected that everyone else would, too.

I'm not going anywhere, big guy.

I wasn't just here to make sure Dylan stayed out of trouble, although that was definitely one of my goals.

Nicole had given me a partnership in ACM, even though I didn't have the funds to buy in.

In return, I wanted to do something to thank her for being more like a sister than a friend. And for trusting me to take care of her mom's business. I really wanted to give Damian his brother back. The *real* Dylan Lancaster. Not the asshole who was currently inhabiting his body.

It was the one thing that would mean everything to Nicole and Damian.

I smiled as I climbed the stairs.

I couldn't think of a better wedding present than that.

EPILOGUE

Damian

Two Weeks Later...

MAYBE IT SHOULDN'T have been quite so easy for two people from different countries to work out how they were going to spend their life together.

But it wasn't difficult at all.

My crazy woman loved England. Hell, she even loved the rain, and didn't mind that it sometimes seemed like London was perpetually gloomy compared to Southern California.

Nicole had wanted to give ACM over to Kylie, but her best friend had refused to take more than a partnership until she could afford to buy Nicole out. I was amazed at how gleefully Nicole had accepted that offer, and had readily given Kylie free rein to run the domestic offices while she stayed a silent partner in the UK. Not that Nicole was planning on becoming a woman of leisure. She wanted to drum up more international business for Kylie whenever possible, and she was planning on returning to corporate law.

One of the things that had made Nicole absolutely ecstatic was finding out that she could actually land a job in London working as a corporate attorney. Essentially, she could practice US law in London, so her résumés were getting sent out to every company that had an available opportunity.

I'd offered to place her in Lancaster International, but all *that* had gotten me was a giant eyeroll and a sweet thanks-but-no-thanks kiss.

I got that Nicole needed to pursue her own goals, find her own way, separate and apart from me, but I didn't want her to go too far. No doubt she'd snag a lucrative job in London. She had too much experience and education not to get her choice of positions.

The only downside about Nicole deciding to stay in England was her love of the water, and the lack of balmy beaches here in the UK.

Luckily, her husband-to-be had access to the entire world at his fingertips, and a private jet to fly us wherever she wanted to go.

As promised, Leo was working on getting me certified for scuba during his brief visits to England, so I'd be able to take Nicole to dive anywhere in the world she wanted to go.

"Is everything okay, Damian? You look deep in thought," Nicole said as she walked into the sitting room and curled up on the sofa right next to me.

I shot her a guilty grin. "I guess I was supposed to be working." I set my laptop aside. "But my mind keeps leading me to more stimulating places."

She scooted closer, and I pulled her into my lap.

I still had a hard time believing this woman was really mine, so any close physical reassurance I could get was definitely helpful.

She made a face. "Do I *really* want to know where your dirty mind has been for the last couple of hours?"

"You love my dirty mind. Admit it, woman."

She smiled. "Okay. Sometimes I do."

I lifted a brow. "Sometimes?"

"Okay, maybe it's a little more often. Is that really where your mind has been?"

"No. I was thinking about us, and how lucky I am to have you." I didn't see a single reason not to be totally honest with Nicole about everything.

Her face softened. "You know I feel the same way."

I knew she did, and that fact still fucking amazed me every single day.

"Did you decide where you want to go for our honeymoon?" I wanted Nicole to choose our destination since I'd pretty much been everywhere.

"I want to go to so many places, so it's hard to make a final decision."

"We'll get to all of them, eventually." I hoped she'd be free enough to travel with me when I had to go. Leaving her behind would be pure hell for me.

She sighed. "I'll think about it more and let you know. Have you heard from Dylan? Is he coming to the wedding?"

"He was invited." My twin was still a sore spot for me. "I can't force him to come. I guess if he shows up, he shows up. It's not going to make or break our wedding. This is about us, not him."

"I know," Nicole said, sounding contemplative. "But I know you two were always close."

"I'm content in the knowledge that I've done everything I can, love. Ultimately, he has to decide what *he* wants."

It killed me to be hands-off with Dylan, but I had no choice if I wanted him to stand on his own two feet. I'd released a substantial amount of money into his bank account, a sum that would probably last him several years.

"I think he'll be okay," Nicole said softly. "Maybe he just needs more time."

I was on board with giving him all the time he needed. I'd restructured the upper echelons of Lancaster to put my executives to work, and decrease my workload.

I could stay hopeful, but be prepared in the event that Dylan decided he never wanted to come back as a partner in Lancaster International.

I tightened my arms around Nicole as I said, "Don't worry about Dylan. That situation is out of our control."

"I'm not worried about Dylan," she corrected me. "I'm worried about you."

Bloody hell! The woman could see right through me. I found that both comforting and frightening at the same time.

"I'm the happiest guy in the world, love. In one more month, I'll be married to you." I took her left hand, and kissed the ring I'd put on her finger a few days after I'd asked her to marry me.

Nicole had wanted a simple design, so all I'd insisted on was having a total of thirteen stones.

It *was* our lucky number, after all.

"I love my ring," she said when I released her hand.

"More than you love me?" I teased.

Okay, I was joking, but maybe I was fishing, too. A guy couldn't really hear those words often enough.

"Not even close," she assured me. "There's nothing and no one in this world I love more than you, Damian Lancaster."

And…there were those three little words I loved to hear so damn much.

Nicole had a little smirk on her face as she leaned down to kiss me, one that told me that she'd known exactly what I'd wanted.

That's the problem with falling for a smart, insightful woman like her.

I'd always have to be on my toes.

"Kiss me," I demanded when she hesitated.

"Bossy man," she said in a scolding tone. "Do you think you can always get exactly what you want?"

I held back a groan of frustration. She *was* going to hold back just because I hadn't asked her nicely.

I reached behind her head. "Yes. Yes, I do."

One pull, and her lips were on mine without a hint of resistance.

And then, I had *everything* I wanted, and more.

The End

Thank you for reading Damian and Nicole's story!
Dylan Lancaster's story, *Tell Me I'm Yours,*
is being released in June of 2021.

Please visit me at:
http://www.authorjsscott.com
http://www.facebook.com/authorjsscott

You can write to me at
jsscott_author@hotmail.com

You can also tweet
@AuthorJSScott

Please sign up for my Newsletter for updates, new releases and exclusive excerpts.

Books by J. S. Scott:

Billionaire Obsession Series

The Billionaire's Obsession~Simon
Heart of the Billionaire
The Billionaire's Salvation
The Billionaire's Game
Billionaire Undone~Travis
Billionaire Unmasked~Jason
Billionaire Untamed~Tate
Billionaire Unbound~Chloe
Billionaire Undaunted~Zane
Billionaire Unknown~Blake
Billionaire Unveiled~Marcus
Billionaire Unloved~Jett
Billionaire Unwed~Zeke
Billionaire Unchallenged~Carter
Billionaire Unattainable~Mason

Billionaire Undercover~Hudson
Billionaire Unexpected~Jax
Billionaire Unnoticed~Cooper
Billionaire Unclaimed~Chase

British Billionaires Series

Tell Me You're Mine
Tell Me I'm Yours
Tell Me This Is Forever

Sinclair Series

The Billionaire's Christmas
No Ordinary Billionaire
The Forbidden Billionaire
The Billionaire's Touch
The Billionaire's Voice
The Billionaire Takes All
The Billionaire's Secret
Only A Millionaire

Accidental Billionaires

Ensnared
Entangled
Enamored
Enchanted
Endeared

Walker Brothers Series

Release
Player
Damaged

The Sentinel Demons

The Sentinel Demons: The Complete Collection
A Dangerous Bargain
A Dangerous Hunger
A Dangerous Fury
A Dangerous Demon King

The Vampire Coalition Series

The Vampire Coalition: The Complete Collection
The Rough Mating of a Vampire (Prelude)
Ethan's Mate
Rory's Mate
Nathan's Mate
Liam's Mate
Daric's Mate

Changeling Encounters Series

Changeling Encounters: The Complete Collection
Mate Of The Werewolf
The Dangers Of Adopting A Werewolf
All I Want For Christmas Is A Werewolf

The Pleasures of His Punishment

The Pleasures of His Punishment: The Complete Collection
The Billionaire Next Door
The Millionaire and the Librarian
Riding with the Cop
Secret Desires of the Counselor
In Trouble with the Boss
Rough Ride with a Cowboy
Rough Day for the Teacher

A Forfeit for a Cowboy
Just what the Doctor Ordered
Wicked Romance of a Vampire

The Curve Collection: Big Girls and Bad Boys Series

The Curve Collection: The Complete Collection
The Curve Ball
The Beast Loves Curves
Curves by Design

Writing as Lane Parker

Dearest Stalker: Part 1
Dearest Stalker: A Complete Collection
A Christmas Dream
A Valentine's Dream
Lost: A Mountain Man Rescue Romance

A Dark Horse Novel w/ Cali MacKay

Bound
Hacked

Taken By A Trillionaire Series

Virgin for the Trillionaire by Ruth Cardello
Virgin for the Prince by J.S. Scott
Virgin to Conquer by Melody Anne
Prince Bryan: Taken By A Trillionaire

Other Titles

Well Played w/Ruth Cardello

Made in the USA
Las Vegas, NV
20 November 2024

12159646R00184